MIDNIGHT RISING

The Lindisfarne Series
Book Three

BY THE SAME AUTHOR

MIDNIGHT RISING

THE LINDISFARNE SERIES
BOOK THREE

JOHANNA CRAVEN

www.johannacraven.com

ISBN: 978-0-6451069-7-8

NORTHUMBERLAND
ENGLAND

OCTOBER 1715

CHAPTER ONE

Silence feels safest. The easy way out. Because Julia Mitchell knows all too well that this could be the last time she ever sees her youngest brother.

The sea between Longstone and the mainland is thrashing against the hull of the dory, churned and restless. Pale sunlight ripples over the water, peaking grey and silver. It's a soupy, wintery half light that makes the morning feel closer to dusk. Julia has her hood pulled up over her head, a shawl bundled around her neck. Keeping out the cold, yes, but also preventing her brother from seeing too much of her grief.

Julia looks over at him, but neither of them speak. What is there to say?

Gentle, soft-spoken Angus has been pegged as a dangerous Jacobite, and has little choice but to hide away in London—out of sight of the British army, but also out of reach of his family. Julia knows that if he was to write to her once he reaches the capital, it would put her and her son in danger.

And so: silence. Speaking will take her far too close to tears.

Angus is deliberate in not looking her way, his green eyes fixed to some distant, intangible point on the mainland. Best this way, Julia thinks. Less painful, somehow.

Her body aches with exhaustion. She had not slept a minute last night, upturned by the news of her brother Michael's death at the hands of the redcoats; and then calmed by hours spent with Nathan Blake on the darkened dunes of Emmanuel Head. The two of them had spent the entire night peering through the telescope she had given him, sharing pieces of their lives while the sky glittered overhead.

But those hours, starlit and fragile, they're marked by betrayal now. Because as she had gone to leave Highfield House, the place had been stormed by village Jacobites, with accusations against the Blakes on their lips. Accusations Julia has spent the last three months trying to ignore.

Government spies.

"Keeping government intelligence at their house," Martin Macauley had told her, as he charged towards Highfield House with a musket in his hand. "Spies coming and going at all hours."

How could she have been so blind?

Ever since their arrival on Holy Island almost four months ago, the Blakes have been under suspicion of spying for the government against the Jacobites. Julia had denied and doubted, convinced herself that everyone was wrong. She needed her friendship with Harriet. And perhaps, even more so, she needed whatever this fragile thing was that was simmering between her and Nathan. Had refused to see what was right in front of her eyes.

She feels like the biggest of fools.

The mainland is coming up on them far too quickly, a sorry cluster of sand-coloured buildings shepherded behind thick town walls. The sea drains of colour in their shadow.

Julia has taken Angus up to Berwick in her brothers' fishing boat. It's a longer journey than the quick crossing to Bamburgh, but from here it will be easier to find transport down to London. And then? She cannot think of it.

Angus has already stayed here in Northumberland far too long. The anonymous chaos of London is the only place he will be safe. But Michael's death, so raw in the harsh light of morning, is weighing almost impossibly heavy on her shoulders. Julia does not know if she has the strength to let another of her brothers go.

Angus hands in the sail, allowing Julia to ease the boat towards the jetty. She reaches for his gloved fingers.

"You'll manage on your own?"

Angus smiles, but it doesn't reach his eyes. "Course I'll manage."

Julia's chest aches. Her youngest brother is barely past twenty, and she can't push aside that fierce swell of protectiveness she has always felt towards him.

"There's a part of me that's glad to leave," Angus admits. "With luck I can put this mess behind me and start again."

Julia nods. She knows Angus had never truly wanted to fight for the Jacobite cause. Knows he had been coerced into joining the rebel army by Michael's blind enthusiasm, and the ox plough that is their eldest brother Hugh. Julia has little doubt that, the day her brothers had fired at redcoats at the protest in York, gentle Angus had not been the one to pull the trigger.

"You'll start again, aye," she says, trying for a smile. He deserves it, after all he's been through: three lightless months in the attic of Highfield House, and weeks marooned out on Longstone with a constant eye on the horizon. "And once all this is passed, you'll find me and Bobby again. Hugh as well, perhaps." She cannot keep the waver from her voice. She reaches for the mooring post, forcing down tears.

Angus puts a hand to her shoulder. "Stay here, Jul. There's no need to come into town. Let's not make this harder than it already is."

He's right, of course, but teetering in the boat, they can manage no more than a brief, unbalanced embrace that is over far too quickly. For the best, Julia tells herself. Any longer and her tears will spill. She kisses his bristly cheek. Lowers her eyes.

She feels the boat tilt as Angus steps out onto the ladder of the jetty, but she does not watch him leave. Does not turn as his footsteps echo against the cold morning sky.

He knows where to find her, Julia reminds herself. One day, Angus will return to Holy Island, and they will climb the dunes with wind in their hair, like they did as children.

No. That memory is far too difficult now Michael is gone.

But she clings to that hope of seeing her brother again, as she guides the fishing boat back down the coast to Holy Island. She clings to it as she makes her way through the narrow streets of Lindisfarne, the maze of stone silver-grey in the weak late-morning light. The sun struggles to reach into the corners of the village, and the shadows sharpen the dull sense of dread beginning to roil in Julia's stomach.

She unlocks the door of her curiosity shop, the fresh holes in her life highlighted by its quietness. Dust floats undisturbed through a shaft of pale sunlight that pools on the floor beside the first row of shelves. Light picks out the gold rim on an old tobacco box.

Julia finds herself standing in the circle of sunlight, willing it to take away a little of her grief. How many hours until her son is due home from the dame school? She is craving his company, craving his boundless energy that is so far undented by the friction of the Jacobite Rising. She has not yet told him about his uncle's death. And she has no idea how to do so. Bobby had adored Michael. Learning of his loss will break him.

Her cat, Minerva, slinks out from between the shelves and rubs up against Julia's skirts. Julia bends, runs a hand across Minerva's back, trying to enjoy the feel of the silky coat beneath her touch.

Once, this was her favourite time of day; when the doors had just been unlocked and she had time to herself to explore the wilds of her shop. To walk the cluttered aisles and admire the pieces of other lives that had ended up on her shelves. A moment to take a breath and celebrate the fact that she was here for another day. Celebrate the fact that somehow, she had made it this far, had built this unlikely life from nothing.

Today, though, with grief over Michael and Angus pouring into her heart, it feels as though it will only be seconds before everything collapses beneath her.

She turns towards the cellar. The door at the bottom of the stairs is swinging open. Unease pulls at her as she hurries down the staircase. The cellar is empty, the blankets on the bed tossed aside. An unlit lantern sits on the floor by the doorway, still giving off a faint stench of tallow. There is a stale warmth to the space that suggests her unwanted guest has only just left.

Julia curses under her breath as she closes the door of the cellar. She pulls a key from her pocket and slides it into the lock to hide the room from prying eyes. And she imagines that day when everything will topple. Feels it creep a little closer.

CHAPTER TWO

His mother had been right to leave Highfield House. Nathan feels that deeply, instinctively. Whatever her hazy, indiscernible reasons for leaving, she had been right to do so. This house; somehow, it has the potential to suck any goodness from the world. Poison the water and pollute the sky.

Twenty years ago, Abigail Blake had fled the family home. Fled Holy Island. Nathan wishes he had that option. Disappear and never look back.

Then again, perhaps it's not the house's fault. Perhaps he only has his own foolishness to blame for his situation. Because he can hardly claim he has any good sense in him when he is standing here outside Julia's door in a desperate hope of making amends. How can he blame anything other than his own stupidity when he has come here by choice? No, perhaps not by choice. Because the need to explain himself to Julia after all she saw this morning feels as crucial as taking a breath.

Spies and muskets and dangerous accusations.

Step through that door, and he knows he can expect a raft of angry Jacobites at worst. A red-hot poker in the eye at best.

He does it anyway.

The bell above the door bellows as he enters. With the high tide, the curiosity shop is empty of customers, and Nathan is not sure if being alone in Julia's presence makes him relieved or terrified. She whirls around from where she stands at one of the shelves, a dusting rag in one hand and a gaudy brass trinket box in the other. A look of unbridled rage makes her green eyes blaze.

"Get out," she says.

"Please let me explain."

"I've no need for an explanation. I've already been foolish enough."

No, he will not let things unravel like this. This balancing game with Julia Mitchell, it is infuriating, it is confounding, but it also undeniably precious. He prays it is not lost forever.

Nathan dares to take a step towards her. "I've not been entirely honest with you," he admits. "But I'm no spy. I swear it. And I wish to tell you everything." The words make something close in his chest, because he knows how dangerous they are. Dangerous, but utterly necessary. If he is to have any chance at resurrecting his fledgling relations with Julia, there can be no more secrets between them. No more lies.

She eyes him. Her red hair is chaos, loose curls escaping from the knot at the back of her neck and clouding around her face. Her cheeks are flushed with anger, eyes shadowed with sleeplessness and heavy with grief. At the sight of her, his heart is pounding. He can feel the resentment radiating off her body.

She slams the trinket box back on the shelf and strides towards the door. Turns the key, locking them in. Then she looks at Nathan with fierce eyes. "Start talking then."

Start talking. Start talking. Really, he has no idea where to begin.

Maybe it's a blessing that his house has been revealed as a meeting place for government spies. Because now the informants will use the house no longer, and he will be freed from the knot of the Jacobite Rising he has found himself tangled in.

But even as the thought comes to him, Nathan knows he's being naïve. Of course it will not be that simple. Because as much as he does not want to admit it, he fears Julia is also deeply entangled in the Rising. And if this attempt at explanation capitulates; if she continues to believe his family are government informants, it could put them in even more danger. This conversation is not just about him and Julia, he realises. It's about putting an end to these foolish rumours of his family spying for the king.

"I'm no spy," he says again, deciding this is as fine a place to begin as any. "No one in my family is. The men that attacked Highfield House this morning were mistaken."

Julia stands with her arms pinned across her chest, her back pressed up against the door of the shop. "Martin Macauley said they were watching your house. He said there have been messengers coming and going. And that they saw one of you delivering government intelligence from William Cotesworth."

"They saw Harriet returning from Lesbury Common," Nathan tells her. "After she helped Michael try to return to the Jacobite army. And they drew their own conclusions." He sees a faint wince from Julia. Regrets having to go near her brother's death.

"And the messengers coming to your house?" Her voice has lost a little of its sharpness.

Nathan swallows. "That part is true."

Julia exhales and reaches for the door handle.

"Wait. Please." He knows what he is about to say could be an enormous mistake. But it's a mistake he needs to make. If Julia is to trust him, he needs to trust her too.

He closes his eyes for a moment; that dizzying point of no return. A dive off a cliff.

"My family are not spies," he says, "but Cotesworth's informants were using Highfield House. I had no choice but to agree to it. For reasons..." He hesitates. "For reasons that are best not to go into."

"No. You cannot tell me your house is being used by government spies, and then refuse to tell me why. At least, you cannot do that if you expect me to believe a word you say."

Nathan nods resignedly. He had expected this much. "The day Donald Macauley disappeared, he forced my sister into his boat and took her out to sea." His chest tightens with the knowledge of what he is to reveal. And what it could mean for Eva if this knowledge falls into the wrong hands. "He accused her of being a spy, and tried to kill her. She defended herself and knocked Macauley unconscious. He fell into the water and drowned." He watches Julia for a reaction, but her face remains almost eerily empty. A slight parting of her lips is the only thing that lets Nathan know she has heard what he said.

"One of the government spies told me he had a way to clear Eva's name. A way to ensure the villagers did not come after her over Macauley's disappearance. In exchange, they asked to use the house as a rendezvous point for the exchange of government messages. I had no choice but agree to it. For my sister's sake."

Julia is silent for a long time. Nathan can practically see her turning this information over in her head, picking at its seams. She toys with the edge of her dusting cloth. Finally, she looks up at him. "Are you telling the truth?"

"Do you truly think I would tell you such a thing if it were a lie? Do you think I would do that to Eva?"

"No," Julia says finally. "I don't suppose you would."

He cannot read her, Nathan realises. The closeness he had felt towards her out on the dunes last night has been washed away by Cordwell and Macauley's accusations. He has no thought of whether she believes him; whether she is angry at him for keeping the knowledge of Donald Macauley's death a secret. No thought of whether, the minute he steps from the shop, she will take this information straight to Donald's son.

Julia stares out the window, her eyes glazed over in thought. Wind pushes against the pane, making the old wooden frame creak. "How did Cordwell and Martin Macauley know what the house was being used for?" she asks. "Why did they attack you?"

"My family has been being watched," Nathan admits. "For some weeks. We've been under suspicion since we arrived here on Lindisfarne. Cordwell and Macauley must have seen the messengers coming to the house. Drawn their own conclusions."

"Did they hurt any of you?"

"No."

Julia sets the rag down on the counter. "I'm sorry I didn't stay to make sure you were unharmed."

"I can hardly blame you for running away as you did," Nathan says with a faint smile. "I'm aware I've been more than a little hypocritical. Given all the trouble I gave you for keeping secrets from me."

"Well." Julia swallows. "I suppose I can understand why you did."

Nathan looks at her for a long second, their eyes meeting. His heart is quick, and he cannot tell if it's his fear of human contact that is causing it, or the heat rising from Julia's body, or everything he has just revealed. Perhaps all three. "You will… keep all this to yourself?"

"Of course."

Nathan dares a small smile. Feels his chest swell when she returns it. "I'd best get back," he manages. "I'm needed at the house."

He decides not to say anything to Julia about the way Harriet had disappeared onto Henry Ward's ship this morning, wild with rage at her family for keeping the truth of who her father was from her. Nathan and Edwin had spent most of this morning pacing in front of the windows, waiting for her to return from Ward's clutches. And she would return, they had told each other, over and over, a feverish chant. Of course she would. As much as Harriet likes to leave most of her mothering duties in the hands of her son's nurse, Nathan knows she would never abandon Thomas completely.

Edwin had been adamant that they go after his wife. Somehow, Nathan had managed to convince him that blundering out to the ship on a misguided rescue mission was not the wisest course of action. Besides, for all Henry Ward's darkness, he is still Harriet's father. And she deserves a chance to know him. Perhaps if they had given her that from the beginning, she would not have run off with him like this.

Eventually, the need to see Julia had overridden Nathan's desire to hover at the window and wait for his sister to show herself, and he had left Edwin to his own devices.

Julia walks him to the door and turns the key. When she looks back to face him, she is close, and he can make out the mist of pale freckles across her cheeks.

"If you…" He lets his words trail off. Doesn't know where they are going. His gaze drifts instinctively to her parted lips and he looks away hurriedly.

There is a hint of warmth in Julia's eyes. "Thank you for telling me all this."

"Everything I've told you is the truth," says Nathan. "You know that, don't you?"

"Yes," says Julia, her fingers curling around the doorframe. "I do."

And that, Nathan thinks, is something well worth celebrating.

CHAPTER THREE

Eva stands at the window of her childhood bedroom, her forehead pressed to the glass. It's late afternoon and the sun is pale; feels as though it barely rose before plummeting back towards the horizon. Beyond the window, the sea is the same ash grey as the sky, the water punctuated by the dark shape of Henry Ward's ship.

Unease is coiled tightly in the bottom of Eva's stomach. She hates the thought of Harriet being out there alone with Ward. Hates the thought of all he could tell her.

Nathan appears around the corner of the house, striding over the dunes from the direction of the village. Eva had had no idea he'd even left. She hears the click of the front door. Hears his footsteps thump steadily into the house.

From the ship out beyond the embankment: nothing. Henry Ward's barque is as still and silent as it has been since dawn, when Harriet had followed her father out there.

Eva knows she ought to have told her sister she was the daughter of Henry Ward the moment she had learnt of it.

Knows she should not have left it to Harriet to find out by overhearing Nathan's words.

But telling the truth had felt like far too much of a risk. One word from Ward and Harriet would know Finn had caused their brother Oliver's death. Eva had hoped it was a secret that would never find its way out. Now, with her sister aboard Ward's ship, such a thing feels like the greatest naivety. She cannot bear to think about what knowledge Harriet might bring back to the house with her. Everything feels dizzyingly close to collapse.

She yanks the curtains closed. The sight of that motionless ship, silhouetted with distance, has her on the edge of madness.

"Perhaps we ought to just tell them," Finn says from behind her, his voice low. He's sitting on the floor by the hearth, brown eyes glassy as he stares into the grate. The firelight casts shadows over his bristly cheeks. "If they hear the truth from me…" He fades out, unable to finish the sentence. Because surely he knows this truth will be just as brutal whether it comes from Henry Ward's mouth or his own. He scrubs a hand across his eyes.

Eva reaches down and runs soft fingers through his hair, wishing she could take away his unease. He has been quiet all day, clearly tossing these thoughts around his head as he worked away at rebuilding the fireplace in her mother's old dressing room.

Eva is craving the emptiness of Longstone. She longs to disappear and leave her sister to her own devices. But she can't push aside the worry. Worry over Harriet's safety, or her own secrets, she cannot quite determine. She only knows she cannot leave until her sister has returned.

"We cannot tell anyone," she says stiffly. "My family cannot find out…"

Finn reaches for her hand and tugs her down to sit beside him. "You know there's every chance Harriet already has."

Eva picks at her thumbnail. Up close to the fire, she feels hot and unsteady. She tugs edgily at her shortjacket. "Harriet is the daughter Ward never knew he had. Surely the first thing they discuss will not be you and Oliver. Why would it be?" But she can hear the desperation in her words. Because the fact that Finn killed Oliver may not be the first thing that Ward tells his daughter. But there is every chance it may be the second, the third, the fourth. Eva knows she is kidding herself if she imagines Ward will keep this a secret. Ever since he had returned to Northumberland, he has been determined to make Finn pay for Oliver's death. What better way to do so than this?

"Let's go back to Longstone," she says suddenly. "Right now."

Finn raises his eyebrows. "I thought you wanted to make sure Harriet got home safely."

"I know. I did. But I cannot just sit here and wait any longer." With each minute, each hour that passes, she is coming to see the danger of staying. Because it's another minute, another hour, in which Henry Ward could tell Harriet the truth. Another minute, hour, in which everything could fall. "Besides," she says desperately, "Angus may have left the island by now. And it will be dark in a few hours. We need to go back to keep the light."

Before Finn can reply, the front door creaks open. There's a muffled flurry of footsteps. Voices.

Eva's stomach rolls. This is it, she thinks. This is the

moment she has been dreading since she learnt the truth of how her eldest brother died. Since she stood at the altar with Finn and committed to honour, obey and keep secrets from her family.

She gets to her feet, sucking in her breath and pushing open the door. She reaches for Finn's hand as she steps out into the passage; a gesture of solidarity. Voices float up the staircase. The smell of overcooked lamb stew turns the air— food their housekeeper had prepared earlier in the day, and that has gone untouched. None of them have been in the mood for eating.

"Are you unharmed?" Eva hears Nathan ask.

"Did you imagine I wouldn't be?" Harriet's voice is oddly level. Expressionless.

Nathan replies only with silence.

Eva looks down the staircase at her sister. Harriet is standing in the entrance hall with Edwin and Nathan, though both men are hovering an uncomfortable distance away from her.

Harriet's cheeks are pink with cold, her chin lifted, shoulders pressed back. She is without a cloak or bonnet, and wearing just a light woollen day dress, her blonde hair in a long plait down her back. There's a new hardness about her, Eva realises. A look in her eyes that goes beyond her typical emotionlessness.

At the sound of Eva and Finn's footsteps on the stairs, Harriet looks up. Her eyes meet her sister's, but Eva cannot read them. Harriet says nothing.

She knows. She must know. This wordlessness, it is all part of some twisted game she is playing. Punishment for keeping the truth of her father a secret. Eva's fingers tighten around the banister. She forces herself to keep walking.

Nathan clears his throat. Rubs a hand across the back of his neck as he calls for the housekeeper. "Mrs Brodie, that stew you prepared earlier. Perhaps you might serve it up for dinner?"

***

This family, Nathan knows, is at risk of fracturing. There have been far too many secrets between them, and he knows he is mostly to blame. This entire venture to Lindisfarne had been built on his own lies. A restoration of the house, he had told his family. In truth, he had been coerced up here by Henry Ward, on a search for the valuable letter his mother had apparently been keeping safe at Ward's request. The valuable letter that Ward now wants back.

Henry Ward has not found his precious letter. But he has found his daughter. And this is arguably more problematic.

Nathan sees clearly now that, just as it was with Julia, the time for keeping secrets from his family is over. He has already done enough damage. He will put an end to all this falsity now, before things are broken beyond repair.

So. They will sit down to a meal like civilised human beings. They will be open and honest with each other. And no one will flee, or lie, or go gallivanting onto a pirate ship.

At least he hopes that will be the case.

"Finn and I need to leave," Eva blurts. "We need to get back before dark. Angus may have left and we need to light the firebasket…"

Two hours, probably three, until nightfall. Nathan knows she is making excuses. He doesn't blame her. "This is very important, Eva," he says, doing his best to conjure up some kind of firmness. "I'd appreciate it if you could stay."

"We can't. I'm sorry." Eva lurches towards the front door, but Finn grabs her hand, tugging her back. For several moments, Eva doesn't speak, eyes meeting her husband's in a moment of unspoken dialogue. Finally, she gives a nod of reluctant agreement. Accepts her fate and creeps towards the dining room like a prisoner approaching the gallows.

Nathan watches after her for a moment. He meets Finn's eyes. Gives him a faint nod of thanks.

They make their way into the dining room, barely speaking, as though driven to silence by the weight of their combined secrets. Mrs Brodie is shuffling her way down the long wooden dining table, lighting candles to brighten the late-afternoon gloom. A fire crackles steadily in the grate, making shadows dance across the dark wood wainscoting of the walls.

Rapid footsteps patter down the hallway and Theodora explodes into the dining room, blonde plaits flying. The children's nurse hurries inside in her wake.

"I'm sorry, Mr Blake," Jenny says, half breathless. "She darted out when I weren't looking."

Nathan gives the nurse a knowing look. "Back to the parlour, Theodora," he tells his daughter. "Mrs Brodie will bring you your stew in there."

Her face wrinkles. "No! I want to eat in here with everyone else!"

He is not in the mood. "Back to the parlour," he says sharply. "No arguments."

Theodora huffs loudly. She drags her feet and looks wistfully over her shoulder as Jenny hauls her out of the dining room, mumbling fresh apologies.

Nathan takes a seat at the head of the table as the housekeeper sets a bowl of congealing stew in front of him. His throat closes in protest.

This high-backed chair in front of the fireplace, it's where he remembers his father sitting. He has never sat here before; the dining table is so vast, there has never been any need to fill this chair. And if he's honest with himself, he has never truly felt worthy. But today, he feels a need to take this seat at the head of the table. He knows he needs to conjure up a little authority. Perhaps sitting in this chair will allow him to absorb a little of his father's influence. Allow him to act like the patriarch of this family he is supposed to be.

Silence hangs over the dinner table. Edwin and Harriet sit on one side of him; Eva and Finn on the other. Nathan has not missed the extra inches Harriet has put between herself and her husband. She has made herself into an island. Disconnected and inaccessible. On the opposite side of the table, Eva and Finn sit shoulder to shoulder, unnaturally close, as though bolstering each other against wherever this discussion is going to take them.

Nathan lifts the bottle of claret from the table and fills the glasses, trying to order his thoughts. He murmurs a hurried grace, then turns to look at Harriet. She picks up her napkin and spreads it carefully over her lap. She lifts her chin, glances around the table with a look of defiance. She knows, of course, that they are all impatient to hear what happened on that ship. Nathan can tell how much she is enjoying it.

He forces down a mouthful of stew. Chases it with a hurried gulp of wine. "Well?" he says. "What did Ward have to say to you?"

Harriet lifts her wine glass and takes a miniscule sip, before setting it carefully back beside her bowl. "Do you not think you ought to be the one answering the questions, Nathan? It seems you have been keeping plenty of things to yourself." Her eyes dart around the table. "You all have. Did not one of you think I might wish to know who my father was? Why did you all think it such a good idea to keep it to yourselves?"

"Harriet, that is enough," Edwin says stiffly. Her eyes flash at him, but she does not respond. Edwin turns to Nathan. "She's right, though, Nate. I think it's time you told us everything."

Nathan nods slowly. At least when he lies down to sleep tonight, he will do so with no secrets on his shoulders. "Ward came to me several months ago," he begins. "He had his lawyers track me down in London. He told me he needed a valuable letter he had given to our mother for safekeeping. Apparently the letter speaks of the Jacobite leanings of someone high up in the Whig party. Prime blackmail material." He feels Edwin's eyes boring into him. "Ward tracked Mother down before her death and wrote to her, asking about the letter's whereabouts. Mother told him it was in a safe at the Bank of England. That turned out not to be true."

He turns his wine glass around by the stem. His family are silent on either side of him, Edwin nodding at him to continue. It's a strange feeling. Nathan cannot remember the last time he commanded such authority from them. "Ward accused me of taking the letter. He believed I sold it for my own purposes. I told him he was mistaken. I was certain Mother had not taken the letter with her when she ran from the house, so Ward was convinced it must still be here. He ordered me to come up to Lindisfarne and find it. When I refused, he made threats against me." His voice drops involuntarily. "And against Theodora."

Edwin sighs. Shakes his head. "You ought to have told us the truth from the beginning. Why lie to us with this nonsense about the restoration?" But the brazenness with which he usually speaks is gone. Nathan senses he too is unnerved by this new hardness of Harriet's.

New? Perhaps it has always been there. Perhaps he has just never looked hard enough. Perhaps the day she has spent in her father's company has given her the courage to bring it to the surface.

Nathan turns to Edwin. "I did not tell you the truth because you would have insisted we fight Ward," he admits. "I know you. And that was a risk I couldn't take. Fighting him is far too dangerous."

"You have it wrong," Harriet says suddenly. "Henry Ward does not wish to hurt you."

"You may wish that to be the case, Harriet," Nathan tells her. "But your father tracked me down in London. He found the house we were renting and came there to threaten me. He forced me to upend my life and come up here to tear the house apart. He made it perfectly clear what the consequences would be if I did not find that letter."

"You've not found it," she reminds him. "And what has he done to harm you? Nothing."

His thoughts collide. It's the truth, he realises. For all his bluster, all his threats, Henry Ward has not harmed a hair on their heads. More than that, if Nathan is not mistaken, Ward had even sought to protect them against the Jacobites who had stormed the house yesterday.

He looks squarely at Harriet. He needs more from her. Needs her to be open; to tell him what had happened on the ship. Needs her to stop playing these infuriating games. "Did Ward say something to you about the letter?" he asks, trying to see behind her eyes. "Is there something you know that you are not telling us? Or is all this talk about him not being dangerous just wishful thinking?"

"Wishful thinking," she snorts. "You really do think me an empty-headed fool." She tears at a piece of bread with long fingers. "The threats do not come from him, Nathan. He is acting on another's bidding."

Finn looks up suddenly. "Whose bidding?"

Harriet glances at him, as though surprised at his question. Nathan is surprised too—he has barely heard a word from him all day. "It doesn't matter who," she says. "You just need to know my father is not a danger."

Nathan rubs his eyes in frustration. "Harriet. If you have that information, you must tell us. Do you not appreciate the seriousness of the situation? Do you not appreciate the trouble this family is in?"

Harriet's laugh is thin, icy. "You are berating me for not telling you important things, Nathan? A little hypocritical wouldn't you say?" Her eyes move around the table before landing back on him. "You need to find that letter," she says. "But you do not need to fear Henry Ward. He does not want to hurt us." She looks down, her voice softening a little. "He loved our mother."

Nathan has no idea if this is true. Though his mother's reasons for escaping Holy Island are hazy, he has little doubt Henry Ward is tied up in them. If Ward had truly loved Abigail Blake, he doubts that love was reciprocated.

Harriet's eyes narrow at Nathan's lack of response. "*You* know he does not want to hurt us, Eva," she says pointedly. "You have been aboard his ship. He told me as much. And did he not treat you with kindness?"

Eva's hand tenses around the handle of her spoon. She has not touched her food. "He tried to kill Finn," she hisses. "We almost drowned trying to escape."

"Well." Harriet brings her wine glass to her lips, then peers across the rim, eyes shifting between Eva and Finn. "Perhaps you did something to deserve it."

CHAPTER FOUR

Eva leans back against the gunwale of the skiff and lifts her face to the sky. The last glow of dusk is turning the sea purple, a fine sheen of rain glittering in the lamplight.

They had been stuck at that cursed dinner table for far longer than she had hoped, and the sun is no more than faint patch of light above the horizon. She prays no ships have come out here tonight to find the ink-dark rocks of the Farne Islands. Prays no one has got themselves in trouble on account of her family's dramas. There are no lights on the sea beyond their own, and she is not sure if that reassures her of its emptiness, or suggests that those ships' lights have dipped beneath the surface.

She curls her fingers around the handle of the lamp, letting her body meet the rhythm of the skiff as it moves on the sea. Even now they have left Highfield House, even now they have made it through dinner without their secrets being spilled, she cannot let go of the unease. The muscles in her back and shoulders feel like iron, and a headache is pressing behind her eyes.

Finn leans back against the gunwale, his gaze drawn towards the inky shape of their cottage, just visible in the disappearing light. "I don't think Ward told her about Oliver," he says finally. "Harriet's clearly furious at everyone. If she knew about Oliver, she'd have spoken of it, don't you think?"

In spite of all they are carrying, Eva can see the difference in Finn now they have left Highfield House. The rigidity with which he had carried himself in the house seems to have drained from his body, and the tension is gone from his voice. She hates that she had put him through such a thing.

She wants to believe Finn is right about Harriet. But she cannot quite bring herself to do so. She lifts her face to the sky, letting the rain dampen her cheeks. "You do not know her like I do. She likes to play games. It is just like her to have this knowledge but keep it close to her chest. Not let it out until she feels it will do the most harm."

Finn leans on the tiller, guiding the boat around the foam-tipped fringes of the archipelago. "D'you think she's right about Ward not wanting to hurt your family? About there being someone else behind these threats over the letter?"

"No," Eva says bitterly. "Do you?"

Finn tilts his head, considering. "Maybe. I know Ward really did care a lot about your ma. It makes sense that he'd not want to hurt your family."

"He threatened Nathan and Theodora."

"Empty threats. He's never hurt either of them. And honestly, I'm not sure he ever would."

Eva uses her free hand to pull her cloak closed. She does not want to consider that there might be someone else, someone unknown, with an eye on her family. At least Henry Ward is something of a known quantity. "How can you even think that way after all he has done? Have you forgotten he almost killed you?"

Finn squeezes her shoulder to calm her. "Of course not. But you said I don't know Harriet like you do. Well, you don't know Ward like I do. And he has a sense of honour. A twisted one, maybe, but a sense of honour nonetheless. I've never known him to lie."

Eva lets out a long breath. "I wish I had your faith in him."

"Besides," Finn says, "there's something different about Ward lately. His confidence, it seems forced. Makes sense if he truly is being forced into this by someone else."

Eva nods faintly. Even if Finn is right, she knows she will never bring herself to trust Henry Ward.

She lifts the lamp, trying to catch the outline of their cottage, and the skeletal shape of the firebasket, half lost against the night. It's a strange thing to see Longstone dark like this. Even on the wettest, wildest nights, when there is no chance of keeping the beacon lit, there is always a fire glowing inside, or at least a lamp on the table. The darkness is unsteadying. A reminder, perhaps, of what their home would look like if they let it be reclaimed by sea.

Eva gathers her skirts in her fist and climbs towards the bow of the skiff, holding up the lamp to guide Finn's way into the moorings. She climbs from the boat, the high tide pushing though the slats of the jetty with each swell of the sea. Finn steps out behind her.

The sea is restless and loud tonight, swallowing much of the island and teasing the stairs at the front of the cottage. Eva carries the lamp around the fringe of the water, guiding

Finn's way towards the coal shed. He loads up a bucket with kindling and coal, then carries it back to the firebasket. The chain groans as he lowers the brazier to the rocky ground. He shovels in the fuel and uses the lamp to spark it to life. Firelight spills across the island, thinning out the darkness.

Eva stares up at the flames, which are roaring against the rain shower. Feels a little of her restlessness drain away. She knows keeping the light has always been a way for Finn to try to atone for Oliver's death, so close to the forefront of their minds after two days at Highfield House. Eva cannot help but feel the same need for redemption. Because she can tell herself as often as she likes that Donald Macauley's death was an accident, but that does not change the fact that she has killed a man. The sight of the blazing beacon, of the responsibility she has chosen to shoulder, to protect the lives of strangers, takes away a scrap of the guilt and regret.

The moment she steps through the door of the cottage, Eva feels tension drain from her shoulders. She is glad to be home. Glad for the familiar smell of woodsmoke and candlewax. For the sight of their wobbly kitchen chairs, the smoke-stained bricks of the hearth, their tin teacups that seem to have found permanent lodgings in the middle of the table. Glad for the creaks of the windows and the faint crackle and groan of the beacon. The soothing lash of the sea. A strange thing, Eva thinks, that this cottage has come to feel like home so quickly, while Highfield House, the very place in which she was born, has always felt like a piece of someone else's life.

The sleeping pallets belonging to Angus and Michael Mitchell are gone, the crates they had sat on around the table no doubt taken back to the coal shed. There's a deep stillness to the place that has not existed for weeks.

Eva sets the lamp on the mantel. "Poor Angus," she murmurs. She cannot imagine how difficult it must have been to have packed up his dead brother's belongings with the long, dangerous journey to London laid out in front of him.

It is a strange feeling to have the cottage to themselves again. It takes Eva back to her first days on Longstone; days when she and Finn were little more than strangers. Hiding secrets from each other, instead of from the rest of the world.

As much as she feels for Angus, she is grateful for the space, the privacy. This precious time alone with her new husband.

Finn comes towards her. He cups her cheek with his rough palm. "My wife," he says. And it makes her smile. This is the first time they have had the cottage to themselves since they married, and right now, there is nowhere she would rather be.

He pulls her into a deep kiss. Eva feels herself sink against him. Feels his broad arms circle her body. She closes her eyes, drinking in every piece of him. The coarseness of his beard against her cheeks, the scent of woodsmoke infused in his shirtsleeves, the warmth of his palms against her skin. She feels herself being lifted onto the table. Feels rough hands sliding beneath her skirts. Hears herself sigh against his mouth.

And this is her choice, Eva thinks distantly, as Finn's lips work their way down her neck. If their secrets spill and everything falls, and she must make the choice between her husband and her family, this is her choice. It is right here that she will stay, with the sea on her doorstep, restless beneath the firelight.

Nathan can see little through the telescope tonight. A faint glint of starlight there; a glimpse of the moon between the cloudbank. Still, the very act of turning his gaze away from the earth has the effect of slowing his heart. Of taking him away from his problems for a time. Of making Ward, and the letter, and that godawful dinner he had insisted on tonight, feel a little more distant.

He yawns. The house is dark and quiet around him. No sound but the groans of beams contracting with the cold; the occasional scrabble of an unseen mouse. No light but the single candle flickering on the far end of his desk. The darkness around him pulls more light from the stars.

A fresh plume of cloud blows across the moon and Nathan stands up from the telescope. He takes the candle and makes his way into his darkened bedchamber. He can make out the shape of Theodora, lying on her side in the truckle bed in the corner of the room.

He sets the candle on the side table and crouches beside the bed. His daughter rolls over to face him. He puts a hand to her shoulder. "I'm sorry, my love. I didn't mean to wake you."

"I wasn't asleep," she announces. "I was lying here thinking about the new story I'm going to write."

"Oh yes? And what is that?"

Her eyes are wide and ridiculously sleepless, though it's well past eleven. "It's about a bold adventurer," she tells him. "Who sails to faraway lands in his magic ship."

"Faraway lands? That does sound like a great adventure."

He tries not to think about the fact that she has likely been inspired by the ship moored outside the window. When he was a child, he had seen Henry Ward as a bold adventurer too.

He keeps his hand to Theodora's shoulder. Despite the flicker of unease the physical contact brings him, there is something reassuring about the feel of her. She is here with him, she is safe. For everything that has unravelled, the threads have not yet slipped through his fingers entirely.

He removes his hand, but stays sitting on the floor beside her bed, watching as her breathing slowly morphs into the deep inhalations of sleep. Nathan leans back against the wall and lets his own heavy eyes drop closed.

Though his much-insisted-upon family dinner was as painful as that poker in the eye, he is relieved to have relinquished himself of his sizeable pot of lies. Even more relieved at not having to maintain this charade of restoring the house. Tomorrow, he will not have to hammer floorboards or rebuild fireplaces, or do any of the other godawful tasks Edwin dishes out to him. For all he cares, the place can sit in ruin until the end of its days. As for Ward's precious letter, well, it is not in the house. That much is clear.

Nathan tosses Harriet's words around his head. He knows better than to take what she says as the gospel truth, especially now, when she feels so angry and betrayed. But he cannot deny that some of her claims had struck a chord within him.

Ward has made threats, yes, but he has never acted upon them. Never done anything to harm their family. Even when he had come to the house and stared down the barrel of Edwin's pistol, Ward had not fired in retaliation.

So perhaps Harriet is right. Perhaps Ward will not hurt

them, Abigail's children. Perhaps he really had cared for their mother too much to do so. Perhaps there really is someone else behind these threats. Someone who is forcing Ward to do their bidding.

The prospect does not quite sit right. From what Nathan knows of Henry Ward, he is far too imposing a man to bend to another's will. But perhaps that is exactly why he had sought to carry on this pretence of being the one behind the threats. Surely it cannot be easy for a man who has been a leader all his life to capitulate to the demands of another.

But in a way, Nathan knows it does not matter. Whoever it is that wants the letter, he cannot produce it.

He looks over at Theodora, her chest rising and falling, a hand splayed out beside her cheek. The urge to run is building up inside him. He imagines he feels the way his mother once felt: that searing need to leave Holy Island—to escape Henry Ward. Because it was Ward his mother was escaping, surely. Escaping so he might never know about his daughter. Nathan can only imagine how horrified Abigail would have been if she knew Harriet had spent the day on her father's ship.

He is certain things had not been simple for his mother, but he is aware they are even more complicated for him. Because he can take Theodora and run, but they will surely be followed—by Henry Ward, or by whichever other nameless, faceless bastards are so desperate for this letter. And even if he did run, how much of his family would he leave behind? Eva has made her life on Longstone, an easy target for Ward and his men if they ever sought to come after her. And Harriet? As much as she has rallied to return to London, Nathan knows she will not take it well if he and Edwin drag her away from the father she has only just come to know.

Nathan knows his relationship with his youngest sister is beginning to fray. Since he had learnt that Samuel Blake was not Harriet's father, he has done his best to make her feel as much a part of the family as ever. But he can sense Harriet sliding apart from them—largely thanks to all they have kept from her.

No, Nathan thinks sickly. He cannot run. He cannot do that to his sisters. Nor can he condemn himself and Thea to a life of always looking over their shoulders, wondering who might be on their tail.

And then, of course, there is the other reason that is making him so hesitant to flee. No, he is not going to think about Julia. Not now. At least, he is going to do his best not to.

He cannot run. But somehow, he needs to get the truth out of his sister. Whatever passed between Harriet and Ward on that ship, he needs to know.

CHAPTER FIVE

Harriet can't quite make sense of why she continues to use her workroom. Since Edwin had condemned her brushes and canvas to the fire after her ill-fated venture to Lesbury with Michael Mitchell, the place has been painfully empty. The table is bare without her brushes and water tray, the armchair made more tattered and wretched by her own misery. Her empty easel stands by the window, holding nothing, mocking her.

But even without her paintings, this is still her space—at least, she wants it to be. The place where it feels most possible to let the real world disappear for a time. Because the real world has become almost impossible to carry.

Now Edwin has forbidden her from painting, now her notebooks have followed her canvases into the fire, she has no idea where to put this chaos of emotions that is thrashing around inside her. How does she navigate the knowledge of her father the pirate? Of his crewmen who have her family in their sights? How does she temper her anger at her siblings for all they had kept from her? Or the aching knowledge that Edwin will likely forbid her from ever seeing Isabelle or any of the others in her artists' circle again? She feels constantly airless, weighed down from above.

A knock at the door, and the muscles in her shoulders tighten instinctively. It's not Edwin, at least. These days, he does not even bother knocking.

"Come in," she murmurs, not bothering to move from the armchair.

When Nathan steps inside, he's wearing a fragile look; a look of uncertainty and faint hope. If he's still angry at her for escaping onto Ward's ship, his expression does not give it away. Harriet is grateful.

"How are you?" he asks.

"Is that really why you're here? To see how I'm faring?"

He knots his hands awkwardly. "In part, yes."

"And the other part?" She knows why he is here, of course. Knows he has come for information about her father and this damn letter. About who might be hiding behind it.

Nathan sighs. He hesitates, as though debating whether to keep pounding away at this pretence of caring. "I need you to speak openly," he says. "About what happened between you and your father on his ship yesterday. I need you to tell me exactly what he told you about the letter, and who it is that is really threatening us."

Harriet examines a fingernail. "And why should I do that?"

"For the good of this family," Nathan says tautly. "I assume that still matters to you."

For the good of this family. That's a hypocritical turd if ever she heard one. *The good of this family* hadn't seemed to matter much when Nathan was spouting lies and swinging hammers to keep up the façade of his mock restoration.

She watches his expression falter, as though he too can see the hypocrisy in what he is asking. He rubs the back of his neck. Continues to hover in the doorway. "Please, Harriet. I know we have all done wrong by you, and I'm truly sorry. But I'm afraid." His voice thickens. "I'm afraid for Thea, and for Thomas, and for you and Eva. I have no idea how I'm to keep everyone safe, because I have no thought of who or what we are really up against."

Harriet picks at a thread on the armchair, not speaking. In spite of herself, she feels a tug of pity towards him. Nathan has always had a propensity for shouldering all the world's problems; for blaming himself for every speck of dirt in the family's treasury. Besides, this is the first genuine apology she has received from anyone about keeping her father from her.

Nathan takes a step further into the room and leans up against the empty table. "What happened between you and Ward when you went aboard his ship?" he asks again.

Harriet looks out the window of the workroom. The ship is still out there, watching the house, as it has been for weeks. "I told you what happened last night."

"No you didn't. You only told us pieces. That pieces that would leave us with the most questions."

Harriet shifts uncomfortably. She had not realised she was so transparent.

In truth, a part of her had feared him, her father, the man who had appeared at their house with a pistol in his pocket. Some part of her was afraid to trap herself by stepping aboard his ship. After all, whether she had his blood running through her or not, Henry Ward was still a stranger.

But there was a part of her that needed to know him. Desperately. She has always felt as though she were on the fringe of her family, the ill-fitting piece. A creative fantasist against her level-headed siblings; sharp-tongued against their compulsive geniality. Ice-blonde against their mousy darkness.

Perhaps, she thought, Henry Ward might help her find some sense of a place in the world. Might anchor her somehow. Give her the sense that she was doing more than being dragged through a life she had no say in crafting. Besides, she had spent the first nineteen years of her life certain she would never know her father. How could she not take this chance she had so unexpectedly been gifted?

In any case, when she had stepped out of Highfield House yesterday morning, her anger at her siblings had been almost blinding, and she felt like she had nowhere else to go. And so, when Ward had invited her aboard his ship, she had accepted without question.

She had felt the eyes on her from the moment her feet touched the polished deck of the ship. The men at the davits murmured; others looked up from their polishing, their carving, their card games. The eyes of Ward's crew told her she was not welcome. A bad omen. She knew the stories: a woman onboard sends a ship to the bottom of the sea. But her father's glare had told the men not to ask questions.

He led her down into the cramped and shadowed depths of the ship, along a narrow corridor that creaked with the shifting of the sea. Into a large cabin unlocked with a key he pulled from his pocket. A table stretched out beneath an ornate black lantern, and embroidered curtains were pulled back to reveal the narrow bed against one wall. The windows at the back of the cabin had been boarded up, and shards of morning sunlight strained through the gaps in the wood, painting a cross-stitch of shadows on the floor. The ship smelled old and sour; sweat and bodies and men who had given up caring. The stench turned Harriet's stomach. Her father made no mention of it, and she wondered if he had ceased to notice.

Ward took the lamp from its hook above the table and lit it with a flick of his tinderbox. The shadows that fell across the cabin seemed to only heighten the gloom.

With a wordless nod, Ward gestured for Harriet to sit. She gathered her skirts and slid awkwardly onto the bench at the table. Her eyes drifted upwards, to where footsteps thumped above their heads.

She folded her hands in her lap, feeling wildly out of place. Her father took the pistol from the pocket within his crimson justacorps and set it on the desk. Slid off his coat and hung it on the back of the chair. He yanked the cork from a half-drunk wine bottle and filled two glasses, setting one in front of Harriet. She glanced at it in disinterest, wishing instead for tea, but unable to find her voice.

Ward took a long gulp of wine, then slid onto the bench opposite her. He looked at her for a long second. A strange thing, Harriet thought, to see herself in the face of this stranger; in his hooded blue eyes, the coils of hair tied at a long and slender neck. Felt as though she had caught hold of a thread that could cause her to unravel.

"How old are you?" he asked finally.

Harriet cleared her throat. "I shall be twenty in June." Her voice came out far softer than she intended. She could practically see his mind whirring, calculating. But surely he knew there was no need for uncertainty. She looked every inch her father, and in a way, she was grateful. It took away the doubt.

Ward stared into his clasped hands. "Abigail never told me," he murmured. "If I had known, I would have..." He trailed off, as though unsure exactly what he would have done. He turned his glass around by the stem, unable to meet her eyes.

"She did not want you to know," Harriet said bluntly. "She did not want me to know either. I grew up believing Samuel was my father until I found his gravestone."

He nodded slowly. Harriet could tell the words pained him, but which part? The fact that Abigail had kept his child from him? Or the fact that he had missed so many years of her life? Perhaps both.

Or perhaps she was just fooling herself. Perhaps she was nothing to her father, this man who crossed oceans in trails of cannon fire. Perhaps she was just one in a long line of achievements he had left in his wake.

She desperately wanted to be something to him. Desperately wanted him to care about her. She wanted to fit into this foreign life, this hatched-light cabin. Because she did not feel as though she fitted into her own life.

She was here on his ship, at least. That had to count to for something. It suggested that, if nothing else, she was a source of curiosity for him.

Harriet knew there were questions she ought to ask. Such as why he had threatened her brother, and what this mysterious letter was all about. But she did not want to bring the rest of her family into this. Right now, she felt painfully disconnected from them. Right now, she wanted this time alone with her father. Were they not owed that, after all the lies they had been put through?

"Tell me about yourself," Ward said. It was a question no one had ever asked her before. A question she had no thought of how to respond to—and one with answers that were not altogether comfortable.

"I want to know about you first," she said. "What manner of ship is this?"

His eyes shifted. "I am afraid I cannot give you the answers that would please you."

"How do you know what answers would please me?"

A faint smile flickered on his lips.

Harriet lifted her glass and took a shallow sip. "A pirate vessel, then," she said easily.

"Much to my shame, yes. The *Eagle* was a successful privateer for many years. But since the war with France ended, there has been no place for privateers. And too many men in my crew support the Stuarts for me to consider offering the king my services against the Jacobites."

It was amusing, almost, the way his eyes lowered in shame. Did he really care so much what she thought of him? But there was something thrilling about this, having a pirate's blood in her. She felt oddly emboldened by the knowledge. It gave her courage, somehow—however misguided and foolish that courage might be.

He told her stories then, of the battles he had waged against the French enemy in the dying years of last century; a time, she saw now, which had been interspersed with visits to Highfield House. And then the stories shifted. Goaded on, perhaps, by the deep interest he saw in Harriet's eyes. Peacetime, and a fleeing to the Caribbean; long hot months spent in the Republic of Pirates. He told her of the men he had gathered on his ship under the black flag. Of his first unlawful attacks against East Indian trade ships in the clear waters outside Nassau.

"The *Albion*," he said, shaking his head. "I'll always remember that name. Full of cotton and silk. We plundered her dry." The candlelight caught the brass buttons on his waistcoat. Made them glitter. "It is not something I'm proud of."

The stories felt faraway. Difficult to grasp, those sun-drenched Caribbean islands, running with stolen gold. Hard to acknowledge as real. After all, Henry Ward's life was so far removed from what Harriet knew to be reality. But there was a sincerity in his eyes that told her the stories were true.

"Where did you meet my mother?" she asked.

"I met her on Holy Island not long after her husband died. She was… not herself then, I suppose you could say."

Harriet frowned. "What do you mean?"

"Well. She was grieving. Concerned about her security. And your brothers and sister's future. She made some rash decisions."

"What decisions? You?" Harriet felt her chest squeeze. She had never imagined herself the consequence of a rash decision.

"I suppose so, yes," said Ward, his eyes drawing downward.

"That is not what you meant, is it," Harriet pressed. "What other rash decisions did she make?"

He shook his head. "It was a long time ago. There's no need to revisit them. I know your mother would not wish us to speak of her mistakes."

Harriet snorted. "My mother would not wish for us to be speaking at all." Her fingers tightened around the stem of her glass in frustration. "'Come midnight, all truths will be revealed.' That's what Mother used to say, was it not? That's what you told me."

Ward nodded faintly.

"And do you not think that time has come? Do you not think we have gone past the point of keeping her secrets?"

Ward didn't answer immediately. He rubbed his smooth jaw. "I know you are angry with Abigail for all she kept from you," he said. "And I confess, I am too. But your mother was a good woman. I do not want you to lose sight of that."

"And what if I already have?"

His eyebrows rose at her brusqueness. "Well. Then that would make me most regretful."

"Did you love her?" Harriet asked boldly.

He lowered his eyes. "I did, yes."

"And did she love you?"

Ward didn't speak immediately. "I believed so, once," he said finally. "But perhaps I was mistaken."

"She fled Holy Island so you'd not know about me."

It was a question more than a statement; a need to piece together these hazy fragments of the past. Ward sighed as he refilled his glass. "It would seem that way." Harriet heard grief in his voice.

"This letter," she began, "you told me it is not you who wants it so desperately. You told me there is another man who is forcing you to do his bidding. Who? Someone else from your crew, I assume?"

The look in Ward's eyes told her she was not mistaken. But he said, "I do not want you involved in this. At least no further than you are already."

Harriet laughed incredulously. "Really? That is all you are going to tell me?"

"Is that why you came here?" he asked. "Because you hoped I would tell you what you wanted to know about the letter?"

"No. I came because I wanted to know who you are. I needed to know."

Ward brought his glass to his lips, studying her closely. "Tell me about yourself now," he said. "I want to know who *you* are."

And where to begin? Surely with *wife* and *mother*, because was there anything beyond that? Surely she ought to tell her father about his grandchild, and his cavalier of a son-in-law who had waved a pistol beneath his eyes. But the words that came out: "I am an artist. A painter. I have been invited to go to Paris to present my work."

Ward lowered his glance. He gave her a faint smile. "Harriet." Said her name carefully, experimentally. "Will you stay a while? Or do you need to get back to your family?"

"I do not need to get back to my family."

She had stayed. Over bread and cheese, and wine that tasted as though it had come from somewhere far away, he had told her more about his travels, his seafaring father, his invitation to the court of William and Mary. Harriet had told him about her childhood in London; about the townhouse in Chelsea where she had been born, and the neat childhood of governesses and painting tutors her mother had built for her. And then dutifully, she had told him about her husband, her son.

As they spoke, she had the distinct sense that Ward was

not allowing her beneath the surface. They were polished stories he told her, empty of emotion, cut and curated for an audience. Perhaps she was not letting him in either—but only because beneath the surface was a far too painful place to go. Perhaps her father felt the same.

But now, as she sits with Nathan in this sorry shell that was once her workroom, Harriet wants to give the impression to her brother that Ward had let her into his secrets. In truth, she has no pieces of useful knowledge to dangle in front of Nathan. If she is honest with herself, she had left her first meeting with her father disappointed by their shallow conversations. By the secrets and truths he refused to share. In so many ways, Henry Ward still feels like a stranger. Not, she supposes, that she could really have expected anything else. Impossible, surely, to overcome almost twenty missed years in a single morning.

"Will I see you again?" she had asked Ward as he had deposited her back on the embankment in front of Highfield House yesterday afternoon.

"Is that what you wish?"

"Yes." The answer made her feel vulnerable. Exposed. She was relieved when he said:

"Then it shall be so."

That vague response had given her hope that maybe one day he would be more than a stranger. That one day, he might let her beneath the surface.

She looks at Nathan. "There is someone else behind the letter. He told me that much. Someone from his crew, I assume. But I do not know who it is," she admits. "Ward said he did not wish for me to be involved."

Nathan glances out the window for a moment before

turning to look back at her. "Is that the truth?"

Harriet bristles. "Yes."

"I see." If he is attempting to hide his disappointment, he is doing a rather terrible job of it. He twists a button on his waistcoat, his brow furrowed in thought. "Do you trust him?" he asks her finally.

"Yes," says Harriet. "I do." She prays she is right to do so. For her own sake more than anyone's.

CHAPTER SIX

He must be a fool to be inviting Ward back into the house. But that is exactly what Nathan finds himself doing.

He scrawls the note quickly, before he can change his mind. He needs answers. Clarity. Needs to know where these threats to his family are truly coming from. And he needs to hear this information from Henry Ward himself.

He makes his way to the tavern, where he has been instructed to leave Ward's messages. He has been forthright—at least as forthright as he can manage; has specified Ward is to come to Highfield House at one tomorrow afternoon. This way, he can ensure Thea and Thomas are out of the house in Jenny's care, plus it will give him time to determine exactly what it is he wishes to say—or time to stew madly over the conversation, in any case.

On his way back to the manor, he collects the mail from the post house. The correspondence he was waiting for has arrived: responses from two potential new watch manufacturers from London. The prospect of rebuilding his failed business is one he is not looking forward to. But at least it gives him a glimpse of a future in which he is free of Holy Island and Henry Ward's grasp.

He has no idea if that future is completely fictitious.

Among the dreary financial outlines of business proposals is something which brings him endlessly more joy: copies of the Kepler star charts he had requested from the circulating library at Cambridge. Nathan remembers these same maps spread out over the desk in the office at Highfield House, back when it belonged to his father. Remembers the two of them huddling at the telescope, translating the ocean of stars to the neat black and white lines of Kepler's charts. Perhaps tonight the sky will clear and he will be able to do so again. A few hours' reprieve from thinking about Ward and the cursed letter.

Nathan hurries out of the post house with the charts tucked under his arm. He glances upwards at the thick bank of clouds. Looking at the stars tonight feels like wishful thinking.

He does his best not to make eye contact with anyone as he strides through the narrow streets. Word must have spread by now about Tom Cordwell and his cohort descending on Highfield House. Nathan wonders what stories are being told. Had Cordwell told the villagers the truth—that he had found nothing in the house? Has it gone someway to easing their suspicion about the Blakes? Or had the appearance of Henry Ward and his wayward pistol added fuel to the fire of the villagers' distrust?

Nathan has barely made it past the churchyard before he hears footsteps thudding behind him. He whirls around to find Joseph Holland closing the distance between them.

Holland is dressed in a long dark greatcoat, a woollen cap pulled down low on his head. His bristly cheeks are red with cold. "We need to speak," he says gruffly.

Joseph Holland is the government spy who had initiated the use of the house, and Nathan is surprised he had not come asking questions the moment he heard about the attack. No doubt he felt that would raise too many questions, especially if the manor is still being watched. How Holland managed to catch him at the very moment he was striding through the village is a question Nathan does not want to know the answer to.

Holland's eyes dart. It's that same wary, hunted look that Nathan had seen in Julia's eyes when he had gone to her shop yesterday. The same look he has seen from so many of the villagers since the Jacobite Rising began. A look of suspicion and distrust, and faintly, of fear. Sensations he knows all too well.

"I'm going on ahead to my cottage," Holland murmurs. "Wait five minutes and then follow me." He is off before Nathan can reply.

Nathan turns in the opposite direction and circles the village before approaching Holland's small wooden cottage at the end of Prior Lane. He checks his pocket watch. Five minutes, as instructed.

Holland opens the door before Nathan knocks. Nods for him to enter. Holland's dog, a scruffy black and white thing with legs far too long for its body, gambols across the room and sniffs Nathan's shoes before winding around the table and settling down on the stones of the hearth.

Despite the pallid daylight, the single room of the house is dark, with shutters closed tightly across the windows and a lamp sputtering in the middle of the table. The place smells of damp and dog.

Nathan sits at a lopsided chair at the table, placing his mail down beside the lamp. The place is freezing, and he makes no effort to remove his greatcoat.

Holland paces, making the floorboards creak. "I heard what happened up at the house. Is your family unharmed?"

"We're all right. Thank you."

Holland takes off his cap and twists it between his hands. "Obviously we can't use the house anymore."

Nathan nods. Doesn't speak, for fear his relief will be too evident.

"Any idea what happened? Any thoughts on how the Jacobites came to know what the house was being used for?" Is there a hint of accusation in Holland's words, Nathan wonders? Or is he just imagining things?

He knows, of course, that Tom Cordwell catching Harriet returning from Lesbury had heightened the suspicions the villagers had had about the family. But there has to be more to it. If his sister is to be believed, Cordwell knew the house was being used for an exchange of messages long before Harriet's ill-advised journey with Michael Mitchell. And though Nathan knows Harriet is not always to be trusted, he is fairly certain Edwin's interrogation the night she had returned from Lesbury had succeeded in getting the truth out of her.

"We've been being watched for the past few weeks," he tells Holland. "Several of us have sensed it."

"Villagers just sitting outside Highfield House and watching for days on end in hope of seeing something untoward?" Holland shakes his head. "I don't believe that.

There has to be more to it. Someone working for the Jacobites must have seen something specific."

Nathan grits his teeth. "You think it was Julia Mitchell."

"Hardly the most outlandish of suggestions. We know her family are active Jacobites. And if I'm not mistaken, she had the good fortune of turning up at the house at the very moment we were meeting."

Nathan curses inwardly. Last week, Julia had appeared on the doorstep while the government spies were gathering beneath his roof. An innocent coincidence, Nathan had told himself, however naively. Julia had claimed she was calling after Harriet, and Nathan had believed—or at least, desperately hoped—that Holland and the other spies had not been aware of her being at the house. He had done his best to get her off the property as quickly as possible, without anyone catching on to her presence. This, he thinks dully, is exactly where he feared such a thing would lead: to baseless accusations hurled in Julia's direction.

"Miss Mitchell had nothing to do with it."

Holland's eyebrows rise—and Nathan's outburst manages to surprise himself just as much. For weeks, he has been as suspicious of Julia as anyone.

But two nights ago, as they had huddled by the telescope together, he had felt something shift. Not just because he had finally managed to break through his fear and make physical contact with her. That night, with no one else around, and any pretence eroded by grief over her lost brother, he had felt a genuineness to her. He had seen a new side to her as she had spoken of her son, her cat, her tomboyish childhood on Holy Island, spent running the dunes and beaches with her skirts tied at her knees. He had glimpsed a softness, a vulnerability he got the sense she rarely allows herself to reveal.

"Careful, Blake," says Holland. "Now is not the time to let a woman cloud your judgement."

Nathan bristles. He feels a swell of anger at Holland, and at himself for being so transparent. For letting his feelings slip without. But beyond it all is that low, rumbling undercurrent of fear for Julia about where Holland's suspicions will lead.

He needs to warn her.

CHAPTER SEVEN

The curiosity shop is empty, the front door locked. Nathan pounds on the side door. Calls Julia's name. Nothing.

He tries the church and shops of Marygate before catching sight of her at the anchorage. She is marching down the jetty in her dark green cloak, a basket of food slung over her arm. He guesses she has just returned from the mainland.

"You look worried," she says. "Has something happened?"

Nathan is fairly certain he has looked worried the entire time Julia has known him. And probably several years before that. He opens his mouth to speak, then stops, glancing edgily over his shoulder. Since the raid on the house, he feels eyes on him everywhere.

Julia hurries towards one of the fishermen's huts dotted along the beach, gesturing for Nathan to follow. "In here." She shoulders open the door and he follows her inside.

It's a bent and tiny place, hung with the smell of herrings and ocean, and creaking loudly with each gust of wind. A small table sits in one corner, cluttered with hooks and tangled twine, and hunks of what appears to be beeswax. Salt-encrusted nets hang from nails along the walls.

Julia puts her basket down on the sandy floorboards and looks up at him expectantly. Nathan stands with his back pressed up against the door. Feels it teeter against his weight. He is acutely aware of the distance between himself and Julia; two feet, perhaps. It's both far too much, and nowhere near enough. His pulse thunders in his ears.

"Joseph Holland," he begins, and that is enough for a look of unease to darken Julia's eyes. He knows she has been wary of him. Knows she has suspected him of spying for the government for some time. "You need to be careful. Keep your distance from him."

"Why? What's happened?" She looks at him squarely. "They are not just rumours, are they. This talk of Holland spying for the government."

"No," Nathan admits. "They're not." The words feel weighted, dangerous. Since setting foot back on Lindisfarne, he has been doing his best to stay out of the Rising. But with every passing minute, he seems to find himself more deeply entangled in it. And he is acutely aware he could be seen to be playing both sides. "Holland was the one who coerced me into letting the government spies use the house in the first place," he says. "And now he's desperate to find out how the Jacobites knew what the house was being used for."

Julia nods slowly. "He thinks I'm the one who told them."

"You came to the house once while the spies were meeting," Nathan admits. "I suspect Holland heard your voice. He knows your brothers are active Jacobites. He suspects you're working for them too."

Julia draws in a breath, as though turning this information over in her mind. "Who else?" she asks. "Who else on the island was coming to these meetings at Highfield House? Who else do I need to be wary of?"

"I didn't recognise the others," Nathan tells her. "They weren't from the island, as far as I could tell. Men Cotesworth recruited from around Northumberland to find the Jacobite nobles. They were using Highfield House because they believed Lindisfarne a key post for the rebel cause."

"I see."

Nathan finds himself taking a step towards her. "You need to watch yourself," he says. "Keep a close eye on Bobby."

There's more he wants to suggest, of course. Outlandish suggestions where he can all but ensure her and her son's safety: close the shop, keep Bobby away from school. And most treacherous—*stay with us.* But of course, he can hardly claim that Highfield House is any kind of safe haven. Not with Ward's ship in the bay and a bullet from his pistol lodged in the stairwell. Besides, it was her being at the house that had landed Julia in this trouble in the first place.

"This was risky," she says. "You telling me this. If Holland were to find out about it, you would be in as much danger as I am."

Nathan allows himself a small smile. Of this, he is well aware. "I could hardly say nothing, could I."

"Many would say that's exactly what you ought to have done." Julia looks up at him for a long, wordless moment, as though debating whether to speak further. The hut creaks loudly above their heads. "Nathan," she says finally, "I am so confused. You have put yourself in danger by telling me all of this. Why would you do that for me?"

He feels his fingers tighten around the star maps in his hand. Hears the steady thud of his pulse become a roar.

Julia continues before he can speak, her voice thin, uncertain. "Sometimes I feel as though… as though you care for me. And other times, it's as though you cannot wait to put distance between us." The intensity of her eyes brings heat to the back of his neck. "I know we've made it difficult to trust one another. But it is not just that, is it. I know it's not." She draws in a breath. "Is it because of my reputation? My past? Does it offend you that I have a child outside of wedlock? I know I couldn't blame you. I—"

"No," Nathan blurts. "It is not that, Julia. It is not that at all." He is not ready for this conversation. His fear of human contact is something he rarely discusses. He has little idea how to even put it into words. But how can he do otherwise when Julia is carrying his imperfections on her own shoulders? Besides, if whatever is between them is to have a chance of turning into anything real, this is something she needs to know.

Her being an unmarried mother had barely even registered with him. When he is in her company, his mind is far too full of determining whether or not she might be spying for the Jacobites, and whether or not he is going to self-combust in her presence, that there is barely room for such things.

And that in itself is somewhat unexpected. The starched and upright man he was in London would never have gone near a woman with such a past. Then again, the man he was in London had never considered going near a woman at all. Somehow, against all odds, his wife, Sarah, had just happened. And then, just as abruptly, she had been taken away.

He looks into Julia's gold-flecked eyes. Reads confusion there; uncertainty. And he knows he needs to be open with her. Here, now. After all the dangerous things he has shared with her these past two days, he needs to share this one more thing. And it is this that most has his heart racing.

"It's not…" He stumbles. Tries again. "It is not that I don't want you around me." His mouth feels dry, his skin hot. It has been so long since he has spoken openly of this. Not since Sarah. Aware he is crushing the star maps between his fingers, he sets his pile of correspondence on the table.

He swallows, choosing his words carefully. He knows that if he misspeaks, he could offend her irrevocably. "I find it difficult to be close to anyone," he says. "Physically… I…" His eyes are down, but on the edge of his vision, he sees Julia nod at him to continue. "When I feel the touch of another person, it's often too much to bear." He knows how foolish it sounds. "I don't know how else to describe it. It's a fear, of sorts, I suppose. One I cannot really make sense of." He scrubs a hand across his eyes. "I'm sorry. I can only imagine what you must think of me. What a madman you must think I am."

Julia frowns. "I don't think that at all." She swallows visibly. "Have you always had such a fear?"

"Since I was a child. I do not know for certain what caused it. Although I suspect my older brother may have had a little to do with it."

Julia nods. Nathan knows she remembers Oliver. She has told him as much; besides, he's sure everyone on Holy Island remembers him. A difficult child to forget. But Julia doesn't speak of his long-gone brother. Instead, she says, "Theodora. Is she…"

"She is my blood daughter, yes," Nathan says, answering her unspoken question. "I never imagined I would have a child. But when I met her mother... it was easy, somehow. Or, easier at least. I did not feel this fear quite so intensely." He looks down. Knots his hands together and squeezes. "Since Sarah died, I've never felt the desire to be near another woman—" Julia shifts and Nathan finds himself reaching for her. Finds his fingers closing around her wrist. He feels a bolt of hot energy shoot through him. Doesn't let go. "Except perhaps with you." The words feel dangerous. As though they could lead him to a path he cannot follow.

For long moments, Julia doesn't speak. Nathan's heart is pumping so hard he is afraid she will hear it. He fears he has said too much. Against her freckled skin, his fingers are blazing.

Julia's lips curl into a faint smile. She holds his gaze for a long, wordless moment, and Nathan is overcome by the sudden urge to pull her close, to feel her body against his own. But that urge is coupled with a sudden wave of overwhelm, and he holds himself back.

"Thank you for telling me," she says. "I'm sure it cannot have been easy."

His thumb traces a faint line across her bare forearm, testing himself. He can feel the smooth plane of her skin, the outline of bone, the fine hairs that dance against his fingertip. He hears loud breath against the background sigh of the sea. Cannot tell if that breath belongs to him or her.

"Where do we go from here?" Julia asks.

Nathan stands motionless, gathering his courage. He takes a step closer. Puts a hand to her shoulder, feels the curve of her, the heat of her body beneath the coarse wool of her bodice. Julia is still. He slides his hand down her arm, over her elbow, over the rough stitching on the sleeve of her shortjacket. His hand is pulsing with energy, blood rushing in his ears. And then, like a dam breaking, it is too much. At least, it is enough. He pulls away.

Julia looks him in the eye. "All right?" There is no judgement there, and he feels a deep gratitude.

He nods. Perhaps he is even a little more than all right. "I don't know where we go from here," he admits.

She smiles. "We shall work it out."

And suddenly there are voices; low murmurs coming towards them.

"I ought to go." Julia snatches her basket and throws open the door. She flies out of the hut without another word, marching, head down, back in the direction of her shop.

Julia stops on the corner of Marygate and watches Nathan slip from the fisherman's hut. With the collar of his greatcoat turned up and rolled papers tucked under his arm, he strides off the beach into the village.

A deep current of guilt runs through her, making her chest ache. After all he has just shared with her, after the danger he has put himself in by confirming her suspicions about Joseph Holland, is secret-keeping the best she can manage? She wishes so desperately that things were different.

She knows her eldest brother is nearby. It was his voice that had made her charge from the hut and put an end to her and Nathan's conversation. She prays Nathan made it off the beach before Hugh has any inkling of who she has been spending her time with.

She hurries back towards the shop, glimpsing the scarlet coats of two militiamen at the other end of the street. Doesn't stop to pick up the apples that escape out the top of her basket and roll into the gutter.

She will not wait for her brother to catch her. Right now, she wants nothing to do with him. And in any case, they cannot be seen in one another's company. Not by anyone. Nathan's warning about Joseph Holland has reminded her that even in a village so skewed with Jacobite support, there are plenty of people who wish the cause to fail. She knows there is every chance that word of Hugh's run-in with the authorities has spread back to Holy Island. Knows there are plenty of people here who would turn him over to the militia if they were to see him. And turn Julia in alongside him for providing shelter to a Jacobite criminal.

She unlocks the front door of the shop, dumping her basket on the floor behind the counter. She will take the food upstairs later. She knows Hugh will not be far behind her, and in the vain hope that he had not seen her at the anchorage, she wants to make it look as though she has been here at work all morning. She unlocks the chest where she keeps her pocket book. Dumps the coins on the counter and begins to count them.

When the bell above the door chimes, Julia doesn't look up. She knows it's Hugh. She has lost track of how many times she has begged him to at least use the side door off the alley when he returns to the shop. Using the front door, where anybody could see him, seems like an act of defiance. Like he is challenging the villagers to turn him in. Michael had been exactly the same. And look where that had led him.

Just after the siege at Lindisfarne Castle three weeks ago, Julia had been awoken in the night by a thumping on the front door of the shop. At first, she had been elated to find herself standing face to face with her eldest brother. After they had fled the conflict in York, in which they became wanted men, Angus and Michael had been separated from Hugh, and Julia had not heard word from him in months. She had begun to believe he was lost to them forever. Finding him on her doorstep had been an astonishing joy. She threw her arms around him, squeezing tightly.

"Where have you been?" she cried, tugging him into the dark shop. "Michael and Angus are waiting for you. They're out on Longstone. They don't want to leave for London without you."

"I'm not going to London. I'm needed here." There was a hardness in Hugh's voice that made Julia wary. Not a hint of warmth in his green eyes.

"Needed how?" she dared to ask.

"You don't need to know." He strode towards the staircase, but Julia darted in front of him, preventing him from going upstairs to her living quarters.

"I do need to know. Tell me, Hugh. Please."

He glanced back at the front door to ensure it was locked. Sighed. "The seizure of Lindisfarne Castle should have been successful," he told her. "Bamburgh and Lindisfarne are Jacobite towns. We've an entire army mustering at Lesbury. But word of the attack on the castle never reached them."

"And what do you plan to do about that from my shop?"

Hugh pulled off his dark wool cap and his thick red hair sprang free. "The Jacobites are using hollow trees and bushes between here and Bamburgh as communication posts. Our messages are being intercepted. We need to know who the government supporters are on Lindisfarne. And who might be intercepting the messages." He clenched his fist around his cap. "It's risky trying to get back to the army. But I can do my part here. Find out who's working for Geordie out on Holy Island."

"You can't stay here," said Julia. "I'm sorry. There are militia in the streets now. They came up from the south last week. If they find you here, we'll both be arrested. I'll not put my child in danger like that."

"Would you rather I return to my own cottage?"

"Of course not. Don't be foolish. If anyone saw movement in your house, they'd be suspicious."

"Then I'm staying here." That unyielding look in his eyes, Julia knew it well. But it had intensified in the months he had been away. Grown harder, colder. Almost made her fear him. He nodded towards the cellar. "I'll sleep down there, if you're so worried about having me in your home. No one will know I'm here."

Once, Hugh had been warm and caring. He had taken her in without question when their father had thrown her into the street after she found herself with child at seventeen, Bobby's father a distant, liquor-hazed memory. It was Hugh who had lent her the money she needed to open the shop; had rented the property for her in his name. But since the death of his wife and child two years ago, he had become fixated on the Jacobite cause. Nothing and no one else seemed to matter.

He had refused to let Julia tell anyone of his being there, not even their other brothers. Michael had died believing Hugh lost to the cause, and when Julia had sent Angus off to

London alone, it had been with lies on her tongue and regret surging in her chest.

This was a cause greater than their own personal trials, Hugh had said. If the Stuarts were to be restored to the throne, as God wished, each man, woman and child had to do their part.

Julia wishes she had the courage to stand up to him. Wishes she had the strength to throw him out of her home. After all, she had been so adamant that her brothers stay away from her shop that she had hidden them in the empty shell of Highfield House. But each time she considers forcing Hugh out, the voice in the back of her head reminds her of everything he has done for her. And she cannot quite find the words.

Has she managed to keep Hugh's presence a secret? Julia cannot be certain of it. Harriet and Michael had both been at the shop while Hugh was hiding in the cellar—Nathan and Eva too. And then there are the blatant lies she had told Nathan about not knowing her brother's whereabouts. Julia had almost convinced herself he could see the untruths behind her eyes.

Today, Hugh is dressed in a long dark greatcoat, his hair tucked up beneath a knitted cap. His square jaw is clean shaven, free of his tell-tale red beard. He's far better at this game than Michael was, Julia thinks dully. With the hat pulled low on his forehead, hiding his fiery hair, she would have easily strolled past Hugh in the street without paying him a second glance. At least if it weren't for the racing pulse and deep dread his presence seems to instinctively stir up within her. She can tell by the look in his eyes that he had seen her with Nathan.

Hugh strides up to her and plants his hands on the counter. Julia can smell the sea on him; guesses he has been on the mainland, exchanging words with the Bamburgh Jacobites that have not left to join the rebel army. She has not seen him since yesterday morning.

"The Northumbrian Jacobites met up with the Highlanders in Kelso," he announces. "We're nearly two thousand strong now." She sees a fire behind his eyes. "Almost enough to outnumber the government troops."

Julia purses her lips. Unless the rebel army is about to storm Lindisfarne, she has little desire to know where they are. "Angus has left," she says. "Gone to London. Alone. I took him over to Berwick yesterday."

Hugh nods. "Good. It's what's best for him. You didn't tell him I was here, did you?"

"No," she says bitterly. "I wouldn't dare."

He nods. "It's for the best, Julia. The less people who know where I am, the better."

"Even your own brother?"

Hugh opens his mouth to respond, then seems to change his mind. He begins to walk down the steps towards the cellar. Looks back over his shoulder at her, a wordless instruction for her to follow. And in spite of every last scrap of self-respect, Julia finds herself following.

Hugh takes the tinderbox from the chair in the corner and lights the lamp, then shuts the door behind them. The room feels suddenly thick and airless, as though the stone walls are closing in.

"You know Nathan Blake," Hugh says.

Julia had been more than a little grateful that Hugh had

not been at the shop when Nathan had appeared yesterday afternoon, begging for the chance to explain himself. This time, she knows she has had no such luxury.

Surely Hugh knows of the rumours pegging the Blakes as government spies. She cannot bear to think on who he might have shared these rumours with. He has no proof, she reminds herself. There is no proof. Because Nathan is not a spy.

She stands with her back pressed to the wall of the cellar. "Yes," she says tautly. "I do know Mr Blake."

"And what did you have to speak about that was so important you saw fit to hide away in a fisherman's hut?"

Julia feels her cheeks blaze. "That is none of your business."

Her mind is still churning from everything Nathan had told her, and she wishes she had a little time to take it all in. Joseph Holland, yes, but that is no surprise. Rumours of Holland's involvement in the government cause have been swirling for months. It is Nathan's other revelation that has most unbalanced her.

Since Bobby had arrived; since the village—and her own father—had labelled her a harlot, Julia has done her best to live up to the reputation. If she is to be perceived that way, why not embrace it? A subconscious thing at first, then a deliberate choice. An act of defiance. An attempt at not caring what people say about her. More than once, when she had opened her cellar to lodgers in the days before the Rising, she had ended up sharing their bed. Empty dalliances, chased away with Queen Anne's Lace, to prevent a brother or sister for Bobby.

And how is it that, after all the trysts and meaningless

entanglements she has found herself in; after all the men she has curled up beneath the sheets with, that single touch of Nathan's hand against her shoulder had set her so alight? She is not sure any man has ever elicited that reaction from her. Bobby's father, perhaps, but he was just a fleeting mistake who had disappeared before he'd even swallowed the last of the whiskey.

She supposes it makes sense, in some strange way. Because Nathan Blake is the opposite of those brash and bawdy men who used to find their way to her cellar. He's a man ill at ease with himself. Self-doubting and uncertain. She had sensed that from the moment he had first walked into her shop to buy a doll for his daughter. A man who seems entirely unaware of his own strength, his own grace. Unaware, she imagines, of how hard her heart beats in his presence.

How can he be anything but strong, given all he is facing? Nathan may not be able to see his own quiet strength, but it was what had drawn Julia to him in the first place. And that need to make him see it himself, well, that is almost overwhelming.

When I feel the touch of another person, it's often too much to bear. Though she could tell the words had not come easy to him— no doubt it is a thing he rarely speaks of—Julia had been almost reassured to hear of his fear. Because while this is an intricacy she had never imagined she would have to navigate, she is relieved to know Nathan is not disgusted by her being an unwed mother, as she had feared.

The hard look in Hugh's eyes sloughs away her thoughts of Nathan.

"It is my business," her brother says, his voice low and slow, "because the Blakes are believed to be working for the government. And you are either sharing Jacobite secrets with him, or you are sharing his bed. Or both."

Julia snorts. "That's quite some conclusion to jump to." When Hugh doesn't respond, she says, "The Blakes are not working for the government. Of that I can assure you. And what is between Nathan and me has nothing to do with you." She meets her brother's eyes challengingly. "If you must know, he was putting himself in danger to ensure my safety."

Hugh's expression suggests he does not believe her. "I would hate to think you were betraying our family, Julia."

"When did the Jacobite cause become our family's cause?"

"When it caused Da to lose his spirit in the battle at Dunkeld. And when Michael lost his life."

"Michael was a fool," Julia hisses. "You know that as well as I do." But Hugh is right, she thinks distantly. This has always been her family's cause. Her father had watched men burnt alive in the houses of Dunkeld, and the weight of it has hung over him ever since. Now Michael is lost to them forever; Angus forced from his family and home. This conflict, bubbling beneath the surface since Julia was in the cradle, has shaped their entire lives.

"Michael was doing what he thought was right," Hugh shoots back. "Instead of hiding away like a coward. Or worse—helping the other side."

"I am not on any side," Julia snaps. "All I want is to keep my son safe."

"Is that what you and Nathan Blake were doing then? Keeping Bobby safe?"

Finding a sudden burst of rebellion, she throws open the cellar door. Hugh catches her wrist before she can charge away.

"Julia." His voice softens slightly. "I'm sorry. I didn't mean to put you on edge."

"How exactly did you imagine I would feel?" she hisses. "I'm being interrogated."

"I'm sorry," he says again. "You know I'm only doing this because I care about you."

She snorts. "No, you're doing this because you've become so passionate about the Jacobite cause you've lost sight of everything else around you."

He seems to consider her words for a moment. "I am passionate about the cause," he agrees. "But I do care about you. You know I do."

Julia is silent. She had known that once, yes. But lately? She's seen little sign that Hugh cares a scrap about her or Bobby. Even the news of Michael's death, told to him with tears running down her face, had elicited little more than a regretful nod. A few steely words muttered about sacrifice and troop numbers, as though Michael were some nameless soldier instead of their own younger brother. Julia has begun to wonder if the empathetic part of Hugh has been scoured away.

He releases his grip on her wrist. "I don't want you to get hurt," he says. "I know how difficult life has been for you. But there cannot be anything between you and Nathan Blake."

Julia glares at him. "It is not your place to decide that."

"It's too dangerous. You can't be associating with government spies."

Julia clenches her hands into fists. Clearly her words about Nathan's innocence have not even registered. "Highfield House was attacked at dawn yesterday," she says tightly. "Did you have anything to do with that?"

"No. It was Tom Cordwell and some others."

Julia grits her teeth. Hugh's knowledge of the situation does little to support his claim of innocence. "Nathan says he's been being watched," she snaps. "He says Cordwell and the others came to the house because they saw the government messengers using it. Was that your doing? Have you been watching Nathan and his family?"

Hugh's silence is all the answer she needs. She knows this is the worst kind of betrayal to Nathan; to be hiding Hugh here after what he has just confessed to. Far worse than anything else she has done to the Blakes. "The government spies think I'm the one who told the Jacobites what Highfield House was being used for," she says pointedly.

Something sparks behind Hugh's eyes. Julia expects some outburst about her safety, but he says, "Who?" Something close to excitement in his voice. "Who's working for the government on Holy Island? If you're so adamant it's not Nathan Blake, tell me who it is."

She snorts. "You were watching the house. Don't you already know that?"

"I saw men coming and going, aye," he says. "But I didn't recognise any of them. They were all dressed as laborers. And did a fine job of keeping their faces hidden. Tell me who they are."

"I've no idea." She cannot speak Joseph Holland's name. It would put Nathan in far too much danger.

Hugh gives a thin laugh. "What happened to you, Julia? You used to be a far better liar."

CHAPTER EIGHT

There has been a debate, Harriet is aware, over whether or not she ought to be told her father is coming to the house this afternoon. It has been going on for much of the morning; she has caught snatches of it through closed doors and around corners. Nathan, clearly still feeling guilty over his secret-keeping, thinks she ought to know; ought to be given the chance to let Henry Ward into her life. Edwin, unsurprisingly, is all for shunting her up to her bedchamber so she might never lay eyes on her troublesome father again.

Well. She listens, and she learns, and she slips out of the house before Edwin and Nathan can make up their minds what to do with her, and when Henry Ward's longboat sighs up against the embankment, she is ready and waiting.

It had crossed her mind, fleetingly, to pretend to be engaged in some other activity: an afternoon stroll perhaps, or removing the dead ivy scrawled across the walls of the house. Something that will make her look less desperate for her father's company.

She decides against it. Her fledgling connection to Henry Ward has already been tainted enough by lies and deceit. She will not poison it further with foolish games.

Showing her father how much she wishes to be a part of his life makes her feel impossibly vulnerable. It is not often that she willingly lets anyone see her weakness. But she knows how easily Henry Ward could weigh anchor and sail out of her life. She could not bear for that to happen.

Ward approaches the house with a deliberate stride, but halts in his step when he sees her. There's something faintly reassuring about that falter. A sign, perhaps, that she matters to him; makes a dent on the vast tableau of his life.

He takes off his cocked hat and passes it between his hands. "Good afternoon, Harriet." His address is stilted; uncertain, somehow, and too formal. The effect of two decades of distance. "Were you out here waiting for me? Surely there's no need for such a thing."

"My husband does not wish me to see you," she admits.

Ward nods, unsurprised. "I'm sure I cannot blame him for that."

Their eyes meet for a silent, stilted moment. "I told Nathan he could trust you," Harriet says finally.

"I'm glad you feel that way."

She hesitates. She thinks to invite him inside with her; show him pieces of her life. Her son, perhaps. What she really wants is to show him her paintings, but thanks to Edwin, those are nothing but ash now. She wants to impress Henry Ward, she realises. Wants to make her newfound father proud of her. How petty, she thinks, chasing the thought away bitterly. Has she not grown up from the child who used to wave her sketches under the nose of her mother, craving validation?

Besides, she is all too aware that Henry Ward has not come here for her. He has come at Nathan's bidding, come to tell the full story. Come to share those midnight truths. To admit, perhaps, that he is not the all-powerful man he once was, and that there are other men at the tiller of his ship. Yes, she has caught pieces of the story, no matter how much Nathan and Edwin have tried to keep her blind and deaf to it.

And so this will have to be enough for now; the fact he is glad to have her trust. Harriet gestures towards the front door and slides a key from her pocket. "My brother is inside waiting for you."

It's Harriet who has let him in, Eva knows. She is making no secret of it, standing at her father's shoulder in the entrance hall with a brittle look on her face. A look that says she has chosen her side.

Eva tries to glimpse behind Ward's eyes. Tries to catch any hint as to whether or not he has spilled the story of Finn and Oliver. She sees only his lifted chin, his hard eyes—a rigid façade of confidence. She cannot bring herself to look at Harriet.

Eva desperately does not want to be here. Desperately does not want Finn here. It feels as though they had escaped just long enough to draw breath before being pulled back below the surface. But when she had come to the house for Thea's lessons yesterday, Nathan had told her of his plans to speak with Ward. And what other choice does she have but to be here? If Ward is to speak of the past, she needs to hear what he has to say.

His eyes move over them, all gathered in the entrance hall like expectant children. Nathan and Edwin, her and Finn. He seems to look down on them, despite being no taller than Nathan and Edwin, and inches shorter than Finn. He greets them only with a wordless nod.

Nathan swallows visibly. "Thank you for coming." He clears his throat and gestures towards the parlour. "Please. This way."

Ward begins striding down the passage before Nathan even finishes speaking. Harriet trails after him, but Edwin steps in front of her, blocking her way before she can enter the parlour. "Upstairs," he murmurs.

The look in Harriet's eyes is so fierce it makes Eva's chest tighten. Harriet looks to her father, as though hoping he might intervene, might allow her to stay. Ward glances over his shoulder at her, but says nothing. Just steps inside the parlour with Nathan. Harriet whirls around and disappears down the passage.

Edwin looks expectantly at Finn. "I'm sure Harriet would welcome her sister's company," he says pointedly.

Finn looks at Edwin, then at Eva. He puts a hand to the small of her back, guiding her into the parlour beside him.

"Thank you," she murmurs.

"If I have to sit through this, I'm not letting you escape it." His half-smile doesn't quite reach his eyes.

Ward takes the armchair in the corner of the parlour without waiting for an invitation. He looks as though he belongs there, Eva thinks sickly. Looks as though those faded blue cushions have been worn smooth with his own weight.

Nathan and Edwin sit opposite him on the settle, leaving Eva and Finn to hover in front of the mantel.

The fire is blazing. Sweat prickles Eva's skin, dampening her shift at her lower back. She shifts her weight edgily, alight with nerves. The fluttering of her heart, her stomach, is almost unbearable. Firelight glows off the dark wood panels of the walls, making the room feel close and cloying, despite the pale sunlight struggling through the windows.

"I was glad to receive your message," Ward says to Nathan. "I'd hoped for the chance to speak with you."

Eva hears a murmur escape her. The men turn to her.

"Do you have something to say?" Ward asks tightly.

Her body turns hot, then cold under his hard blue eyes. "Just that you are hardly one to wait for an invitation."

A few months ago, she would never have spoken out like this. Would have kept quiet in an attempt to veer away from conflict. But conflict has become such a part of her life of late that she is no longer so afraid of it. Still, she knows the only place her outbursts can lead here is to her and Finn's secrets being spilled. Perhaps she ought to have been sent upstairs with Harriet.

Ward seems unfazed by her blundering. "I promised your brother I would not come to the house uninvited," he says firmly. "And I am a man who keeps his word. As I'm sure your husband will tell you."

Eva swallows. Feels herself take an involuntary step towards Finn. He shifts his hand slightly to graze his knuckles over hers. She can sense the tension in his body.

"Well," Edwin shoots an irritated glance at Eva, before turning back to Ward, "now that you're here, I think we would all appreciate you giving us a full explanation of the situation we're facing."

Nathan shifts awkwardly on the settle. He is well dressed today, Eva notices, in a deep blue waistcoat embroidered with gold thread. Brown hair powdered and tied with a matching ribbon. To give him confidence, perhaps. It does not appear to be working.

"You've not told us the truth about this letter," he tells Ward. "I need to know who is behind it. And why."

Ward leans back in his chair, curling his weather-worn hands around the arms. "Those are quite forward requests, Mr Blake. Rather hypocritical of you to demand such openness from me when you yourself have kept so many secrets. Did you not imagine I might care to know I had a daughter?"

Nathan bristles. "Can you blame me for not telling you about Harriet after the threats you made towards me and my child?"

"I suppose not." Ward's eyes shift to Eva and Finn. "Although I cannot help but wonder if your silence might have come from more selfish reasons."

"You've been threatening our family," Eva snaps, the words tumbling out before she can rein them in. "Can you really be surprised that we kept such a thing from you?"

"Indeed I can't." Ward's eyes pierce her. "Mrs Murray."

She falls silent, cursing herself for her outburst. The drumbeat against her ribs is dizzying. Ward's threat, unspoken, presses down on her, making the air unbreathable. Finn meets her eyes in silence.

Ward looks their way for a long second, before turning back to Nathan. "I will tell you what you wish to know, Mr Blake," he says. "But perhaps once I do, you will understand why I kept the truth from you for so many months."

Eva feels Nathan glance at her. Unease in his eyes. He nods for Ward to continue. Eva hears the faint creak of the floorboards in the passage outside the parlour. She knows Harriet is listening.

"When I met your mother a little over twenty years ago, she had got herself in trouble," says Ward. "The first Jacobite Rising had failed some years earlier, and the cause was struggling to find its feet. After your father died, Abigail involved herself in the cause, raising money, as it were."

Nathan's hands tighten around his knees. "Mother was not a Jacobite."

"No," says Ward. "But she was in desperate need of money after your father's death. Samuel had little wealth to leave her. Her settlement was terribly small, and she had no rights to sell the house. She aligned herself with the Jacobites on this island, under the guise of friendship. The Jacobite cause was languishing after Dundee's failed rebellion. Their morale was low and they desperately needed funds. Abigail volunteered to visit the noble Jacobite families around Northumberland, raising money for the cause. She kept a large percentage of that money for herself."

"No." The word falls out of Eva's mouth on its own accord. "You're lying. She would not have done something like that. She was a good person."

Ward's eyes soften slightly, and his expression of sympathy hits her hard. "She was a good person in many ways, yes," he says. "But not all. I'm sorry, Eva. It brings me no joy to tell you this." She hates the sincerity in his voice. Hates that that sheen of bravado has come down, to reveal an authenticity beneath. Because it makes it so hard to doubt him. So hard to brand him a liar. And beneath it all is that thorn Eva has been doing her best to ignore: that she has been questioning exactly who her mother was since she learnt Harriet was Henry Ward's daughter.

Eva looks at Nathan, willing him to protest. Willing him to drop some piece of information from their childhood that will prove Henry Ward is wrong about this. But the look in Nathan's eyes, it's almost as unsettling as Ward's sympathy. Almost as though these words have triggered some forgotten memory within him. Does he remember their mother making fundraising trips around the county? Does he remember her spending time with the Jacobites on Lindisfarne?

"The letter I have been so eager to get my hands on was written to me by a Scottish nobleman I sailed with in my youth," Ward tells them. "I knew the value of the letter immediately, especially given it contained the signature and seal of a prominent member of the aristocracy. I knew how much damage it could do if it fell into the wrong hands. And how much the Whig party would pay to ensure that did not happen.

"Your mother found it among my belongings one night. Offered to hide it in the house. She argued that it would be much safer locked away here, than travelling around Europe aboard my ship. I regret that I agreed."

He turns to look out the window, his eyes growing glassy. "I assumed Abigail took the letter with her when she left the island, given its value. And when I contacted her before her death, she told me she had put it in our safe at the Bank of England. That turned out to be a lie."

Nathan shifts forward on the settle. "Why did she lie to you? What did you do to her?"

Ward's eyes flicker at the accusation. He does not speak at once. "I suppose something made her change her mind about what was between us," he says finally. "But I know no more than you do. I've not seen her since the night your brother died."

Eva's heart thunders at the mention of her brother. She stares at her feet, unable to meet Ward's eyes. But Ward's thoughts are not with Finn and Oliver, she realises—at least not at this moment. They are with Abigail, and whatever had been between the two of them.

"Given you have been unable to find the letter," Ward tells Nathan, "I can only assume she sold it and used the money to fund her new life in London. And that she was too afraid to tell me the truth when I asked after the letter before she died."

Eva's stomach rolls. Her childhood in London had not been filled with wealth, but nor had it been penniless. She and her siblings had grown up in her late father's townhouse in Chelsea; had never been cold or hungry, had never walked the streets with holes in their boots. The three of them had been well educated: herself and Harriet with sought-after governesses, Nathan at Tenison's, and then at Cambridge. Eva had always assumed such a life had been possible because of the settlement her father had left Abigail after his death. But is it possible that life had been paid for with the funds from a stolen Jacobite letter?

"Why do you want the letter so badly now?" Finn says suddenly. "Why come for it after twenty years? Is because you want to offer your crew immunity like you told me?"

Ward rubs a hand over his shorn chin. Eva catches a hint of shame in his eyes. "My crew is largely English," he says.

"And like all Englishmen in this day and age, they are divided."

"You have Jacobites in your crew," says Nathan.

"Indeed. One particularly fervent supporter of the Stuarts is my quartermaster, John Graveney. He has been a part of my crew for more than two decades." He looks at Finn. "Perhaps you might remember him."

Finn says nothing.

"Mr Graveney is—or rather, was—a loyal member of my crew. When we were in Nassau several years ago, he came across correspondence that Abigail had written to me while she was living at Highfield House. In it, she speaks of the theft she committed against the Jacobites she pretended to be working for."

His words catch Eva by surprise. "You kept her letters," she murmurs.

"They were precious to me," Ward admits. "But I can see now that it was foolish to do so. When my quartermaster discovered the damage Abigail had inflicted on the Jacobite cause, he became determined that she be punished for her crimes. See the money she stole returned, and justice done. Of course, such a thing is no longer possible. At least from Abigail herself."

"He wants the money our mother stole," Nathan says dully.

Ward nods. "Indeed."

Nathan gets to his feet and strides to the window. He stares through the glass for long moments, his hands folded behind his back and his shoulders rounded. Eva can practically see the weight of the situation pressing down on him.

"You're Graveney's captain, Ward," Finn snaps. "Do you not have control over what he does?"

"I have control over him as a member of my crew, yes," says Ward. "But not as a man." He looks at Finn pointedly. "You ought to understand that better than anybody."

Eva sees the clench of Finn's jaw. Sees the rapid rise and fall of his chest. After a moment of silence, he asks, "How did Graveney learn of the letter?"

"I told him of it," Ward admits. "I hoped it would appease him. I truly believe it has the power to offer my crew immunity. The Whigs have far more influence than they did twenty years ago, when the letter was first written. And the man it speaks of is still holding office."

"So, what?" Edwin demands. "You plan to blackmail the authorities with the information in the letter in the event of your pirate crew being captured?"

"Indeed." More poorly hidden shame in Ward's voice. "Without the threat of capture in British waters, my crew could make great wealth. Wealth that Mr Graveney could funnel back into the Jacobite cause, if he chose to do so." He lowers his eyes. "I hoped such a promise would be enough to keep him away from your family. But without the letter, I cannot say what he will do."

"Why not tell us all this from the beginning?" Nathan asks. "Why let me believe you were going to kill me? Come after my child?"

Ward sighs. "It brought me no pleasure, Mr Blake. But whatever you might believe, I loved your mother. And I know she never wished you to find out what she had involved herself in. It was something she was not proud of."

"Why tell us the truth now?"

"Is that not obvious?" Ward says tautly. "I have just learnt I have a daughter. I do not wish her to see me as a monster I am not." His voice hardens. "And given all Abigail kept hidden from me, I am less inclined to keep her secrets. Especially when doing so reflects so poorly on me."

Nathan leans back against the window. "The letter is not in the house," he says finally. "Whether it's you or your quartermaster that wants the damn thing, it doesn't change that."

Ward nods. "Mr Graveney knows you have been unable to find the letter."

"And?"

"And he wishes repayment in another way. He wants the money your mother stole to be returned to the Jacobite cause."

"There is no money," Nathan says thinly.

"That's an argument you can attempt to make, Mr Blake," says Ward. "But I'm afraid Graveney is unlikely to believe it when you are sitting in the biggest house on Holy Island."

CHAPTER NINE

Finn follows Ward out of the house, letting the door thud shut behind him. A fine, misty rain has begun to billow in across the sea. "How many?" he asks. "How many men will side with Graveney to force this money from Eva's family?" Their boots sigh over the soft earth of the dunes.

Ward presses his lips together. "Enough."

"You can't let him take the house," Finn hisses. "It's all they have."

"Do you really think any of this is my choice? Do you really think I'd choose to be here, floating around this cursed house for weeks if I had an alternative? Don't you think I hate this place as much as you do?"

His outburst catches Finn off guard. "You don't want to be here?"

Ward turns away. Lowers his voice. "Of course I don't. There's nothing here for me but bad memories. But Graveney and the other Jacobites... they're determined that the Blakes pay for what their mother did. They want the letter. Or payment, in its place."

"Fight them," Finn snaps. "When have you ever let your crew do something against your will? Surely you can't support Graveney taking the house."

"Of course I don't."

"Then put a stop to it!" Finn hisses.

Ward looks down. "I'm afraid it's not that simple."

And Finn sees it clearly now; sees that Ward's captaincy is not as secure as it had once been. He has a ship full of angry Jacobites seeking justice for Abigail Blake's twenty-year-old crimes, and he's made promises of immunity that he cannot deliver on.

Finn looks out to the ship lying at anchor beyond the house. It's barely visible behind the fresh curtain of mist. "You fear Graveney will mutiny, don't you. And you think if you leave Lindisfarne without the letter it'll turn your crew against you."

Ward doesn't answer. He doesn't need to.

For the first time in his life, Finn sees through Ward's brassy façade to the flawed and frightened man that lies beneath. There is something unsteadying about Ward's weakness being on such glaring display, especially with the fate of Eva's family depending on him.

"So your captaincy is more important to you than the family of the woman you loved," Finn says bitterly. "Is that the kind of man you are now?"

He sees something flicker behind Ward's eyes. Anger. He knows he has gone too far.

"I could sail away from this house right now without the letter or the money," Ward says. "But how long do you think it would be before Graveney and his supporters wrestled the captaincy from me? And the first thing they would do would be to come right back here to Holy Island and force the house from Nathan in exchange for the money his mother stole." His eyes bore into Finn's. "I'm trying to keep Abigail's family safe. That is all I've ever wanted to do."

Finn says nothing. Ward is right, he realises. He hates that he is right.

"Do you really think this is acceptable, Finn?" Ward asks suddenly. "For you to be sitting at their table? Giving your input into these matters? Do you really think you ought to be a part of this family?"

Finn swallows. "Eva and I are married," he says. "It's time you accepted that."

Ward laughs thinly. "Don't tell me what I ought to accept, lad. You know me better than that."

Finn's stomach knots. "Abigail deceived you. She left this island so you'd never know about Harriet." He knows Ward does not need the reminder. "And you're still pressuring me to leave Eva as you think her mother would have wanted?"

"Yes. Because it's the right thing to do. You do not belong in this family, Finn. Surely you can see that." Ward looks at him pointedly. "My offer still stands. Join my crew, and I will let the punishment due to you over Oliver's death slide."

"I am not going to join your crew, Ward. I've no intention of leaving my wife. So if you mean to kill me, just do it." He folds his arms. "What exactly are you waiting for?"

Ward chuckles dully at Finn's clumsy boldness. "I'm waiting for you to see sense and take up my offer. It would bring me no pleasure to kill you, Finn. You know that."

"Because you want my support against Graveney?"

Ward ignores his barbed comment. Raindrops glitter on

the shoulders of his justacorps. "You can't go your life without being held accountable for what you did. Sooner or later, the truth is going to come out."

The muscles in Finn's neck tighten. One word from Ward to his daughter and the truth about Oliver's death will spill. If he has not told Harriet already.

As if reading Finn's thoughts, Ward says, "Fetch my daughter for me. I wish to say goodbye to her before I leave."

"Can you sail this boat to the North Pole?" asks Theodora. She is clambering over the benches of the skiff, which is beached high up on the embankment. Ward's longboat lies barely thirty feet away. The rain has eased to a fine drizzle, making the grass of the dunes glitter.

"You'd have to find it first," says Finn. "And you might get a little cold."

Theodora's shoes skid over the wet palings of the boat. His hand darts out and grabs her arm to keep her upright.

"Careful, Thea," Eva says edgily. She glances back to where Harriet is talking to her father just outside the house.

Theodora ignores her. "What about the South Pole? I think the adventurers in my story would like to go there. I bet there's sea monsters."

Eva gnaws at her thumbnail, trying to gauge Harriet's expression. Her face is too hard to read from side on. Ward presses Harriet's hand between both of his for a moment, before turning from the house and striding towards his longboat.

Theodora follows him with her gaze. Eva steps

protectively in front of her, trying to block her view.

"Who is that?" Thea asks, peeking out from behind her. When she gets no response, she pulls at Eva's skirts. "Auntie Eva? Who is he?"

"He's no one," Eva says tautly.

Despite all he had told them about not being the one behind the threats over the letter, trusting Henry Ward is not something that comes easily. Harriet glances their way, then disappears inside.

"Wait for me," Eva tells Finn suddenly. "I'm going to speak to her. I want to find out what she and Ward were talking about."

She grabs Theodora's hand and tugs her back into the house behind her. Sends her niece upstairs, before making her way tentatively down to the workroom, where she feels certain Harriet will be hiding.

She knocks, but steps inside without waiting for an invitation. With the fire almost out and the lamp unlit, the room is a misery of shadow.

Harriet doesn't look surprised to see her. "Come for more information, have you?" She wipes away the condensation on the window and watches as Ward's longboat glides back towards his ship. Her damp hair is frizzing slightly around her face, escaping the confines of the long plait down her back.

"Of course not." Eva knots her hands. "Well. Perhaps a little." She shakes her head, hating how on edge she is around her sister these days. "I just wish to speak with you." And yes, she had come here so she might manage a glimpse beneath Harriet's prickly shell, to determine whether Ward has told her about Finn and Oliver. But as she stands opposite her, Eva realises this is about more than that. It is about rebuilding their fragile relations before they are frayed completely. If Harriet knows how Oliver died, such a thing will be impossible. But if not, perhaps she has a chance to keep her sister in her life. Eva suddenly realises how much she longs for that to be the case.

"Speak with me about what?" Harriet asks tautly. She doesn't turn away from the window.

Eva toys with the splintering edge of the table. "I wondered if you might like to come back to Longstone with me," she says hopefully. "I know I spoke about showing it to you one day. The rain has almost stopped and the sea is quite calm."

"No thank you."

"Very well. Then perhaps we could have tea?"

Harriet turns to look at her. "Why?"

"What do you mean, why?" Eva takes a step forward, closing the space between them. "I'm sorry," she says, "for not telling you about Ward. It was wrong of me."

Harriet eyes her closely, making Eva's heart quicken. She has always struggled to read her sister, but now such a thing is near impossible. She hates this roiling in her stomach when she is around Harriet. Hates that she cannot trust her. Ward's daughter or not, it does not change the fact that Harriet is Eva's only sister. And she cares about her far too much to let their relationship be destroyed by this.

Perhaps it is too late. Perhaps Harriet knows about Finn and Oliver, and their sisterhood is already in pieces. But until Eva knows that for certain, she is not going to stop trying.

"Come on," she says, in the firm voice she used on her flighty younger sister back when they were children. "It is not doing you any good being down here. Let's go to the parlour.

I'll have Mrs Brodie bring us some tea."

Harriet stiffens. "Your husband is waiting for you."

"He'll not mind waiting a little longer." Eva knows he'll be particularly willing to wait if she can determine just how much her sister knows.

Harriet sighs heavily and follows Eva down the passage towards the parlour. Eva rings the handbell on the side table; asks Mrs Brodie for a pot of tea. For long moments, they sit silently beside each other on the settle, Harriet perched on the edge, her back rigid and her eyes unreadable. Eva knots her fingers. This suddenly feels like a terrible idea.

"Why did you not tell me?" Harriet asks abruptly.

It feels like a test. "Because I believe Henry Ward is a dangerous man," Eva admits. "He dragged Finn aboard his ship a few months ago. Tried to kill him for something he did back when he was a child." She is sailing far too close to the wind, she knows. But if she is to have any hope of resurrecting things with Harriet, she needs to give her something other than empty lies.

"What did he do?"

"He fought with someone," says Eva, trying to keep her voice level. "He was just defending himself. He did not deserve to be punished for it."

Harriet snorts. "You would say that, wouldn't you."

Mrs Brodie shoulders open the door, a tea tray in her hands. Eva murmurs her thanks as the housekeeper sets the pot on the tea table and fills two cups.

Eva picks up her teacup, letting the warmth seep into her fingers. Once the door has closed behind Mrs Brodie, she says, "I do not want this business to destroy what is between us, Harriet. You are my sister and I want you in my life."

Harriet takes her cup from the table, but doesn't drink. "Why does it matter?" she asks. "In a few months, I will be back in London and you will be up here, more than a week's journey away. We are hardly going to be at each other's supper table every Sunday." She lets out a faint, private laugh. "Assuming you have a supper table, that is."

Eva sets down her teacup. Tries to swallow the hurt and anger. "So that is all I mean to you then? I'll be forgotten once you return to London?"

Harriet sighs, with a faint hint of regret. "I did not mean it like that. I just meant... Well. Once I leave, are you and I ever going to see each other again?" Her words feel too dramatic, too weighted.

"I certainly hope so," Eva says. "Is that not what you want too?"

Harriet gives a snort of humourless laughter. "I can promise you, Evie, once I get out of this place, I shall not be returning."

"Very well. But I can come and see you in London from time to time." She swallows. "If you wish it."

Harriet seems to consider her question. Then she nods faintly. It's a meagre, hollow promise, Eva knows, but one that clearly shows she does not know the truth of how Oliver died.

It feels like an enormous victory.

CHAPTER TEN

"I assume you're going to the authorities with this," says Edwin, following Nathan out of the house. "It'll be easy enough with the militia in the village."

Nathan curses under his breath. He had hoped to slip out without Edwin noticing. Had hoped for an uninterrupted hour to drift around the island and let the chaotic thoughts in his head fall into some kind of order.

He has no idea what he is supposed to think of Ward's claims. He does not want to believe his mother was a thief. But he cannot deny that Ward's story had pricked at some hidden thread of memory. At some unnameable unease that always comes when he thinks of his childhood. His mother's vague, insubstantial answers to his questions, perhaps. Her long absences from the house.

In a way, he is glad she is not here to see what her choices have led to.

But he cannot go to the authorities.

"Ward and Graveney have not done a thing to us."

Nathan tucks his hands into his pockets and strides with his head down. "The authorities are not going to go after them based on threats that may amount to nothing."

Edwin raises his eyebrows. "Is that what you believe? That this will come to nothing?"

"Of course not. But you know that's how the militia will see it."

"These men are pirates, Nathan," Edwin says. "You're telling me you don't think the authorities will be interested?"

Nathan doesn't reply. He never ceases to be amazed by his brother-in-law's ability to make him feel so small and foolish. Edwin quickens his pace to keep up with him. Gulls swoop above their path as they trudge towards the village.

"Ward's men are watching us," Nathan says finally. "Their ship is right outside our house. Who knows what they'll do if they see us going to the militia? I can't take that risk."

Edwin walks in silence for several paces. Nathan expects a retaliation; a recitation of all the reasons why this is the wrong thing to do. But Edwin says:

"Very well. You may be right."

Nathan gives a humourless laugh. "I'm surprised to hear you say that." He folds his arms across his chest, bracing himself for what's to come. He knows Edwin's solutions will revolve around pistols and counter-threats. And while Nathan can see that this is likely the way forward, he aches for a peaceful resolution.

Edwin says, "We need this Henry Ward removed from our lives."

"By killing him, you mean?"

"Well, he's hardly going to go on his own accord, is he.

He's made that perfectly clear." Edwin digs his hands into the pockets of his coat, his shoes sighing through the mud on the edge of the village. "I know you don't have it in you to kill a man, Nate. But for the safety of this family, I can assure you I do."

Nathan is a little taken aback by the blasé tone to Edwin's voice. He suspects it's little more than bravado. He has known Edwin for almost a decade, and has never known him to so much as swing a punch at another man. Then again, he has brandished a pistol at Henry Ward before. Not that he had the courage to pull the trigger. "Does it not faze you that he is your wife's father?"

"No," Edwin says matter-of-factly. "Quite honestly, we'd all be better off without him in our lives. Harriet especially."

"Killing Ward is not going to solve the problem," Nathan says irritably. "You heard what he said; he's not the one behind these threats. And even if he is lying about that, he has a whole crew behind him. Or at least part of one. We can't fight all those men."

Edwin makes a noise in his throat. He doesn't respond with suggestions of duels and pistol fire, and Nathan feels faintly relieved.

"Then we leave," Edwin says finally. "We pack our things and we leave Lindisfarne as quickly as we can."

"They'll be watching the house. They'll expect us to run."

"Then we leave in the night."

Leave in the night. Just as his mother did. How many times in his life is he to be forced from Highfield House on account of Henry Ward?

"What of Eva and Finn?" Nathan says. "This is their home now. Are we just to leave them to the devices of Ward and his crew?"

Edwin keeps his eyes down. "Eva and Finn can make their own choices."

Nathan is aware, suddenly, of two men walking behind them along the row of stone fences on the outskirts of the village. He feels a tug of unease as he realises the men are gaining on them. Deliberately so.

They're unremarkable men, both grey and leathery, in colourless sailor's slops and cavalier boots. They fall into line beside Nathan and Edwin, forcing Nathan into the muddy grass on the edge of the path.

"Can I help you?" Edwin says brusquely.

He doesn't need an explanation, Nathan realises. He knows instinctively who these men are. "Mr Graveney," he says dully.

"You're him then are you?" says Edwin. "The man seeking to make his fortune off our family?"

"Rather, the man seeking to reclaim what was stolen from the Jacobites." Graveney is the older of the two men; taller than his crewmate, with a narrow face and eyes pitted in the hollows of his cheeks. A patchy grey beard hangs in threads down to the top of his chest.

Nathan feels something sink inside him. The dull knowledge that this man is not a figment of Ward's imagination. Not a fictitious vessel to make him look better in his daughter's eyes. He wonders why Graveney has chosen to show himself now. Perhaps he's grown tired of waiting for Henry Ward to produce the letter. Decided to take matters into his own hands.

John Graveney has a self-righteous look about him. That proud glow in his eyes that Nathan has seen in the faces of other Jacobites when they spout words like *true king* and *by the grace of God*. The glare Graveney gives him is one of a victim towards a criminal. Nathan can't help but shoulder a little of his mother's guilt.

"I don't have the letter," he says, expressionless.

"So I hear." Graveney's voice is gravelly. "But a family as wealthy as yours no doubt has other ways to repay your mother's debts."

Nathan says nothing. There's little point, of course, telling this man how empty his family's coffers are. Because the fact remains, he is the freehold owner of Highfield House, and the pocket of land that surrounds it. No doubt Graveney is aware of this. No doubt it's the house he's seeking. After all, these men seem to have little difficulty in finding out all they wish to know about his family.

Graveney digs his hands into the pockets of his greatcoat, as casual as if they were discussing the weather. "You have until the end of the week," he says. "Saturday. The letter or the house."

Nathan glances at Edwin. He's silent, staring at the two men, a muscle ticking in his jaw. Nathan grits his teeth, hating his own rote nod of acceptance.

Graveney and his crewmate turn down the path and disappear. Edwin watches after them. "We need to leave," he says finally. "Tonight. I'm going home to pack our things."

Nathan feels the pit in his stomach widen. Edwin is right, of course. Leaving is the only way forward. The only way to ensure his child's safety. His own safety. And as much as he hates the thought of leaving Eva out on Longstone in Ward's purview, Edwin is right: she and Finn can make their own choices.

But, "Saturday," he says desperately. "We have six days."

"Six days to do what?" Edwin hisses. "You've been looking for this letter for months. You know it's not in the house. Your mother probably sold the damn thing years ago."

"I know. I just..." He trails off. He cannot bring himself to speak of that sickening parallel of being forced from the house once again. For weeks, the urge to run has been building up inside him. But now it's becoming a reality. And he is beginning to realise that running is not what he wants to do at all.

He knows it's foolish to stay, but he cannot bear the thought of history repeating. Nor can he bear the thought of walking away from this fragile thing he and Julia have begun to build. "Just give me these six days." He looks at Edwin pointedly. "If Graveney can give me that time, surely you can too."

Edwin lets out a breath. "What in hell happened to you? A few months ago, you were desperate that none of us were even in the house with you. And now you're refusing to leave?"

Nathan doesn't reply, making Edwin scrub a hand across his eyes in frustration.

"Six days," Edwin says tautly. "And then we're leaving. All of us."

"As you wish." Nathan turns suddenly and begins to stride away.

"Where are you going?" Edwin demands.

And Nathan does not feel the need to answer.

The sight of her husband makes Harriet's heart jolt. What is he doing here in the village? She thought he and Nathan were locked away in the office at Highfield House, piecing together their plans to rid the world of her father. She darts down the nearest alley, catapulting through a puddle and soaking her stockings to the shins.

It's no use. Edwin has seen her.

His footsteps echo on the cobbles as he rounds the corner to face her. "What are you doing here?" he demands.

"A walk." The lie is so clumsy she would almost have laughed if he had believed it. He rubs his eyes. Looks around them at the narrow lane leading towards the anchorage and tavern. A hunched old man drowning in a long black cloak watches them from a corner as he brings a pipe to his lips. Edwin puts a hand to Harriet's shoulder, ushering her away.

"That is not the kind of street you ought to be seen on," he says. Harriet watches the realisation dawn on him. "Were you going to the tavern? To get word to your father?"

"No."

He sighs. Holds out a hand. "May I see the message?"

What would he do if she refused, Harriet wonders distantly? He would cart her back to the house no doubt, probably put her behind locked doors. Any chance of getting word to her father, of telling him how much she longs to speak to him, would be gone. Probably forever.

Reluctantly, she pulls the note from her pocket and presses it into Edwin's palm. He unfolds it. Reads slowly. Harriet turns away, huddling into her cloak. She feels as though she is burning under his scrutiny. It's not the fact that he has caught her that makes her feel so unbalanced; it's the fact that he might sense the vulnerability she knows is all too evident in her words to Henry Ward.

I would very much like to spend more time with you…

Know you a little better…

Very important to me…

Edwin crumples the page in his fist. "Things have changed, Harriet. We cannot stay here any longer. We shall be leaving for London by Friday at the latest."

Harriet feels suddenly breathless. A return to London. She cannot make sense of why the idea leaves her feeling so hollow. Is this not what she has longed for? "Why?" she finds herself asking.

A look of hesitation passes across Edwin's eyes, as though he is debating how much to share with her. "Because it's not safe here," he says. "There are men in your father's crew who are threatening our family."

Harriet's thoughts begin to race. She knows there is little point arguing about the intentions of Ward's crew. Knows she has little chance of convincing Edwin to stay. Besides, is that even what she wants? All she knows is that the need to speak with her father has just become even greater.

"If we are to leave, will you not give me this last opportunity to get to know my father?" Edwin opens his mouth to speak, but Harriet presses on before he can get a word out. "Once we leave Holy Island, he will be out of our lives. Can you not just give me this one chance? Please?" She hates imploring him like this. But she is desperate. She needs to be a part of Henry Ward's life. Needs that sense of belonging. Needs to matter to him. He is a man with his own ship, she thinks distantly. Surely he has the means to travel to London to spend time with his daughter when he wishes to. Surely her leaving Lindisfarne does not have to mean cutting her father out of her life.

Edwin looks down at the wet cobbles, deep in thought. Finally, he says, "One meeting. At the house. With me in attendance." He crushes her note between his fingers. "I shall rewrite the message and deliver it to the tavern myself this evening."

CHAPTER ELEVEN

There's a heaviness to Nathan today; Julia can sense it from the moment he steps into her shop. There are customers floating around between the shelves, picking up items to examine them before setting them back in other places. Julia knows this type of customer—the ones that are here to kill time as they wait for the rain to stop or the coach to arrive or the tide to fall. Knows they will leave without spending a penny.

She looks across the counter at Nathan. There's a new intensity to his blue eyes, and it makes her desperate to speak to him. But she knows she cannot do so with other people in the shop. At least, she cannot speak to him openly.

"Good afternoon, sir," she says to him brightly, avoiding Nathan's name in case Hugh, tucked away upstairs, should catch hold of it. "Feel free to look as you wish."

Nathan gives her a faint nod of understanding. "Thank you." He makes his way to the bookshelf, giving a wide berth to Minerva, who is stalking silently along the perimeter. He stands with his hands folded behind his back, eyes scanning the worn spines. He pulls out a title and flicks mindlessly through its pages.

Finally, the customers thank her and leave. Julia locks the door behind them. Nathan slides the book back onto the shelf as she comes close to him. She stops short of reaching for his hand as she longs to. She smells a faint hint of rosewater on him, and the cold, briny air.

"Are you safe?" he asks. "There's been no trouble from Holland?"

"No." Their voices seem to carry in the empty shop—carry all the way upstairs to where Hugh is hiding. Whatever Nathan has come here to say, Julia does not want her brother to hear it. She nods towards the cellar. "Down there," she whispers.

Nathan frowns. "Why?"

"Because it's safer. More private." Her voice comes out strained. The words sound too suspicious, or perhaps too intimate. She feels her cheeks colour violently. And she can't help darting a glance up towards the living quarters. She doesn't hear a sound from Hugh. But she knows he will be listening. If he has any sense that Nathan is here, he will try to catch a word from him, in an attempt to determine who the government spies might be. Julia will not give him the pleasure. Will not betray Nathan like that. At least not any more than she is betraying him already.

Nathan nods, not asking more questions. He follows her down the narrow stone staircase. Julia pushes open the door of the cellar and steps inside. She pulls the tinderbox from the pocket of her apron and lights the lamp. Orange light fills the space, falling over Hugh's bed in the centre of the room, blankets tossed messily across it. A look of confusion passes over Nathan's eyes.

"Is someone is staying down here?" he asks.

"I used to rent the room out to lodgers," says Julia. "For the extra money. I've not done it since the Rising began. Too dangerous." It's not a lie, she tells herself. Just a half-truth. But that does nothing to stop the tug of regret in her stomach. The room is too warm; smells cloying and inhabited. But Nathan says:

"I'm glad." He looks up to meet her eyes. "Why did you bring us down here now? You've never felt the need to do so before. And you've spoken to me about the Rising in the past."

Julia hesitates. "I'm coming to realise we need to be careful speaking of these things," she says. "Cordwell and Martin Macauley and the others that came to your house... They're fools, making their Jacobites sympathies so obvious, especially with the militia around. I'm sure it's only a matter of time before they'll be raiding houses and throwing people in prison like they're doing in Newcastle." She realises she is talking too quickly. These reasons, she supposes, are all valid. If not entirely the core truth of the matter.

Nathan nods.

"You did not come here just to ask about Holland, did you?" says Julia.

He sighs heavily. "No." He perches on the edge of the bed, curling his hands around his knees. "There's something I need to ask you. About the past."

And more of the story comes out. A lost letter; a privateer turned pirate; threats made against his family in the wake of his mother's betrayal of the Jacobites. More of the things

Nathan Blake has been carrying on his shoulders since long before he came to Lindisfarne, Julia sees now.

"A letter?" she says. "That's what you've been doing in the house?" She dares to sit beside him on the bed. Is relieved when he does not shift away. He turns to face her, his knees inches from hers. Lamplight flickers against his shorn cheeks. Makes his blue eyes shine.

"My secrets seem so foolish now," he says. "But when I decided to keep them, I truly thought it was for the best."

Julia smiles wryly to herself. She understands that more than he could know.

The telling of this story, she realises, it seems to be loosening something inside him. Because as he has been speaking, his hand has drifted from his thigh to her own curled fingers, resting on the bed between them. His thumb traces light circles over her knuckles. Energy flickers through her.

"This man, John Graveney, he seems determined to punish us for the damage our mother inflicted on the Jacobite cause," Nathan says.

"I can understand that. The Jacobites are passionate men and women. They fail and they keep coming back. And they do not let go of grudges. I can see why this Graveney would do such a thing, especially now, in the midst of the Rising." She meets his eyes. "Not that I wish him to succeed, of course."

Nathan nods slowly. "I don't suppose your family knows anything of this letter? Your parents were on the island the same time as mine. You never heard them speak of it?"

"I'm sorry, no. I was only seven when Ma died. And Da, well... if he knows anything, I'd be the last person to know.

I never heard him mention it when I was a child, and we barely speak these days. When Bobby arrived, he was so ashamed he left Holy Island to get away from me. I went to see him yesterday to tell him about Michael. Didn't even ask me inside."

"I'm sorry." The disappointment in Nathan's eyes is poorly hidden.

A creak at the top of the stairs makes Julia's chest tighten. Nathan's eyes pull towards the sound.

"Is someone in the shop?" He stands from the bed. Julia bounds awkwardly in front of him and pulls open the cellar door. She scrambles up the stairs ahead of Nathan.

The shop is quiet, but she can sense Hugh is here. Can feel him breathing beneath the faint shift and crackle of the fire. In any case, she would have heard his footsteps if he had attempted to go back upstairs. Nathan strides purposefully between the shelves; opens the side door to peer out into the alley. Julia looks over the counter. Sees her brother crouched on the floor like a naughty child. She glares at him; receives a mocking smile in return.

"There's no one here," she says, trying to keep her voice level. She hurries across the shop towards Nathan, steering him away from the counter. She opens the side door again, scooping up Minerva before she dashes out into the lane. Nathan follows her into the alley, eying the cat warily. Julia laughs a little. "It's just a cat, Nathan. Not the devil's spawn."

He looks down into Minerva's golden eyes. "One and the same, if you ask me." He shakes his head. "Forgive me. I'm sure that thing's very dear to you."

Julia smiles. "*That thing* is, yes." She shoulders open the door and tips the cat back into the shop. Minerva stalks away with her tail in the air.

Julia turns back to face him. He reaches out tentatively, his fingers brushing lightly against hers. Wind tears through the alley, lifting the dark waves of hair from his neck. "I ought to get back," he says.

Julia nods. "Thank you for telling me all that you did. And I'm sorry I couldn't help you."

Nathan steps closer, making her breath catch. He presses his palm to her cheek, his other hand wrapping around her wrist. His skin feels warm against her own.

Julia hears her rapid breath; feels her chest straining against her stays. He tugs her closer. But as his nose grazes hers, he releases his grip on her suddenly. Steps away. The distance between them feels cavernous.

Nathan squeezes his eyes closed, shaking his head at himself. "I'm sorry," he mumbles. "I'm so sorry."

Julia pushes away her disappointment. "It's all right," she says gently. "Of course it's all right."

He swallows. "Thank you for being so patient with me."

Julia nods; gives him a faint smile. All that Nathan Blake is carrying. She is not sure if she is adding to it or taking it away.

Nathan murmurs his goodbye and Julia steps back inside. Closes her eyes for a moment. Her heart is fast. Unease, fear, and something else entirely. She locks the door behind her. Turns to see Hugh leaning against the counter, hands on his hips, shirtsleeves rolled up over his broad freckled forearms.

"This letter you were speaking of," he says. "I may know something that could help you."

Julia's stomach tightens. She had assumed that, hidden in the cellar, her and Nathan's voices were low enough to not be heard. Her brother has clearly become a master at catching other people's conversations. Had he been standing on the stairs with an ear to the door?

"There are rumours among the English Jacobites about the dissenter in the Whig party," he says. "I've heard men speak about him at a meeting in the Rose Tavern in Bamburgh. If those rumours came about because of this letter, it may well still exist."

Julia folds her arms. "Those rumours could have come from anywhere. Especially if there's any truth to them. This letter was written twenty years ago."

"True. But it seems your dear Mr Blake is in quite a situation. Is it not worth following a lead, however hazy?"

Julia strides upstairs to the living quarters in a desperate attempt to get Hugh out of the shop before anyone— especially Nathan—sees him. He follows her upstairs and sinks into a chair at the rickety wooden table.

She sits opposite him, toying with a half-drunk mug of tea left to grow cold in the middle of the table. "Why should I believe a word you're telling me?"

Hugh stretches his long legs out in front of him. "Is that where we've ended up? At complete distrust?"

"Can you blame me?"

He smiles wryly. "I suppose not. But I'm telling the truth about this."

For a long time, Julia doesn't speak. She suddenly remembers she left the lamp burning in the cellar. "Why?" she presses. "Why would you do this? Why help Nathan? You've made it more than clear what you think of him."

"Because I can tell you care about him."

She feels her cheeks heat. "Somehow that makes me even

less likely to believe you."

Hugh leans back in his chair, surprise on his face, as though her words have struck him. Surely he cannot be surprised that there is little trust left between them. "I've never seen you like this around a man before," he says.

"Like what?" Her response comes out sharper than she intended.

He smiles, ignoring her brusqueness. "You let your guard down around him. As though for a moment, you realise you don't have to do everything under the sun all on your own."

Julia looks down. She hates that Hugh has seen all this. Hates it because it means he has been watching her and Nathan more closely than she realised. But she also hates it because she knows he is right. Ever since Bobby was born, she has carried an impossible weight on her shoulders. Not that she would change a moment with her son. But sometimes the strain of it is too much. There have been far too many nights that she has lain awake, doubting her ability to put a roof over her child's head. Far too many nights she has gone to bed hungry. Far too many nights when the fire has burnt out from lack of coal, her feet frozen inside wet stockings and shoes full of holes.

Since her father had cast her from his home; since Bobby was born and she had sworn to herself that she would make a good life for him, she has prided herself on her independence. But she cannot deny that sometimes, fleetingly, she wishes she had someone to share her troubles with. Someone who might ease the strain of this precarious, weighted life she has built.

It's ludicrous, of course, imagining herself up in Highfield House, building that life with Nathan. Nothing about the two of them align. He is rungs above her on the social ladder, and would surely support the king against the Jacobites if forced to make a choice. Besides, even now, with their distrust for one another fading and her heart and body alive for him, she is still keeping secrets that could turn him away from her forever.

But that does not stop her from wishing it. Or even daring to think it might be possible.

"Besides," Hugh goes on, "if I tell you what you wish to know about the letter, perhaps you might tell me what I want to know about the government spies."

This feels far more like the Hugh she knows. "I don't know who the government spies are," Julia snaps. "I already told you."

"You did." Hugh gives a short laugh. "But I know you're lying. I can only assume your Mr Blake knows who they are, given they were gallivanting around his house. And the two of you seem to be in the habit of sharing things with one another."

Julia says nothing. What her brother is asking—for her to betray Nathan's confidence by revealing Joseph Holland as a spy—is galling. But in a strange way, it makes her believe he might actually be telling the truth about the letter.

If they were to find the thing, against all odds, it would ease the strain on Nathan and his family. Get Henry Ward and his quartermaster out of their lives.

Julia wants desperately to trust her brother. But she knows that could turn out to be an enormous mistake.

"Do you really think me that kind of person?" Hugh says, as though reading her thoughts. "That I would deliberately put the man you care about in danger?"

"I do when that man is rumoured to be a government spy. You've made it perfectly clear what you think of him."

"Well." Hugh gets to his feet and takes the poker from up against the wall. He jabs at the dwindling fire in an attempt to coax it back to life. "In that case, I'm sorry. I didn't realise you saw me that way."

Julia gets to her feet. "I'm re-opening the shop," she says brusquely. "Don't come down there."

Hugh nods wordlessly. As she reaches the top of the stairs, he says, "They're meeting on Thursday at noon. The men I heard speak of the Whig dissenter. The Rose Tavern in Bamburgh. Perhaps they can tell you what you wish to know."

Julia doesn't reply, but his words keep circling through her head as she goes down to the cellar to blow out the lamp. As she returns to the shop and unlocks the front door. Minerva stalks silently out from between the shelves and Julia scoops her into her arms. She presses her cheek against the cat's silky fur.

She hates that she cannot trust her brother. But really, what else can be expected? They have always been a family of liars, of manipulators.

But was that genuineness in Hugh's eyes when he had promised he would not hurt Nathan? Would he truly lie and risk the safety of the man she has come to care for?

She desperately hopes the answer is no.

CHAPTER TWELVE

"Are you sure you'll be all right?" Finn asks, for at least the fifth time. He tosses the empty peat sacks into the boat, ready be filled by the farmers he is working for today. "I don't have to go, if you're unsure about being out here alone."

Eva stands on the jetty, shivering at a gust of icy wind. The sunrise is just peeking over the horizon, painting a corridor of gold light across the water. A thin line of smoke rises from the firebasket, its scent mingling with sea. "You do have to go," she says. "You've already told them you'll be there. Besides, we need to put food on the table." She looks at him pointedly. "Through honest means."

He grins. "I'd not dream of doing anything else."

Eva gives him a crooked smile. "I'm sure."

He holds up his hands in surrender. "I've not thieved so much as an apple in months," he says. "I swear it."

"Or a lump of coal?"

"Or a lump of coal."

She laces her hands through his and tugs him close. "In

that case, you'd best get on. You don't want to be late." If she is honest with herself, there's a part of her that's nervous about being alone on Longstone. It's unease at Ward's nearness, yes, but it's also unease wrought by the island's deep isolation. That sense of being hemmed in by sea, with just the birds, the seals, the fish for company.

But there is money to be made and their lives to live. Besides, what Ward would achieve by coming after her alone, Eva cannot fathom. The fear rooted inside her is for Finn's safety, not her own. She presses her cheek against his broad chest. Wraps her arms around his waist.

He looks down at her, and seems to catch something in her eyes. "Are you certain?" he asks again, a faint frown creasing his brow.

"Of course." She smiles, trying to force away her anxiousness. "Would you like to see me sail around the island once more, just so you can be absolutely, positively sure I can do it?"

He chuckles. "I trust you. As long as you feel comfortable taking the skiff out on your own if you need to leave for any reason." A sudden seriousness in his eyes. "If you see Ward's ship, get in the boat and go straight to your family's house. Or if you see anything else that makes you uncomfortable."

"I shall be fine," Eva assures him again. "Now go before you are late."

He tucks the edges of his scarf into his greatcoat then holds his lips to hers. "Get a little sleep."

Eva nods. With Finn off to work this morning, she had taken the watch since just after midnight, and her body is aching with tiredness. A few hours' sleep, she tells herself, then the day will be too full to spend any time or energy on thoughts of Ward and his crew. There's bread to make and bedsheets to wash, and water to be collected from the rainwater barrels behind the cottage. Then there is her needlework—mending and embroidery for mainlanders, met through the men on the farms. Doing her own part to put food on the table.

Earning coin with her own hands is strangely thrilling, she has realised. An upturning of her pre-emptively lived life in which her sole reason for being was producing Matthew Walton's children.

So yes, she tells herself again. Not a single moment to spend in fear of Henry Ward.

She stands on the jetty and watches as Finn pulls the longboat away from the island. Henry Ward's longboat, she thinks distantly. They had taken it from his ship the night he had tried to kill Finn. A few days ago, Finn had found it roped to the moorings at Lindisfarne, left there by Michael Mitchell on his way to re-join the rebel army.

Eva watches the boat disappear behind the scarps of the Pinnacles. She draws in a breath. Closes her eyes.

When she opens them, thick shards of sunlight are breaking through the clouds and turning the rockpools gold. And there is something magical about being alone on this island, she realises. As though she has opened her eyes to find herself in an otherworld. She finds herself walking the shallow crags of rock, peering into the pools to watch the miniature forests of green and yellow that dance in the low tide. Inhaling the sea salt and the tangible scent of cold. It feels almost as though she is experiencing it all for the first time.

Longstone is anything but silent. All around her is the constant lash of the sea, the chorus of birds and seals, the wind rattling the chain of the firebasket. And yet there's an impossible stillness here too; devoid of voices, of footsteps, of human breath beyond her own.

Twin feelings war inside her head: that she belongs out here in this cottage with Finn; and that the two of them have made their home in a place that was never meant for humanity. An intrusion in a wild place. To save lives—or is to atone for their own mistakes?

In the madness of the past weeks, Eva has barely had a chance to breathe, barely had a chance to look in detail at this life that has so unexpectedly become hers. She was never supposed to be a woman with callused hands and coal-streaked aprons, wearing soft and pliable jump stays that let her bend and crawl and haul firebaskets into the sky. Was never supposed to wear petticoats quilted against ocean air. And yet somehow, inexplicably, this is also exactly how she is supposed to be living. She longs to settle into this life without the threat of Ward and his crew. Longs to treasure this wild place without an undercurrent of fear.

The stillness is even more intense inside the cottage, with the sound of the sea muted. She rinses the breakfast plates in the trough, tucking them neatly away in the sideboard. Then she stumbles wearily into the bedroom. Unlaces her stays and climbs beneath the blankets Finn has left warm and rumpled.

Her mind races behind closed eyes. Because she can pretend all she likes that she and Finn are alone out here; that they have this island to themselves and the rest of the world is distant. But she knows it is all fantasy. Because not six miles away, Henry Ward's ship is lying at anchor, filled with men who wish to punish her family for her mother's crimes. Six days, Nathan had told her. Six days, and he will be forced to run. No—five days, with the rising dawn.

Eva gives up on sleep.

She slips out of bed and wraps the blanket around her shoulders. With her shift bunched up in one hand, she teeters barefoot across the rocks and stands at the edge of the island. She sees the first vessels of morning dotted across the leathery, sun-streaked ocean, and they bring a tug of unease. Herring boats, she tells herself. Nothing more.

"Enough," she says out loud. Because she cannot build a life out here if she is to panic at every boat on the sea. She cannot settle. Cannot treasure. She reaches down and picks up two loose fragments of rock that are glittering like onyx on the edge of the pool. She carries them inside and sets them on the mantel between the lamp and old quadrant. She returns to the bedroom, tugging her stockings on over frozen feet. Draws closed the curtains and tucks herself beneath the bedclothes, in an attempt to make her wild place feel safe.

CHAPTER THIRTEEN

Harriet had assumed Edwin lying when he said he was going to leave the letter for Ward, inviting him to the house. But here she and her husband are in the parlour, waiting for the knock at the door.

Harriet has no idea if this is just a game. She doubts Edwin wrote the note to her father. Doubts he left it at the tavern for Ward to collect. All too easy, she knows, for them to wait out the hour, and then for Edwin to blame Ward's absence on his reluctance, or his busyness, or his failure to collect the message.

They sit in silence, side by side on the settle. The clock on the mantel ticks away the seconds. Harriet smooths her skirts, deliberate in not looking Edwin's way.

"I thought we might talk about things moving forward," he says finally.

"I thought we were here to speak with my father." She turns to face him. "Is this where you tell me you never sent the message?"

113

She sees Edwin's jaw clench. "I sent the message, Harriet. I cannot be held responsible if your father decides not to come."

She folds her hands. Shoots a surreptitious glance at the clock. At least if her father does not show himself, she can blame Edwin. Convince herself he is lying when he says he delivered the message. It's a far easier prospect to swallow than the alternative: that her father might not wish to spend time in her company.

"Very well," she says bitterly. "Speak to me about things moving forward. Speak to me about the wonderful life we are going to have once we return to London."

Edwin sighs. "You'd rather we be angry and miserable for the rest of our lives? Is that the kind of home you want our son to grow up in?"

"You destroyed my artwork," Harriet snaps. "How can I be anything but miserable when you have taken away the one thing that is important to me?"

She sees Edwin flinch at her choice of words, but he chooses not to comment. "Well," he says after a long silence, "perhaps once you prove yourself trustworthy, things can change. I have no desire to make you unhappy. I just wish for you to show some responsibility."

Harriet says nothing. Just stares down into her clasped hands. The appeal is a reasonable one; some part of her can see that. But there is another part that is preventing her from being reasonable. Some part that wants to retaliate; to be as difficult as possible. Her husband makes her this way, she knows. If she is to be treated like a child, so she will act as one. Or is it the other way around?

When the knock at the door comes, she is so flooded with

relief she leaps instinctively to her feet. Edwin grabs her hand and tugs her back down to the settle. "Mrs Brodie will answer the door."

Harriet obeys—largely out of gratitude that Edwin had in fact delivered the message. It was not what she expected.

Her heart begins to pound when she hears her father's deep baritone in the entrance hall as he addresses the housekeeper. His footsteps echo down the hallway, growing louder as he approaches the parlour.

The door clicks open, and here is Henry Ward, hiding Mrs Brodie in his shadow.

Edwin stands. Offers him his hand. "Thank you for coming," he says, managing to sound remotely sincere. "My wife was very eager to speak with you."

Ward nods slowly, as though taking his time to determine the correct response to this. He eyes Edwin closely; shakes his hand with an expression that's impossible to read. Then, to Harriet's satisfaction, he turns away from her husband and looks squarely at her.

"Harriet." He nods in her direction. Lowers himself into the armchair.

She is disappointed, of course, at this sorry excuse for a greeting. Not that she has any intention of letting Edwin see that. She offers her father her most beatific smile. "Good morning. Thank you for coming." She has no idea how to address him. *Mr Ward* feels far too formal. *Father* feels impossible.

"Was there something in particular you wished to see me about?" Ward asks her.

"No," she admits. "I just... I rather hoped for the chance to speak with you. Get to know you a little better." She feels her cheeks flush. She can sense Edwin's eyes on her—and she is well aware she has never let him see this side of her before; this uncertain, needy side that craves validation. She can't bring herself to look at him.

Mrs Brodie reappears with a tea tray and sets it tentatively on the table. Her eyes dart to Ward, and Harriet can tell his presence has unsettled her. Is Mrs Brodie still shaken after the raid on the house? Or is it just the malaise of unease her father manages to inflict on people? She sets his teacup down on the side table beside the armchair and vanishes from the room.

Ward sits rigid in the chair, making no attempt at the tea. "Perhaps you might like to show me some of your work?" he says to Harriet. He clears his throat. "Your paintings?"

She feels a too-fleeting jolt of happiness. But, "I'm afraid I don't have any of my work here with me." She wonders if Ward can read the bone-breaking glare she gives to Edwin.

Her husband turns away from her cold eyes. Shifts uncomfortably.

"I've plenty of pieces in my workroom in London," Harriet presses on boldly. "When we return, I—"

"Nathan and I have made a number of changes to the house recently," Edwin cuts in. "I've replaced much of the old wainscoting here in the parlour. Painted a number of rooms. In addition to all the running repairs, of course. No doubt the place is quite different from what you remember."

What is he playing at? Harriet is sure the state of the house is the furthest thing from Henry Ward's mind. Edwin is keeping Ward away from their plans, she sees then. He does not want him to know they are planning to return to London. No doubt he fears Ward will alert his men. Send them after their family in a last desperate ploy for Abigail's letter.

She sips her tea with mildly trembling hands. She hates that Edwin has such distrust for her father. But really, what else can she expect?

"I see," Ward says thinly. "You must have some skills to have undertaken such a task yourself."

There's a difference to him today, Harriet notices. A difference from the bold, authoritative man he had been each time he had come to the house before. Each of those times, he had drawn everyone's attention. Turned heads. Incited fear.

Today, as he listens to Edwin rambling on about replacing cantilevers, Henry Ward does not feel bold and authoritative. At least, not to her. Today, he just feels like a normal man.

He is different, too, from the way he was when it was just the two of them alone in his cabin. He had seemed a little uncertain of himself then also—unbalanced by the discovery of her. But that day, she had at least had glimpses of genuineness. However fleeting and far between. But right now, the man her father really is has never felt so far away.

It's Edwin's presence, of course, that is changing things. Edwin, with his faux sincerity and rotting cantilevers. An irony, Harriet thinks, that her husband might conjure such unease in her father, rather than the other way around.

She had wanted to speak to Henry Ward again in the vain hope he might be more open with her. That he might let her beneath the surface and she might come to know who he really is. How hopeless that seems now.

She cannot force him to be more unguarded with her, of course. But she can be more unguarded with him. She can let him in, and hopefully encourage him to do the same. Even if that means letting Edwin see her for who she really is. Harriet pushes aside the dread that prospect brings her.

"I am very glad you're here," she blurts. "It means a lot to me."

A faint smile flickers on the edge of Ward's mouth, but it's an uncertain, transitory look.

"I would very much like to hear more about the time you spent with my mother," Harriet continues hopefully. "Did you come to the house a lot?"

Ward hesitates before speaking. Brings his teacup to his lips and takes a short sip. "As often as I could. My visits were sometimes months apart, thanks to my obligations during the war." He turns his gaze towards the window. "And your mother and I... I suppose we only really knew each other for a little under a year." He blows out a breath. Picks at the stitching on the arm of the chair. "I admit, it seems far longer."

Harriet smiles faintly. It pleases her that her mother might have made such an impact on her father. That Abigail Blake had proven impossible to forget.

Ward rubs a hand across his chin. His eyes have taken on a faraway look and Harriet wonders what he is thinking. Are his thoughts back in the past? In those months he had spent at Highfield House? Those months he had spent falling in love with her mother?

Harriet can see an ache in Ward's eyes. A reminder that whatever had once been between them, Abigail had fled the house so Henry Ward would not find out about his child. Harriet feels a faint satisfaction that they might be sitting here together; that she might be defying her mother like this. How might life have been different if she had grown up knowing her father?

Ward gets suddenly to his feet. "Forgive me," he says. "I shouldn't be here. I'm sorry."

"Don't be foolish," Harriet says desperately. "Of course you should be here. I…"

She gets to her feet, but he strides past her to the door of the parlour, making no more attempt at a farewell. Harriet turns hot eyes to Edwin, trying to manage a little rage at him. But as much as she tries to blame her husband for Henry Ward's leaving, she knows it's nothing more than hollow, misguided frustration.

———— ◈ ————

Nathan is in his office reading through the deeds of the house when he hears Julia's voice. She's in the entrance hall, speaking with Mrs Brodie. His heart pounds—did anyone see her approaching the manor? He pushes the thought away. Surely now the spies have ceased to use this place, it's of no matter if Julia is seen here. Maybe his heart is pounding for an entirely different reason.

Nathan is well aware that, although he had told Julia almost the entire story about his mother's letter and the threats of Ward and his crew, he had neglected to tell her of John Graveney's ultimatum. Neglected to tell her that in five days' time, there is every chance he will be forced to run from Holy Island, just as his mother was. There is every chance he might never see her again.

He had left out this part of the story on purpose. He does not want Julia to see this fledgling thing between them as something that is about to die. He wants her to see it as something that is just beginning.

That's how he wants to see it too. However naïve and foolish that makes him.

He steps out of his office and makes his way down the stairs.

A faint smile flickers on Julia's lips at the sight of him. She is wrapped in her threadbare cloak, a blue shawl bundled at her neck. She takes off her bonnet and squeezes it between her hands. Shakes her head politely at the housekeeper when she offers to take it away.

Nathan thanks Mrs Brodie, and nods for Julia to join him in the parlour. He closes the door behind them.

"I need you to not ask questions," Julia says, before he can speak. Her eyes are down, her voice low. She sets her bonnet on the tea table and reaches for his hand. Nathan has the sense that she is doing it to test his trust in her. He nods slightly, urging her to continue.

"The dissenter your mother's letter speaks about. Someone has told me there's word of him among the Jacobites in Bamburgh. I know it's the smallest of chances, but it's possible these rumours came about because of the letter."

At once, Nathan's mind is racing, questioning where this information has come from. And also whether he dares to believe it. "Was it your father who told you this?"

"My father? No. I told you, we barely speak."

Nathan nods. He has been unable to shake the possibility that Julia's father might know something about the letter. Elias Mitchell had been an active Jacobite in the years Abigail had apparently been stealing from the cause. A likely candidate for someone who might have information about the letter and its whereabouts. But he trusts that Julia is telling the truth about barely speaking to him. She has always been brutally up front about her broken relations with her father. Where else the information might have come from, Nathan does not dare think about. He is coming to realise that the best way to deal with Julia, and the chaos she causes within him, is to ask as few questions as possible.

"I'm told these men are meeting in the Rose Tavern in Bamburgh on Thursday," she says. "Perhaps it's worth asking them some questions."

Nathan turns the thought over in his mind. He wants this scrap of hope. Needs it. The end of the week is approaching far too rapidly. He begins to pace in front of the simmering hearth. "I'll not ask questions," he promises. "Just tell me one thing: is this information I can trust?"

"I believe so, aye."

His heart is quick; always, his heart is quick around Julia— a product of his feelings for her, and the way she pushes at the edges of his fear. But right now, it is fast because he wants to believe this. Wants the chance of a future in which he is not left penniless by his mother's mistakes.

He wants the chance of a future with Julia Mitchell in it.

"Thursday," he repeats. "The Rose Tavern." And he finds himself agreeing.

CHAPTER FOURTEEN

"Look at you," says Julia that afternoon. "Willingly climbing into my boat without a look of blatant dread on your face."

"Oh, the blatant dread is still very much there," says Nathan. "I've just learnt to suppress it somewhat."

She smiles. "What is it you hate about the sea so much?" she asks, as if the wind weren't howling hard enough to strip a forest bare.

Nathan focuses on the Longstone firebasket out ahead. In the whitewash of daylight, the unlit basket is just a shape in the cloud, solid against the wild roll of the water. Julia's question is a complicated one, because there are far more things he does hate about the sea than those he doesn't. Prime among them is that hideous somersaulting of his stomach, and a sense of giving up control. "I suppose I feel less vulnerable with my feet on solid ground," he admits. "Comes with being a Londoner, I suppose."

"But you're not a Londoner," she reminds him. "This is

where you come from."

"Yes. That's true." It's something Nathan barely acknowledges. He is not quite sure why. But he is dimly aware that he had not hated the sea as a child. He has faint memories of his father's fishing boat lying on the embankment outside Highfield House. Of being excited to scramble over the gunwale and watch the land grow distant. But Londoner or not, Nathan can't deny he feels far more comfortable without reams of ocean beneath him.

Julia's eyes glaze over as they approach the glistening crags of Longstone. "How is Harriet faring since Michael's death?" Her voice is suddenly soft.

"You've not spoken to her?"

Julia shakes her head, her face half hidden beneath the shadow of her bonnet. "It's petty of me, perhaps. But I'm not sure I could face her after... well... all that happened to my brother."

Nathan nods. He understands, though he is faintly regretful. He's sure Harriet would benefit from her friendship with Julia.

"She's... well, she's Harriet," he says uselessly. "To be honest, I often struggle to know what's going on in her head at all. But I'm sure she regrets what happened to Michael."

Julia nods. She eases the dory up against the Longstone jetty. The boat thuds softly into the worn wooden posts, and she winds the mooring ropes without speaking. Her eyes have darkened suddenly, as though her grief is once again fresh. The last time she had been out here, Nathan imagines, she had been coming to deliver the news of Michael's death to Angus. Coming to take him away to the mainland and send him off to London.

"I'm sorry," he says. "I shouldn't have asked you to bring me out here. I'm sure the place reminds you terribly of your brothers."

She gives him a small smile. "It's all right. I suspect you wouldn't have made it far without me."

He gives a gentle laugh. "Of that I can assure you." He clambers awkwardly from the boat and teeters across the slippery rock of the island.

Before they can make it up the front stairs, the door swings open and Eva steps out. She is without shoes, her hair hanging in a messy plait down her back, and her dark blue skirts streaked with flour that has escaped the confines of her apron.

Her eyes dart between Nathan and Julia. He can tell she is surprised to see them together. "Has something happened?" she asks. "I can only guess you'd not be jumping in a boat for a social call, Nathan."

He gives her a thin smile. "Everything is all right. Well. It's as good as can be expected. Given the circumstances."

Eva holds open the door as they make their way up the stairs and into the cottage. She eyes Julia with a mix of curiosity and wariness.

The house is warm, and fragrant with the smell of baking bread and woodsmoke. Wind whistles under the door, and makes the window frames creak. Eva has coated the entire table, and much of the floor in flour, a trail of white footprints leading to and from the door. A bread loaf sits cooling on a rack atop the sideboard, oddly shaped, but golden brown, and would smell delicious, if he didn't feel like he was about to lose his breakfast. Nathan glances around the tiny living space: navigation tools and rocks on the mantel, what looks to be a small net of some sort bundled into a corner. Kettle and cooking pot sitting on the hearth. He realises he is fascinated by this abrupt turn his sister's life has taken.

"Where is your husband?" he asks.

Eva reaches for a cloth and attempts to dust the flour from the table. "He has a day's farm work in Bamburgh. He'll be back this evening."

Nathan takes a step back to avoid the cloud of flour that is fluttering onto the floorboards. "I don't know how I feel about you being out here alone."

"It's a good thing you don't have a say in the matter then, isn't it."

He sees Julia cover a smile.

"There's no need to worry," says Eva. "If anything happens and I need to leave, I can manage the skiff on my own. Finn has made sure of that. Repeatedly."

"I see." Nathan pulls out a chair and wipes the flour off the seat before lowering himself onto it. Julia stays hovering a few yards back from the table.

"I've information on Mother's letter," Nathan says.

Eva's dark eyebrows rise. "What information?" The look she shoots Julia is more than a little suspicious.

Julia presses her lips into a thin line. "I shall be outside," she says. Before Nathan can protest, she throws open the door and disappears down the stairs.

Nathan turns to his sister. "Really?"

"I didn't say a word. She left of her own accord."

He shifts uncomfortably. "Make us some tea, will you? My stomach is rolling."

Eva takes the kettle from the hearth and hangs it on the hook above the fire. She turns back to face him. "What information do you have?"

Nathan hesitates. Is he being foolish by repeating what Julia told him about the letter? By allowing himself to believe it? Believe in her? Really, what choice does he have? They've gone far beyond the beginning of desperation.

More to the point, is he really going to let this hideous journey out here be for nothing? If he was going to have doubts, he might have had them before he left dry land.

He tells Eva. The talk of the dissenter. The meeting at the tavern in Bamburgh. He is dimly aware he is keeping his gaze turned downward, refusing to look her in the eye.

Eva goes to the sideboard and pulls out the teapot and tea tin. Nathan can practically see her thoughts whirring as she spoons the leaves into the pot. "This information came from Julia?"

"Yes."

"Then I—"

"I know what you're about to say," he cuts in. "But what choice do we have other than to trust her?"

Eva takes the kettle from the hook and fills the teapot. "Who told her?" she asks finally.

"I don't know," Nathan admits. "She wouldn't say."

Eva lets out her breath. "I am trying to trust her, Nathan," she says tautly. "For your sake. I really am. But she does not make it easy."

"I know," he admits. "But do you not think this is worth following up on? If it could put an end to all our trouble…"

"And what if it's a trap?" Eva demands, setting the kettle back on the hearth. "What if she's sending you into the path of more Jacobites who want to punish you for letting the government spies use the house?"

"Cordwell and Macauley found nothing. I've no reason to believe the Jacobites will be after us. Their failed raid on the house may well be the best thing that could have happened for us."

Eva sighs. She fills two cups and sets one in front of him. "You are going to go anyway, aren't you."

"Three cups," Nathan says tautly. He glances out the window at Julia, who is leaning up against the posts of the jetty, her eyes turned out to sea. Wind is blowing her cloak out behind her like a wave. "If you're going to cast her out of your house, the least you can do is offer her a cup of tea."

Eva sits and folds her hands in front of her on the table. Nathan can tell the third cup of tea is not going to be forthcoming.

"I am going to go anyway," he tells her. "I just thought you ought to know about this." He sips his tea. It's weak and tastes vaguely salty. Cheap stuff smuggled over from Guernsey, he guesses. He's seen it sold at Bamburgh market for pennies. "And I rather... Well... I hoped I might convince Finn to come with us."

Eva gives him hard eyes. "If you are so certain this is not a trap, why do you want Finn to go with you?"

He falters. Really, he had wondered that himself when he had asked Julia to bring him out here today. Had wondered that as he had watched Longstone emerge from the cloud. Had cursed himself for that faint doubt of Julia he is unable to wash away.

After Sarah had died, Nathan had not for a moment imagined ever finding someone else. As far as he was concerned, Sarah had been the only woman he would ever feel comfortable being around. The only woman he would ever want. Now she was gone, Theodora would be his everything. All he needed.

But he cannot deny those thoughts have changed since Julia has come into his life. He has fallen for her. Hard. He knows there is no point denying it, at least to himself. Perhaps he had fallen for her the moment he had first stepped into her curiosity shop and seen her bright smile light the shadows of the island.

But even beneath these most astounding of feelings, is that uncertainty he cannot break. Heaven knows he has tried hard enough. He knows he and Julia can have no future together if he cannot manage complete trust.

He has done his best to silence his doubt. To convince himself that asking Finn to come to Bamburgh is merely a matter of wanting extra support—rather than an extra pair of eyes on Julia. And a way of getting that support without being forced to asked Edwin, who will only berate him for his foolishness and tell him to pack his bags for London.

"These are unsettled times," he tells Eva, hoping he sounds somewhat convincing. "Safety in numbers and all that. Besides, I'm sure Finn is just as eager to be rid of Ward as I am."

"Why do you say that?" she asks defensively.

Nathan raises his eyebrows. "Are we not all eager to be rid of him?"

Eva sips her tea. She wraps her hands around the cup, as though trying to steady herself through its warmth. "I shall pass on your request," she says finally. "And I'm sure Finn will be happy to help you." She looks pointedly at Nathan over the rim of her cup. "But I'm coming too."

CHAPTER FIFTEEN

Traipsing out to Bamburgh to pick up the traces of a twenty-year-old piece of correspondence feels like a fool's errand. A thing of deep desperation. But that's where they're at now, isn't it? Deep desperation?

Besides, Finn is well aware of the whisper at the back of his mind—and, these days, more often at the front of his mind—that tells him he owes a debt to Nathan Blake for taking his brother. And—perhaps equally as unforgiveable in Nathan's mind—his sister.

Finn is still furious at Ward for refusing to fight John Graveney. If Ward was willing to take up arms and confront the men who are threatening his captaincy, they would all be free of this mess. Abigail Blake's letter could be packed off to the past—and so could Henry Ward, and all he represents. Finn knows the memories of his childhood on Ward's ship will never disappear completely. But surely they'll be less potent with his former captain gone.

Ward is more of a coward than Finn remembers. Has he

always been like this? Has time and age weakened him? Or had Finn just idolised him so much as a child he'd been blind to his flaws? Seen him as a hero he was not?

Here they are in this shuddery rented wagon, with the sea rolling past on their left and the grey-stone maze of Bamburgh peeking over the horizon. Finn has taken up the reins, if for no other reason than to put Eva in the box seat beside him and stop her so obviously spouting her distrust of Julia Mitchell.

She glances over her shoulder to peek at Nathan and Julia inside the wagon. "What do you suppose they're talking about?"

"Well." He lowers his voice and leans in conspiratorially. "I'm fairly certain I heard her ask him if he thought it was going to rain. Can hardly believe the nerve of that lass."

Eva looks at him witheringly. "I'm glad you find all this amusing."

He laughs.

"Do you trust her?" she asks.

Finn smiles to himself. He's answered this question at least ten times. "She's given me no reason not to."

"Well, I suppose it was not your house she was hiding her brothers in."

"Aye, it was. I remember bloody Angus draining the last of my moonshine. On more than one occasion."

She laughs a little. "You know what I mean."

"What are you afraid she's going to do?" asks Finn, tugging on the reins to slow the horse as the path veers down a mud-caked hill. "All we're doing is asking a few questions. Questions I think we all know are going to come to nought."

Eva shoots another quick glance over her shoulder. "But

where did the information about the letter come from in the first place? How are we expected to trust her if she cannot be honest with us?" She sighs. "I suppose I'm just worried about Nathan. He's been through so much. And for him to feel this way about someone, it is such a rare thing. It's taken him an age to trust her. If it turns out she's deceiving him, I cannot bear to think what it will do to him."

"Maybe the fact that he's taken an age to trust her means he's finally decided she's trustworthy," says Finn. "Your brother doesn't seem like the kind of man to leap into things without thinking."

Eva sighs. "I suppose you're right." She sounds more than a little begrudging.

He grins. Nudges her knee with his. "In that case, you might want to make your distrust for her a little less obvious."

The tavern Julia has directed them to is a dubious-looking place on the fringe of the anchorage, all dark windows and low awnings, and stone walls thick enough to keep secrets. Finn has heard of the place of course—the lads he works with on the farms are full of stories about the moonshine here that'll blow your head clean off—but he has always stayed away. Gunpowder moonshine or not, the Rose is known to be a Jacobite tavern, and the last thing he needs is to be caught here by the redcoats and locked up on suspicion of treason.

Julia climbs out of the wagon as Finn is tying the horse to a hitching post a safe distance from the building. Nathan follows close behind her.

"I ought to be the one to go inside," Julia says. "I can ask the barkeep if he knows anything of the letter."

"No." Nathan leaps in before Eva can get out whatever

distrustful words Finn can see hovering on her lips. "Absolutely not. I did not intend for you to put yourself in danger on my account."

"There's nothing dangerous about asking a few questions. Besides," she lowers her eyes, "my family are known Jacobites. The barkeep will trust me."

"I'm coming with you, at least."

"Nathan." She looks at him pointedly. "They'll trust me. And they won't trust you. Everyone on Holy Island knows who you are. There's every chance you could be recognised here in Bamburgh too. Do you really think they'll take it well if you're seen to be asking about Jacobite secrets?" She buttons her cloak and pulls the hood up over her fiery hair. "The rest of you stay out here and keep watch for the army. And mind the wagon. I'm sure there are a few people inside who'd like to make off with a fine-looking horse like that one. Heard there's been a lot of thieving out this way lately."

Eva flashes Finn wide, desperate eyes. He can read the meaning in them: that there is no way in hell she trusts Julia enough to let her go off and ask questions on behalf of their family.

"I'll go with you," he says.

Julia presses her lips together and Finn knows she has caught on to his and Eva's wordless conversation. "Fine." She doesn't bother to protest.

Finn follows Julia towards the tavern, past a bank of old wooden houses that seem to be holding each other up.

"You shouldn't be here either," she says, not looking at him. "The people on Lindisfarne like to gossip. If any of them are here, they'll know you're married to one of the Blakes."

Finn sidesteps a mound of horse dung on the edge of the

road. "I'll keep my distance. But Nathan's right—it's dangerous for you to be visiting the place on your own."

Julia snorts. "I'd thank you for your chivalry if it weren't so obvious your wife put you up to this."

Finn chuckles. "Eva's just concerned about her brother is all. She doesn't want to see him get hurt."

"Well, you can tell her that hurting Nathan is the last thing in the world I wish to do." Her voice wavers slightly, and Finn hears a deep sincerity.

"All right," he says. "Let's get in and out of here as quick as we can, aye? I don't fancy being here when the redcoats next pay this place a visit."

Julia nods. Shoves open the door. "Wait a minute before you follow me."

Finn watches through the grimy window as she makes her way into the tavern. Waits a moment before stepping inside.

The tavern is almost empty, with a few men clustered around a half-baked fire and a bored-looking young woman wiping out cups on the other side of the bar. The air is thick with the smell of woodsmoke and old, soured ale. Surely no place to collect information on a letter from the long-dead past.

Julia approaches the counter and speaks to the young woman. The woman nods, gestures to someone unseen. An older man shuffles in from another room. Julia leans over the bar to speak with him.

Finn takes a step closer, hoping to catch a piece of their conversation. He doesn't trust Julia Mitchell either, he realises. At least, not entirely. He can't tell if it's instinct, or if Eva has just gotten in his head.

He cannot hear what Julia is saying, but he sees her face

fall. Sees her mouth a dejected thanks.

She sidles away from the bar. "The barkeep doesn't know anything of the letter," she murmurs. "But we ought to wait a while. The men I'm hoping to speak to, they ought to be here soon."

"How d'you know that?"

She doesn't answer. "Stay out of my way," she says, eyes darting towards the door as it creaks open, letting in two old men in tarred greatcoats. "If anyone recognises you as Eva's husband, they'll likely tell these people to keep their mouths shut."

Nathan can't see much from inside the wagon. The windows of the tavern are far too small and grimy to see through, and the wagon is too far away. Probably for the best, he tells himself. He is not sure he wants to watch Julia at work among the Jacobites. He is too nervous about her safety, he tells himself. Nothing more.

"All right." He slides out of the wagon and looks up at Eva. "Given you insisted on being here, you can come with me."

"Where are we going?"

He hesitates. "There's someone we need to speak to."

"I thought we were here to keep watch."

"We'll not be long. And this is very important. It could give us more of a lead on the letter than these men at the tavern."

Eva's eyes dart towards the crooked stone building. "What about the horse? Julia said there were thieves around."

"We shall have to take our chances. I'm not leaving you here alone."

He starts walking in the hope that Eva will follow. And that she won't prod at his ridiculously vague explanation of what they are doing. Of course, he has no such luck. She is full of questions Nathan responds to with stilted silence, until he steps into the post house and asks after the man he is seeking.

"Elias Mitchell?" Eva hisses, once Nathan has gathered directions to the man's house and emerged back onto the street where she is waiting. "Julia's father? Does she know you're planning to pay him a visit?"

"Of course not. She barely speaks to the man." Nathan keeps his head down, voice low. Shame prevents him from speaking any louder. He can't bring himself to look at Eva.

"So you are keeping things from her," she says. "Is that because you believe she is still keeping things from you?"

Nathan quickens his pace, irritated. "She's not keeping anything from me. And I'm only keeping this from her because I know things are difficult between her and her father. She'd not appreciate me speaking to him. But I need to. Elias Mitchell was part of the Jacobite movement when Mother was involved with them. There's a chance he may know something about the letter."

"I see." Eva nods.

Nathan raises his eyebrows. "Do I take it you actually think this a decent idea?"

She shrugs. "You've certainly had worse."

Nathan follows the directions he was given through the winding streets of Bamburgh. He feels horribly on edge as his footsteps clatter against the cobbles, past a boarded-up shopfront and a blood-splattered pillory. He knows this to be a Jacobite town, much of the land owned by Thomas Forster, a Jacobite commander. Knows the redcoats have had their eyes on the place since the Rising began.

He wonders, sometimes, how all this happened. Six months ago, he had been a flailing watch merchant, with nothing more interesting in his days than his sorry failures in his business. Sometimes this all feels as though he has stepped into someone else's life by mistake.

And yet, at the same time, buried deep, there's a distant sense of coming home. A home that is anything but easy. These months he has spent on Lindisfarne, breathing briny air and looking at the stars, have reminded him that this place, so long forgotten, has always been a part of him. Buried deep, yes. But perhaps beginning to make its way towards the surface.

He has seen it in Eva's eyes; that look that says, against all odds, that this is where she belongs. He wonders if there has ever been such a look in his own eyes. Is he carrying these same thoughts, so well hidden he can barely make them out? After all, he and Eva were born Northumbrian children, their nursery windows speckled with German Ocean salt. Is it so surprising they feel drawn back to the place?

There is more to it, of course. Because Nathan knows it is love that has made Eva plant her feet back in Northumbrian soil. And there's a part of him that's afraid he might be drawn here for the very same reason.

Either way, the thought of leaving—of being forced from Lindisfarne, just as his mother was—makes something ache inside him. When he had first been dragged up here by Henry Ward, all he wanted was to return to London. Thoughts of escape had never been far from his mind. But now, the thought leaves him feeling hollow. He knows how much Theodora loves it here, and in spite of everything, there's a part of him that comes alive when he steps out into the cold air of Emmanuel Head. A part of him that wants to spend his life peering at stars and auroras in the clear skies of Lindisfarne, unimpeded by London smog.

It's so unexpected he can barely wrap his mind around it.

He has still not said anything to Julia about his leaving. Doing so will make it too real. But he is well aware they are nearly out of time. The day after tomorrow, John Graveney and his men will be at the door. Leaving feels at once both inevitable and impossible.

Elias Mitchell's cottage is a grey and tilted stone hovel, a sea of brambles keeping visitors from the door. It's a sad and sagging place—or perhaps just made that way by Nathan's knowledge of Mitchell's family: one child lost forever, a daughter disowned, two sons gifted to the rebel army. Nathan feels a pang of regret. Mitchell has already lost so much to the Jacobite movement; surely he'll not help the children of the woman who had stolen from their cause—especially so soon after Michael's death.

But he has come this far. Risked this much. There is little point leaving now.

He steps onto the path, leaving Eva hovering beside the low stone fence. She wraps herself in her cloak.

"You go ahead and speak with him. I'll keep watch."

Nathan nods. He can tell she is reluctant to hear any more brutal truths about who their mother was. He is reluctant to do so too. But he knows it cannot be avoided.

Brambles on the edge of the path snag on his coat and breeches as he fights his way to the door. He knocks firmly. Footsteps sound through the house and the door swings open.

The man that stands in front of him is sharp-eyed and tall, with sallow cheeks beneath a fog of grey stubble. Nathan sees hints of Julia in his green eyes and pale, freckled skin, but there's a rigidity to him that is far removed from his daughter's brightness.

He puts a thick arm out across the doorway, as if to prevent Nathan from stepping inside. "Yes?" He looks him up and down.

Nathan swallows. "My name is Nathan Blake. My mother was Abigail Blake." He sees something pass across Mitchell's eyes.

"I don't think I want anything to do with the son of Abigail Blake."

"Why not?" he dares to ask. He knows the answer, of course. But he wants to hear it from the man's mouth. Needs confirmation that Henry Ward was not speaking in lies.

"Because your mother was a thief and a liar."

Expected or not, the words still strike a blow.

"I'm sorry for what my mother did," Nathan says. "I've only recently learnt of it. And now my family is in trouble because of her crimes."

Mitchell scratches his bristly chin. "Is that so?" His expression is unreadable.

"I wondered if you ever heard my mother speak of a letter," Nathan tries. Even as he speaks, he knows there is little point. Elias Mitchell had thrown his daughter into the street with a child growing inside her. He is clearly not a man prone to sympathy.

"Never heard her speak of a letter," he says brusquely. "But even if she did, I'd know better than to believe her."

Finn sits in the corner of the tavern, an untouched glass of ale on the table in front of him. From where he's sitting, he can see Julia pacing up and down in front of the bar. She has her gaze pinned to the door. Looks painfully obvious. Finn wants to tell her to at least buy herself a drink and stop looking so damn suspicious, but he knows she'll not welcome his intrusion. At least he can tell Eva that Julia is so terrible at this whole business, there's bugger all chance she's a Jacobite spy.

At a table a few yards away, pieces of conversation catch his attention: *treasure fleet* and *lost gold* and *New World*. He can't help being drawn to these stories of the sea. His years on the *Eagle* have left a deep-rooted mark upon him, in more ways than one. Not, of course, that he has any desire to climb aboard a ship again—least of all, Henry Ward's. That simple life beneath the Longstone light, that life he had once done everything to escape, is now the only existence he wants. Nonetheless, he can't help but be intrigued.

He slides onto the empty stool at the table the stories had flown from. Three men are sitting around it, capped heads bent towards each other. "This true?" he asks. "A treasure fleet's gone down?"

One man turns and scowls at the interruption. But another says, "So I hear." He chuckles. "Why? You thinking of going after it?"

Finn smiles thinly. "Nah. Just curious."

"Two Spanish fleets went down in a hurricane off the coast of Florida over the summer. More than a thousand dead. They was taking their gold and silver back to Spain. Now it's lying in the water, there for the taking. They say it's just washing up on the beaches. Anyone with two oars and a piece of driftwood is heading over there to see what they can find."

The door creaks open as the man speaks. Once, twice, three times. The tavern is filling slowly, Finn realises. Men in tartans. Men with Jacobite cockades pinned to their caps. Old men, mostly, a woman or two among them, the men of fighting age all off marching with the rebel army. Julia's eyes dart. Have the men she's been waiting for arrived? Does she even know who they are?

She makes her way to a cluster of people in the corner of the tavern. Finn keeps one eye on her, but can't help focusing on what the men at the table are telling him. *Lost treasure fleet* and *washing up on the beaches* has caused his mind to race. Because the wealth from these Spanish treasure ships, well that would surely outweigh whatever paltry sum the sale of a ruin like Highfield House would fetch.

"Army!" shouts a man at the window. Yells and thuds as people scramble to their feet. Stools thump to the ground, tin cups bouncing across the flagstones.

The door cracks open and soldiers charge inside. Four men; no, five. More outside, perhaps. Finn hears the crack of a pistol. Feels wood shards against his cheek as the bullet lodges in the rafters above his head. Gunpowder burns the air.

He grabs Julia's elbow and tugs her towards the door.

Keeping to the edges of the tavern, he clambers over fallen chairs. Spills into the street with a tangle of men around him. He runs towards the wagon, looking over his shoulder to make sure Julia is following. He hears a window breaking inside the tavern. Hears a woman scream.

He lurches forward, panic jolting through him when he finds the wagon empty. The horse is thrashing against the hitching post, spooked by the sound of gunfire. Finn grapples with the reins, pressing a hand to the horse's neck in a desperate attempt to calm it.

He hears Eva call his name. She and Nathan burst from the tangle of streets and race towards the wagon.

"Where have you been?" Julia presses.

"We—"

"Militiamen were watching us," Nathan cuts in. "We thought it best to leave."

The look on Eva's face tells Finn her brother is lying. He doesn't push the issue. Not now, with bullets flying across the tavern. He scrambles into the box seat, reaching out a hand to help Eva up. She'll tell him where they've been later, he knows, once they're tucked away on Longstone and the rest of the world has fallen aside. And as for Nathan's reasons for lying to Julia, Finn is fairly sure that the less he knows, the better.

CHAPTER SIXTEEN

Julia finds Hugh in the cellar, dozing on the bed with his legs dangling off the mattress and one arm folded beneath his head. The room is hot, the air thick with the smell of her brother's pipe smoke and sweat. She yanks the blankets off him and shoves his shoulder hard. Hugh murmurs with shock as his eyes fly open.

"What in hell, Julia?"

"Get out," she demands.

He sits up, rubbing his eyes. "What?"

"I said, get out." This time, she will not let herself be swayed by him. This time, her anger is so vivid, so all-consuming that it washes away everything else her brother has done for her.

"Where exactly would you like me to go?" he asks, an amused smile flickering on his lips.

"I don't care. I don't want you here. I can't even look at you after what you did." She hears her voice rattle with emotion.

The amusement disappears from his eyes. "What are you on about?"

"Don't, Hugh. I've had enough of these games."

The bed creaks as he stands. He rubs blearily at his face. "I honestly don't know what you're talking about."

Julia closes her eyes. No. She won't let herself believe him. Won't let herself fall for this.

"Jul?" he says. "Is everything all right? Are you in danger?"

And that concern in his voice, it's so real, she finds herself saying, "I went to the Rose Tavern with Nathan today. At the very time you told me to go. Just as the redcoats turned up."

Something flickers across Hugh's eyes. "I hoped you wouldn't go with him."

"Why?" Julia hisses. "Because you led him into a trap? Because you hoped the redcoats would catch him?"

"Because it was dangerous," Hugh says tautly. "Can you really be surprised the army was watching? Bamburgh is a Jacobite town." He shakes his head. "Surely you can't be so naïve as to think that was my doing. How could I possibly know when the redcoats would turn up?"

"I don't know," she snaps. "I've no idea what you're involved in. I'd not put anything past you."

Hugh chuckles humourlessly. Shakes his head.

Julia had been terrified to climb back into the wagon with Nathan after the army had stormed the tavern. He would blame her, surely. Would demand to know where the information about the Rose Tavern had come from. Demand to know why she had led them into danger. And then things would fall, and splinter, and crumble beyond repair.

"I didn't know the army was going to show themselves," she had said, unable to look him in the eye. "I swear it."

"Of course you didn't. How could you?" Nathan reached across the bench seat and pressed a hand against her clasped fist, forcing her to look at him. "This was always going to be risky. That's why I did not want you to go in there in the first place. I'm just glad you're safe."

His words, Julia thinks now, they're so similar to Hugh's. Perhaps she is being unreasonable, blaming her brother for the army's appearance. But she'll not allow herself to be blinded by his games. Because at the back of her mind is the unsettling knowledge that Hugh has it in him to hurt others. He had pulled the trigger on a soldier—and who knows what else he has done?

Once, Hugh had been compassionate and kind. A loving husband and father. A loving brother. But with his wife and child in the earth, he has changed. His passion for this cause has taken over his decency.

Julia knows that in Hugh's eyes, he is doing nothing but good. Acting with honour to see the God-divined king upon the throne. And she fears that, for all his words about not putting the man she cares for in danger, he would not hesitate to put a bullet in Nathan's chest if he believed he was hampering the Jacobite cause. Would not hesitate to throw him into the path of the redcoats.

The knot in her stomach grows tighter. She ought to tell Nathan that Hugh is here. But all she can think about is how much will topple if she does so.

For the first time in her life, she is beginning to glimpse a future with a man, rather than just a half-remembered night of shame. She knows Nathan's trust in her is still flimsy; surely if he is to find out Hugh is here—that he has overheard his secrets, and that he is pressuring her for information on who the government spies are—it will shatter that trust for good.

"I had no idea the army was going to storm the tavern today," Hugh says. He sits back on the bed and reaches down to pull on his boots. "I'm your brother, Julia. I'd never put you in danger like that."

"But you would put someone in danger if they were suspected of spying for the government. Like Nathan Blake."

He holds her gaze. "Jul. I would *never* put you in danger. Even if you were gallivanting around the place with that dandy. I told you about the letter because I wanted to help him. Because I can tell how much he means to you."

She snorts. "You told me about the letter because you hoped I'd tell you who the government spies are."

"Well. That too." The smile returns to his lips. "You can't blame me for trying."

CHAPTER SEVENTEEN

Wrecked ships, sunken treasure, Floridian beaches glittering with gold.

Finn has slept little tonight, thoughts of what he learnt at the tavern circling through his head. He lies in bed in shifting darkness, the glow of the firebasket through the shutters painting stripes of orange light across the floor. He rolls onto Eva's side of the bed, soaking up the warmth she has left beneath the blankets.

He knows better than to believe these stories at face value. But if they are true, if these Spanish treasure ships really have gone down with their wealth littering the beaches, this is a precious piece of knowledge.

Even the smallest cut of such a haul would give Graveney and his supporters far more than they would gain from taking Highfield House from Nathan. And make a far better substitute for the immunity Ward has promised his crew.

Before he and Eva had returned to Longstone tonight, Finn had scrawled a note to Henry Ward; deposited it in the

Lindisfarne tavern. Instructions for him to meet him there at noon tomorrow. He hopes he's not too late. He is well aware that tomorrow is Friday. Well aware that Nathan Blake is running out of time.

Finn slides out of bed, giving up on sleep. He is to take the watch in a few hours anyway, and would rather spend the night in Eva's company than tossing and turning in the darkness. When he steps out into the living area, he finds her at the table in a pool of lamplight, her dark head bent over her sewing. He watches her wordlessly for several moments, her needle darting in and out of the fabric, fingers flying. The floor creaks beneath him and she turns in surprise.

"What are you doing awake?" she asks. "It's barely midnight. I can stay up for a few more hours."

He makes his way over to her; wraps his arms around her from behind and presses his head into her neck. "I think I've slept all I'm going to tonight."

She reaches a hand up behind her to brush her fingers through his tangled brown hair. She holds up the shirt she is hemming. "Look how crooked this stitching is. Hope the fellow who owns it has poor eyesight."

Finn squints. It looks as straight as an arrow to him. "You're tired," he says, planting a kiss below her ear. "Rest."

Eva ties off her sewing and puts the shirt down on the table in front of her, but continues toying with a loose piece of thread. Finn uncorks the whisky bottle on the sideboard and sloshes a sizeable gulp into her teacup.

She smiles up at him. "I'm not sure that will help my crooked sewing."

"Probably not," he agrees. "But might help you relax a little."

"Mmm." She sounds unconvinced.

Finn nods at the cup. "Drink up." She takes an obedient mouthful.

He goes to the table and breaks a chunk from the bread loaf. Eats it at the window, looking out across the dark sea.

"Anyone there?" Eva asks edgily.

"Dark water. Seems even the herring fishermen are staying away." He wonders how many times tonight she has gone to the window to look for Ward's ship.

Finn turns away from the glass. He slides onto a chair at the table, deliberate in blocking Eva's view out the window. He stretches his legs out in front of him. "Where'd you and Nathan really go today?"

Eva takes another sip of her tea. "To speak with Elias Mitchell."

"Julia's father?"

"Estranged father," she says with a wry smile.

Finn chuckles. "I can see why Nathan dished out that load of rubbish about the militia."

"He hoped Mitchell might be able to tell us something about Mother's letter. Given he was active in the Jacobite cause when she was... well, involved with them."

"And?"

She shakes her head. "Nothing of any use. Just confirmation that Ward was telling the truth about everything Mother did." There's a heaviness to her voice. Finn presses a hand to her knee and squeezes gently.

"I so desperately wish I could speak to her," Eva murmurs. "Ask her why she did what she did. Ask her what really happened the night we fled."

Finn raises his eyebrows. "You don't think she fled

because of Ward? Because she didn't want him to find out about Harriet?"

She fiddles with the hem of her sewing. "We left in the middle of the night. Why would she have done that? It does not make sense. There has to be more to it."

"Maybe Ward arrived unexpectedly," Finn suggests. "Maybe she saw him coming to the house and had no choice but to run before he found her. Maybe she worried that if he saw her, he'd know she was carrying his child."

Eva sighs. "Perhaps you're right. But there's no way we'll ever know for sure. I have to make peace with that." She looks past him, straining to see through the window.

It's doing her no good being out here, Finn can tell. He's sure she's thinking of nothing but Henry Ward and his connection to her family.

There's a part of him that wants to whisk her away from the island; take her someplace without an uninterrupted view of sea. But do that, and this uninterrupted view of sea turns dark. A treacherous passage of water likely to become a graveyard—and Finn knows neither he nor Eva could live with that on their conscience.

"These treasure ships," she says suddenly. "Do you really think they'll be enough to tempt Ward and Graveney away from Highfield House?"

"I don't know," Finn admits. "I hope so." He regrets telling her about the treasure ships; about his plan to meet Ward in the tavern tomorrow. He had done so in an attempt to give her a little hope and optimism. But he can tell it's just given her more to dwell on.

He reaches out and tucks a loose strand of hair behind her ear. "Get some sleep, Evie. Forget about Ward for a while. I can manage out here."

She hesitates. Looks out at the window again. "You'll tell me if you see anything out there?"

"If I see anything important, aye. But you need to rest. You've hardly slept in days."

She nods, getting wearily to her feet. "All right." She bends to kiss his lips and Finn feels a tug of desire. Considers tumbling her into the bedroom and making her forget about Ward in a completely different way. No. She needs to sleep. He squeezes her fingers and gives her a smile he hopes looks somewhat convincing. Eva takes another gulp of whisky-laced tea. She disappears into the bedroom on silent feet, closing the door behind her.

It's the stillest, deepest part of the night when Finn sees the lights bearing down on the island. He steps out of the cottage and peers across the water at the ship emerging from the dark. The firebasket gives out just enough light to tell him he will not have the luxury of speaking to Ward in the tavern this afternoon.

He waits on the jetty. Watches as a longboat is lowered from the *Eagle*. Watches as it approaches the island, oars sighing rhythmically through the water.

Ward is alone. Interesting, Finn thinks. When he has come for him in the past, he has always sent swathes of men to do his bidding. Finn is not sure if this solo visit makes him more or less wary.

For a second, he considers waking Eva. Considers keeping his promise to tell her of any news. He pushes the thought away quickly. Let her sleep. Let her have a few uninterrupted hours not filled with anxiety over Ward. She'll be furious if she finds out, of course. But it's a fury he's willing to carry.

Finn stands on the jetty with folded arms as Ward ties the longboat's hawser to the moorings. Climbs out with one step. He is dressed in a thick black greatcoat and cocked hat, a grey scarf bundled at his neck and a queue hanging in coils down his back.

"You couldn't wait a few more hours to speak to me?" Finn asks bitterly. His breath plumes out in a silver cloud before disappearing into the darkness.

"Waiting around for the days to pass will do no one any good." Ward glances down at his stolen longboat, roped to the other side of the jetty. "Glad you're making good use of my property." He begins to stride towards the cottage, but Finn grabs his shoulder, pulling him back.

"No. We can speak out here."

"Very well." Ward rubs his gloved hands together to warm them. "You have something to tell me, I assume? I hope you've finally come to your senses and will agree to come back to the *Eagle* with me."

"No, Ward. If you want that, you'll have to force me." And Finn knows, as he speaks, that there is every chance of that happening. Every chance of Eva waking up alone on the island, with no word of explanation from him. His stomach turns over at the thought.

Ward looks unsurprised. "Why did you wish to see me?"

And Finn tells him of the two lost Spanish treasure fleets; of the wealth now lying on the ocean floor. "Perhaps you can't offer your crew immunity," he says. "But surely the chance of enough wealth to see them through their lives is a fair exchange. It would restore their faith in you as captain, aye?"

151

Ward is silent for a long moment, eyes glazed over as he looks towards the dark shape of the *Eagle*. How close is he to losing his ship, Finn wonders? How many men would side with him if he found the courage to fight John Graveney?

"This could all just be hearsay," Ward says finally. "The ramblings of a few drunkards in a tavern."

"It could," Finn admits. "But is a prize like this not worth taking a gamble on? You find even a scrap of this haul and Graveney will have far more than he'd get from the sale of that ruined old house. Your captaincy would be secure again, and you'd have no need to fight for it."

Ward rubs his jaw. Finn can tell the idea has intrigued him. But he says, "Going after these ships is a risk. Two months to the New World, if we're lucky. And there's no certainty we'll find a thing. But the house is there for the taking." Before Finn can argue, Ward says, "You know that's how Graveney and his supporters will see it."

"And what about how you see it? You're the damn captain."

"And I'm doing my best to keep it that way." Ward digs his hands into the pockets of his coat, rounding his shoulders against the cold. Wind swirls off the sea, sending a volley of sparks fluttering down from the firebasket. "This is not just about the money," he says. "Graveney and his supporters are staunch Jacobites. They want the Blakes to pay for Abigail's crimes."

Finn lets out his breath. "You can't let him take the house. Eva's family would have nothing left to their name." He looks out at the lamplit ship, then back at Ward. "If you chose to fight Graveney, how many men would side with you? Half?"

Ward eyes him, and Finn doubts he is going to answer the

question. But he says, "More, I should hope."

"Then why are you being such a damn coward?" The words fall out before Finn can stop them. He can tell there's a part of Ward that desperately wants to fight Graveney. But he's afraid of losing. Better to be captain merely in name, Finn supposes, than to fail trying to take back his power.

He is bitterly disappointed in Henry Ward. The very same way, he imagines, that Ward feels about him.

Ward chuckles dully. "I must say, your loyalty to the Blakes is quite something. Trying to make up for past mistakes, are you?"

"Does it not matter to you that it's your daughter's family Graveney is trying to steal from?" Finn demands, pushing past his question. "You're so determined to see me away from Eva because you think it's what Abigail would have wanted. But do you really think she'd expect this cowardice from you? You're just sitting by and letting these men take Highfield House."

"Abigail lied to me. Deceived me. I'm no longer so inclined to put my captaincy on the line for what she would have wanted."

Finn scrubs a hand across his eyes in frustration. "Then why in hell are you trying to force me from my wife?"

Ward takes a step closer. In the light of the firebasket, Finn can see the deep creases around his mouth and eyes. "I taught you many things when you were a lad," Ward says. "And one of them, I hope, was decency. Owning your mistakes."

And at once, Finn is a child again. He is huddling at the table in the *Eagle's* great cabin, listening to Ward's footsteps click back and forth across the floorboards in front of him.

Listening to the captain berate him in that that steel-hard, expressionless voice. A scolding for losing his temper. For forgetting to scrub the back of the range. For sloppy handwriting. Oversleeping. *Aye, sir. Sorry, sir.*

Finn feels himself bow his head. Lower his eyes. The same reaction he'd had to Ward's reprimanding as a child.

"You're ingratiating yourself into the Blakes' lives," Ward continues, "all the while, lying to them about how their brother died."

"I've told them no lies."

"But no truths either."

Finn closes his eyes. He's right, of course. And this rationale, it's far worse than Ward trying to wrestle him away from Eva out of some long-ago loyalty to Abigail. It goes much deeper than that, Finn realises now. Perhaps it always has.

He looks at Ward squarely. "I am not going to leave Eva," he says. "Are you going to kill me for it? Because if you are, then just do it. Let's put an end to this." He hopes Ward can't hear the uncertainty in his voice. Finn is unsure what he is more afraid of: Ward putting a pistol to his chest and forcing him back aboard the ship, or Ward telling Nathan and Harriet how their brother died.

Ward holds his gaze for a long moment, and the tug of fear in Finn's stomach intensifies. Perhaps it's neither of these things he's so afraid of. Perhaps it's the possibility of his life ending tonight. Ward has tried to kill him before; under the rulings of the ship's articles, yes, but it proves he is not above such things. But somehow, Finn also senses that Ward will not do so again. Perhaps the act of keel-hauling the boy he had taken under his wing had been harder for Ward than he anticipated.

It's his history with Henry Ward that's saving him, Finn realises. It's those reading lessons, those open discussions about fear and courage, those nights spent on deck with a quadrant at his eye, learning to read the stars. Those scoldings at the table as Ward tried to turn him into a better man. He wonders how long such an amnesty will last.

"I'm not going to kill you, Finn," Ward says finally. "I'd not shoot you in front of your own home and leave your body for your wife to find. But my offer still stands. Come with me now and your crimes will be forgiven. I swear to you that I will never speak of them again."

"Come with you now? So I can be another body to help you fight Graveney? Is that what you mean?"

Ward says nothing. But Finn can tell by the look in his eyes that his guess is an accurate one. He would be valuable to Ward, yes. One more man to take his side; to help him secure his captaincy. Help rid him of John Graveney.

Finn lets out a desperate laugh. "I'm just one man, Ward. Do you really think having me fight for you will make a difference?"

"Every man counts."

Finn shakes his head. "I'm not coming with you. I'm not going to fight for you."

"Not even if it meant getting John Graveney away from your wife's family?" Ward looks at Finn for a long second, a faint smile flickering in the corner of his mouth. "It would seem as though we both want something from one another."

For a moment, time hollows and distorts, and Finn feels a falling sensation in his stomach. He swallows hard. "So if I re-join your crew, you'll fight Graveney and his men? Get them away from the Blakes?" The words feel impossibly heavy.

"I can't assure you we will be victorious. But I can assure you I will fight him."

No. He does not want to hear this.

But isn't this what he asked for? For Ward to fight for the Blakes? For Ward to turn on Graveney? Thoughts pound against his head. He feels hot and sick.

Ward's eyes spear him. "You have my word, Finn. You make your sacrifice, and in return, I will make mine."

The words strike him. Ward is a selfish coward, yes. But so, Finn realises, is he. He glances up at the firebasket. The flames have dwindled to a faint coppery glow and the basket needs refilling. The shadows across the island are becoming ink-dark. "I'm not going to leave Eva," he says again.

"Even if it meant helping her family?" Ward raises his eyebrows; a questioning, probing look Finn has seen from him all too many times. A look that makes him question himself. "Don't you owe them this?"

Finn feels painfully on edge as he goes to the shed for the coal. He refills the basket, then stands on the rim of the island, watching Ward's longboat glide back towards his ship.

You make your sacrifice, and in return, I will make mine.

Don't you owe them this?

He hates that Henry Ward's words always manage to work their way inside him. Right now, he knows they are having such an effect because they are right. Finn has kept secrets from the Blakes. Has sat around their table, has slept beneath their roof, made himself part of their family. All after taking their brother from them.

The realisation swings at him suddenly.

He cannot leave Eva. But he does need to tell her family the truth.

Telling them will give Henry Ward once less piece of ammunition against him. But that is not the argument that has him climbing into the longboat with the first blue light of dawn. It's the dull knowledge that Ward did teach him decency. And keeping this secret from Eva's family has not been the decent thing to do. He cannot change the past. But he can do the right thing now.

He rows away from the jetty before he can change his mind. Before Eva wakes and makes him doubt everything.

He hates that he is doing this without telling her. But Ward is right. He cannot sit around the table with the Blakes and pretend nothing had happened. Because yes, Henry Ward had taught him to be a better man than that.

He knows her family finding out the truth is the thing Eva fears the most. But he also knows Ward is right when he says the truth will not stay hidden forever. And Finn would rather they hear it from him.

CHAPTER EIGHTEEN

Nathan pokes at the fire in the parlour, willing the flimsy flames to warm the room. The house is full of blue shadow in the early morning, the walls radiating cold. Even Mrs Brodie has not shown herself yet.

He is not surprised his foolish venture to Bamburgh came to nothing. His mother's letter is from a past so distant that any knowledge of it can be based on no more than flimsy hearsay. He is just as unsurprised at Elias Mitchell's reaction to his turning up on his doorstep. He is just relieved Julia had not questioned his clumsy lie about being watched by the militia. He cannot bear to think how angry she would be if she knew he had been to see her father.

One day soon, he will stop lying to her. Once Henry Ward and his men are a memory, he will speak nothing but truths to Julia for the rest of his days.

But he is running out of time to make *the rest of his days* a reality. The six days Graveney had promised him are nearly over. And as much as it pains him, Nathan knows that is for the best. As he had lain sleepless in bed last night, he had stared down at Theodora in the truckle bed beside him and been hit with an enormous swell of guilt. Edwin is right—they need to get out of this house as soon as possible. Get their children to safety. Nothing else matters.

The knock at the door startles him. It's barely dawn—and these days, a knock at the door is rarely good news. He finds Finn on the doorstep, a look of deep unease in his eyes. Nathan's mind goes to freak waves and boating accidents, and all the other godawful things that might have happened to his sister out on Longstone.

"Has something happened?" he asks. "Eva, is she—"

"Eva's well," Finn cuts in. "But there's something I need to speak with you about." There's a desperate, lingering panic in his eyes; the same look Nathan is sure he himself has been wearing since Henry Ward first appeared on his doorstep. He nods, gesturing for Finn to enter.

Finn hesitates. He glances up at the bleak façade of the house, then digs his hands into the pockets of his greatcoat, his shoulders rounding. "Can we speak outside?"

Nathan has never seen him so uneasy. "As you wish." He takes his coat from the hook in the foyer and slides it on. Steps out of the house without a word and closes the door behind him.

Finn begins to pace, his boots sighing through the damp grass. His breath clouds, before disappearing into the pearly sunrise. "There's something I ought to tell you," he begins. "Something I regret not telling you earlier. It was wrong of me. But I've been too much of a coward to tell you the truth."

And Nathan understands, suddenly, the reason behind the panic in Finn's eyes. The desperation. The regret.

"I know about you and Oliver," he says.

Finn stops pacing. "What?" He hesitates. Opens his mouth to speak, then stops. "You recognised me?"

Nathan smiles wryly. "No." He wraps his arms around his body; shivers. "Ward told me before you and Eva married. He wanted me to put a stop to your wedding."

Finn stares at him. "But you didn't."

"No."

Ward had come to the house a few days before Eva's wedding, having overheard word in the village of her impending marriage. Told Nathan exactly who she planned to bring into the family.

Nathan knows he had not given Ward the response he was expecting. He had not gone tearing out to Longstone for revenge, or to drag Eva home. Perhaps that was what he ought to have done. Perhaps that was, as Ward had insisted, the right thing to do. The thing that Abigail would have wanted.

But Abigail is not here. The decision was not hers to make. And angry as Nathan was at Eva for bolting out to Longstone in the first place, somehow, it had felt wrong to deny her happiness on account of their cruel brother—even if it meant abandoning his last hopes of her marrying Matthew Walton. Nathan cares for his sister deeply. Is not sure he ever felt anything for Oliver other than fear.

Finn stands motionless for long moments, his gaze turned to the grey stone walls of the house's second storey. He knows the place perhaps better than anyone, Nathan thinks. Knows of the priest hole that had allowed him to hide, the passage in the wall that had given him an escape. He can only imagine the nerve it must have taken him to step back through the door again.

"Why?" Finn asks after a long silence. "Why allow Eva to marry me?"

"She loves you," Nathan says simply. "If she is able to look past what happened, then it seemed wrong for me to not do the same." He lets out a long breath, looking past Finn to the slate-grey roll of the sea. "I know what Oliver was like. And I saw what happened between the two of you that night. I know it was hardly a case of cold-blooded murder."

"That doesn't change what happened."

"No. That's true."

Finn looks at him for a long second. "Thank you."

Nathan nods. The muscles in his shoulders are tight, a dull coil of unease in his stomach. His body's eternal reaction to speaking of this piece of the past. In London, Oliver had been pushed to the back of his mind, the trauma he had inflicted along with it. Here in Highfield House, that past is harder to ignore. Still, he keeps the door to Oliver's old bedroom locked. Still, he can barely bring himself to step inside it. If by some miracle he finds a way to remain here on Lindisfarne, he will force himself to open that room up. Let the sea air blow through and take the memories with it.

"I wasn't sorry, you know," Nathan says suddenly. "About what happened to Oliver." The words spill. "At his burial, everyone approached me to tell me how sorry they were for my loss. And I realised I was glad he was gone." The moment he speaks, he feels his shoulders slump forward; feels that dread in his stomach begin to uncoil. This is a truth he has never admitted to. A truth he has been carrying somewhere hidden for the past twenty years. Speaking it makes him feel like a terrible person. But at the same time, it makes the weight on his shoulders grow a little lighter. Makes the memories of his brother lose their potency. He takes a long, slow breath, feeling the cold air fill his lungs, anchoring him to the present. For a long moment, neither of them speak, the wordlessness punctuated by the hush of the sea.

"I'm sorry," Finn says. "For not speaking to you about this much earlier."

Nathan smiles wryly. "I can understand why you didn't." He turns up his collar, huddling in on himself against the cold. "If I'm honest, I hoped it would be something this family would never speak of. Much like Oliver himself."

Finn's eyes turn downward. "Who else knows?"

"No one," says Nathan. "Just myself and Eva. What point would there be in telling anyone else?"

"What about Harriet?"

"It's best that she doesn't know," says Nathan. "Things are fragile enough between her and the rest of the family."

"I'm sure Ward will tell her if I don't."

Nathan shakes his head. "From what I can gather, Ward is not in the habit of sharing things with her. As much as she might wish otherwise."

Finn is silent for a long time, as though turning this information over in his head. There is something in his eyes that is not quite relief, not quite dread. No doubt he had expected to leave Highfield House with his secrets spilled; with the weight of them off his shoulders, but the consequences laid out in front of him. Nonetheless, Nathan is adamant that Harriet not know of this. He fears it would be the incision that would sever her from the rest of the family forever. She had never known Oliver, and the few times he has been mentioned in the past, they have always veered away from speaking of his true nature. His true death.

Succumbed to smallpox. Quick and unremarkable. Oliver Blake has become just an average boy who died an average death. Nathan knows Harriet will not see things the way he does.

"Has there been any sign of Ward these past few days?" Finn asks finally. "Or Graveney?"

Nathan is glad for the change of subject. Although the thought of Ward and Graveney is hardly more pleasant than the thought of his older brother. "No. I've not seen them since Graveney approached me in the village."

"What will you do?" asks Finn. "If he comes for the house?"

"*When* he comes for the house," Nathan says dully. "He told me I had six days. That was five days ago."

Finn nods. "What will you do?" he asks again.

"I will give it to him," says Nathan. "What else can I do? Edwin has offered to put Thea and me up for as long as we need it." Speaking the words aloud make his shoulders sink forward. He will be penniless. Forced to rely on Edwin's charity until he can scrabble together some form of income. Once he is safely away from Lindisfarne, he can attempt to sell the house, of course, but he does not dare think about how long it will take to find someone willing to purchase such a faraway wreck. Rebuilding his business will be an impossibility with no money to his name. As will staying here on Lindisfarne to make a future with Julia.

He turns these thoughts over, feeling the weight of them.

"There may be another way," says Finn.

Nathan feels a faint flicker of hope. Pushes it aside before it can take root. "You know something of the letter?"

"No. But there's a chance Ward can give his crew the wealth they want, without taking the house from your family." And the story he tells is a fantastical one, filled with sunken ships and gold lost in New World hurricanes. True, Finn claims, at least as far as he can tell. Either way, it is a story Henry Ward believes.

"Ward came to Longstone last night," Finn says. "I told him about these ships. I could tell he was intrigued. He's afraid that if he doesn't give his crew the wealth and immunity he promised them, they'll overthrow him as captain. He thinks he has a chance of regaining the crew's trust if he takes them to Florida to salvage the gold. But he knows Graveney wants to stay and punish your family for what your ma did."

Nathan frowns. "How does any of this help me?"

"I'm not saying you ought to stay and fight Graveney," says Finn. "That's your choice to make. But Ward wants Graveney gone, and if he commits to going after these treasure ships, it'll likely give him fresh support from his crew. If you chose to stand up to Graveney, there's a chance Ward might support you."

The thought stays with him long after Finn leaves. Stays with him as he forces down breakfast with Theodora; as he pens his lacklustre responses to the watch manufacturers. And with it comes a strength he was not expecting.

Refuse to hand over the house. Stay and fight. It's not the kind of thing he has ever done in his life. But perhaps he has grown tired of being shaped by others' bidding.

Graveney will not kill him—the knowledge comes to him suddenly, in bright colours. It's a bold, brazen thought, but Nathan trusts it. He is the one who must sign over the deeds to Highfield House. If he is to die without doing so, the manor will pass into Theodora's dowry. For the place to be more to him than a pile of crumbling brick and stone, Graveney needs Nathan alive. It's an oddly empowering thought.

Over and over, Nathan has told himself he hates this house. Its poisonous past and its priest holes and passages. Hates it for the stress it has caused him; the sleepless nights. But he realises now he has been wrong. It is not hatred for the house at all. It is hatred for Ward and Graveney. And yes, for Oliver—because he may as well admit that now. Perhaps even for this darkest side of his mother and all the pain and stress her mistakes have caused him. This house, this island, salt-streaked and windblown, is not to blame.

Nathan realises then what he has known in the back of his mind for days: he is not going to give this house up. He is not going to flee like Abigail did. This is home. He is not going to give up on a future with Julia; a future of his own making.

He knows this is madness. But he also sees now what he had failed to see before: that he is not the only one who despises John Graveney.

There's a chance Henry Ward might support you.

"How big a chance?" he had asked Finn that morning.

"I can't be sure. It's a risk, for certain. But maybe one worth taking. Ward's afraid Graveney will mutiny. But if Graveney failed to get the letter, and failed to get the house from you, the men'd be unlikely to support him as captain. Especially if Ward's offering to take them to Florida to salvage the treasure ships. There's every chance he might support you in order to make that a reality."

"Support me how?" Nathan asked, mind already

beginning to run. "You think he and his supporters would fight Graveney on my behalf?"

"Maybe," said Finn. "He wants Graveney gone as much as you do."

A risk, for certain. But yes, Nathan thinks, it is a risk worth taking.

CHAPTER NINETEEN

"What do you mean you are staying?" Edwin demands later that morning. He paces in front of Nathan's desk, footsteps clopping against the floorboards. "Are you mad?"

"I need you to get Thomas and Thea out of the house," Nathan says, surprising himself with his calmness. "Harriet too."

"Don't be a fool," Edwin hisses. "I'm not leaving you alone to face these bastards. They're going to be on the doorstep tomorrow. And unless you have your mother's letter, or the deeds to the house for them, they'll likely put a bullet in your chest."

"I'm well aware of the situation." Nathan runs the soft end of a quill along his fingers. "But I'll not be facing Graveney alone. I'll have Ward's support." Edwin does not need to know that that support is no certain thing. Once Harriet and the children are out of the house, he will send for Ward and list all the reasons why he ought to raise arms against Graveney and get these men out of their lives.

In truth, Nathan would like to have Edwin here at the house with him, in case Ward's support falls through and Graveney appears on the doorstep as promised. Though he feels certain Graveney will achieve nothing from killing him, Nathan knows there is little chance of him coming out of this completely unscathed. If he could ever use a trigger-happy ally, it is now.

But he needs Theodora out of the house. Needs Edwin to take her back to London with Thomas and Harriet.

Edwin pulls the chair from the corner of the room and sinks into it. He leans forward on the desk, looking at Nathan intently. "Come back to London with us, Nate. Let Graveney have the house. Like I said, you and Thea can stay with us until you've found your feet again."

His patronising tone makes Nathan bristle. "No. Thank you for the offer. But I can't rely on your charity."

"Is accepting my charity worse than Theodora growing up as an orphan? Because that's where this is headed."

Nathan shakes his head. "Graveney won't kill me. He'll achieve nothing from that. He needs me alive to sign over the deeds to the house."

"And you don't think he can force you to do that?"

Nathan pushes away a swell of fear he can't bring himself to acknowledge. "He needs me alive," he says again.

Edwin rubs his eyes. "Ward has been doing Graveney's bidding for months, trying to get the letter from you. What makes you think he'll suddenly turn around and support you?"

"Finn tells me he has a way of gaining his crew's trust again. A way of giving them the wealth they want."

Edwin snorts. "I'm not sure I'd trust Finn any more than

I'd trust Henry Ward. If his reputation is anything to go by, he's hardly the most honest of men."

Nathan doesn't speak at once. He is well aware that this is the height of foolishness. But something seems to have split open inside him—whether wrought by Julia, or by months of fear and threats, or by years of feeling weak and ineffective, he doesn't know. He only knows he cannot roll over like this.

"My mind is made up," he tells Edwin. "Will you take Harriet and the children back to London or not?"

Edwin sighs heavily. Gives Nathan a look full of disapproval. But he says, "Of course."

"It's looking like we've got more support coming from the south," says Hugh, leaning up against the stones of the fireplace and bringing his teacup to his lips.

Bobby looks up in interest from where he is sitting cross-legged on the settle.

"The Lancashire Catholics are ready to rise. About time, wouldn't you say, lad? Thought we'd never hear from the cowards."

Bobby nods enthusiastically. "About time, aye. The cowards."

"Stop it," Julia hisses at Hugh. "He doesn't need to hear all this." Once upon a time, she had loved how much Bobby idolised his uncle. Now it just makes her angry.

Hugh raises his eyebrows. "You going to raise him to support the Hanoverian, Jul?"

Julia fills a bowl of porridge for Bobby. Herds him to the table. "It's dangerous for him to know these things," she says, voice low. "If he said something to the wrong person..." She glances back over her shoulder at her son. His dark head is hunched over his bowl, and he's shovelling porridge into his mouth. He shows no inkling of having caught on to their conversation.

Julia takes two more bowls from the shelf. "It's already too much to ask to expect him to keep quiet about you being here. And now you expect him to keep quiet about the rebels' plans too?"

"I don't think you give the boy enough credit," says Hugh, folding his arms across his chest. "He knows these things are not to be spoken of openly."

Julia spoons porridge into the bowls, sloshing the colourless liquid over the side in her anger. "I know my son better than you do."

"Are you certain about that? I've been in his life since the day he was born. I'm the closest he's ever had to a father."

She grits her teeth. It's a razor-sharp barb, and entirely intentional. That reminder Hugh so often drops at her feet of all she owes him. She stands by the hearth and forces down a mouthful of porridge, not bothering to sit at the table. It sticks in her throat, made dry and tasteless by her complete lack of appetite.

She hears a knock at the side door. Glares at Hugh. "Not another word to Bobby about the Rising." She lifts her voice a little. "In fact, not another word from either of you. Could be anyone at the door. Understand, Bobby? Silence."

Her son nods obediently, flashing her a milk-smeared smile. Julia hurries downstairs, realising halfway to the door she has brought her porridge spoon with her. She flings it on the counter, cursing under her breath as it clatters to the floor.

When she opens the side door to find Nathan in the alley, it is all she can do not to sink into his arms.

"You look upset," he says. "Has something happened?" His voice drops. "Has Holland—"

"No." She steps out into the lane, pulling the door closed behind her. Shards of late-morning sun are struggling between the dark stone houses, but they're providing little warmth. Julia stands as close as possible to Nathan, without making contact with him. "Nothing's happened. There's been no sign of Holland. I've been doing my best to stay away from him."

"Good."

There's something different about Nathan today. A fresh blaze in his eyes. She is afraid of what might have caused it.

"May I come inside?" he asks. "There's something I wish to speak to you about."

Julia hesitates. Despite her warnings, she knows there's no way Hugh and Bobby will stay silent enough for her to invite Nathan into the shop. And she already knows Hugh is capable of eavesdropping into the cellar. "Bobby is still sleeping," she says, cursing herself for the lie. "If you don't mind, perhaps we could stay out here…"

"Of course." Nathan takes a step closer to her, his thighs brushing the soft swell of her skirts. "I've just come from the tavern," he says. "I've left word for Henry Ward asking for his help to get Graveney and his men out of our lives."

Julia frowns. "What are you talking about? Do you really imagine you can do such a thing?"

"I have to." Nathan reaches suddenly for her hands. Squeezes. "I am not going to let these men scare me from my home. I'll not be forced to flee like my mother did. This is where I want to be, Julia. Here on Lindisfarne. With you."

She feels a jolt in her chest. His words are so forthright, so open, they catch her by surprise. And there is joy at first; deep, searing joy, but beneath it, something far closer to dread. From what she has heard of this Henry Ward, she hates the thought of Nathan's safety depending on his support.

And perhaps even more terrifyingly, how long will it be before Nathan learns what she is hiding? Can she get Hugh out of her house before Nathan discovers he is here? Before he learns what he has been trying to do?

Nathan falters. "Is that what you want? Have I been too forward?"

Julia dares a smile. Dares to feel a little of the happiness his words elicit. Dares to imagine that life of having someone by her side. "Of course that's what I want." She presses a light palm to his cheek. Feels the faint stubble beneath her fingertips. Feels his body shift with breath. After a moment, she pulls away. "But I'm worried for you. For your safety."

"These men won't hurt me," he says. "They need me alive."

"Are you certain of that?"

He gives her a faint smile; no, she reads in it. He is not certain. But he is doing it anyway.

Her stomach loops. A part of her wants to talk him out of it. But another part of her wants to support him unwaveringly. Wants every chance at making him stay.

"You are not going to change your mind about this, are you."

"No. I can't." He pulls her close. His fingers intertwine with hers, and he stands motionless for a moment, as though allowing himself to grow comfortable with the contact. His breath tickles her nose. "Edwin will take Harriet and the children off the island. But I can't run. I won't run."

There's a hardness to his voice Julia has not heard before. A new depth. A new resolve. It thrills her, frightens her—a deep concern for his safety.

"Be careful," she says, her voice catching. "Please be careful. If anything were to happen to you—" Before she can finish the sentence, he is kissing her hard. His lips are on hers before she can fully make sense of it, and she reaches out instinctively to grip the top of his arm. Desire uncoils from deep within her.

When he pulls away, his breath has quickened, his chest rising and falling beneath his greatcoat. She sees the flush of his cheeks, the heat in his eyes. *All right?*, she wants to ask— but she does not want to break the silence.

He gives her hand a final squeeze before stepping back and putting distance between them. "I shall be careful," he says. "I promise."

CHAPTER TWENTY

"No," says Harriet. "I'm not leaving." She is planted in the armchair in her workroom, watching with hard eyes as her husband paces the room. This is a stupid place for pacing, she thinks. Two steps across and two steps back.

"You cannot be serious," Edwin says. "All I've heard from you since we arrived here is how much you wish to be back in London."

"Things have changed," she snaps. Surely he can see that. Of course he can. He just doesn't care.

"I understand you have just met your father," he says tautly. "But he is the very reason we cannot stay in this place. For some ungodly reason, your brother is intent on fighting these *pirates*. Surely you can see that we cannot leave our son here."

"I am not afraid of the pirates," says Harriet. "My father will see to it that they do not hurt me. Or Thomas." Even as the words come out of her mouth, she can hear their naivety. They earn the snort from Edwin she expected.

"You barely know the man, Harriet. How can you make any such assurances? Besides, if Henry Ward truly does care for you, it will make you a target for the men he is to fight against."

If Henry Ward truly does care for you... She can hear the doubt in Edwin's voice. Or is that just her own uncertainty making itself known?

A return to London. For weeks, months, it was all she wanted. A thing she had longed for with every breath. But now she feels like she has little to return to. After her escape to Lesbury, Edwin will never allow her to see Isabelle, or any of the other artists in her circle. And she has no painting to lose herself in. What can London offer but bleak grey reminders of her every mistake?

Edwin had spoken of trying to resurrect things between them; trying to rebuild some sense of happiness in their lives. But how can she rebuild something that never existed?

She knows returning to the capital is inevitable. And really, she does not want to stay here on this scrap of an island any more than she wishes to return to that miserable London townhouse to be *wife* and *mother*. But she cannot leave yet. Not while she and her father still feel like strangers.

"Pack your things," Edwin says, turning towards the door without looking back at her. "We leave tonight."

Harriet waits. Listens to his footsteps echo down the passage, up the stairs. Waits until she hears the bedroom door thump shut. Then she takes her cloak and gloves from where she had tossed them on the table. Slips out through the kitchen into the vast expanse of white-haired dunes.

When Eva finishes Theodora's lessons, she makes her way upstairs to Nathan's study. Knocks lightly on the door.

The knowledge that Nathan might have known about Finn and Oliver, might have kept silent all this time, is astounding. When Finn had returned to Longstone this morning, he had told her everything. Told her of his need to unburden himself of the secret.

She understood. She is not angry; not really. Perhaps things would be different if not for this most unexpected of outcomes. But she understands the weight Finn has been carrying on his shoulders. For twenty years—and never more so in the months since they had met and married.

Finn had told her, too, of Henry Ward's visit to Longstone last night. About Ward's interest in the Spanish treasure ships. About the renewed possibility of Ward fighting Graveney. And Nathan's refusal to back down.

This is not the brother she knows.

For years, Eva has been nudging Nathan to stand up for himself, to show a little anger. But right here, right now? She knows well that he could die for it.

She finds him in his desk chair, poring over what look to be astronomical charts. She is not surprised. When he was younger, he had always sought solace in the sky when the real world was pressing down too heavily upon him.

He gives her a faint smile. Nods at her to enter.

She slides into the empty chair opposite the desk. She hardly knows where to begin. There is so much she needs to say.

"You knew," she says, "all this time, and you did not say anything?"

Nathan runs a finger across the star chart as though

tracing a passage through the sky. After a moment, he says, "Oliver's death is not something I wish to speak about any more than I'm sure you and Finn do."

Eva looks him in the eye. "Thank you, Nathan. For not putting a stop to our wedding. I know you were well within your rights to do so. And I know how much you were counting on my marriage to Mr Walton."

Nathan leans back in his chair. Smiles wryly. "Agonising over your marriage to Walton seems rather trite now, I must say."

Eva holds the silence for a moment. "Is it true, then? You're considering standing against Graveney? Refusing to hand over the house?"

"I'm not considering it," says Nathan. "It's what I've decided to do. I'm sending Theodora back to London with Edwin and Harriet. And I've asked Henry Ward for his support."

Eva's stomach tightens. Some distant part of her had hoped her brother would see sense and change his mind. "These men are trained to fight, Nathan. How can you hope to defeat them?"

"Graveney will achieve nothing from my death. If he's to profit from this family, he needs me alive." His eyes draw downward, back to the tableau of stars. "I cannot just stand by and let these men take our family's home."

He's determined, Eva sees. For years, he had despised this house. Had done nothing but let it rot. But now there is no changing his mind. It is as though all the knocks of the past few years have collided to lead him to this.

"Is this because of Julia?" she asks.

Nathan is silent for a moment, as though debating

whether to answer. "I've just had enough of acting on another's bidding."

Before Eva can respond, the door cracks open and Edwin charges inside. He is flustered with anger; red-cheeked and hot-eyed. Perhaps it's not anger, Eva thinks. Perhaps it's fear. Given all Nathan is risking, he would be right to feel it.

Edwin makes no attempt to acknowledge her. "I'm having Jenny take Thomas off the island," he tells Nathan. "Immediately. I've told her to take him to Bamburgh and find lodgings there until I come for them."

Nathan frowns. "What about Harriet?"

Edwin blows out a breath. "You tell me. She's taken herself off on another of her little runaway jaunts." He slams a fist into the wall, making the muscles in Eva's shoulders tighten. "I've been far too lenient with her. I thought that the best way to handle her. The best way to make her happy. But things can't go on like this. It's high time I treated her with a firmer hand." He glances then at Eva and she sees a flicker of regret in his eyes—regret, she assumes, that he had let her see his outburst.

For several moments, Nathan doesn't speak. "Perhaps now is not the time to be making such decisions," he says finally, with a calmness that is so uncharacteristic it makes something coil in Eva's stomach.

"I cannot wait for Harriet to show herself," Edwin says tautly. "Not when Graveney and his men could turn up at any moment."

"I agree," says Nathan evenly. "I don't want anyone in danger because of my decisions. Especially not the children. We'll manage Harriet when she decides to show herself." He presses his shoulders back, lifts his chin. "Have Jenny take

Thea too."

Edwin nods. "All right. But she needs to be ready to leave in an hour so they can catch the low tide. I don't want my son spending another night in this house."

CHAPTER TWENTY-ONE

Theodora's tantrum is painfully predictable. "No!" she wails, as Nathan goes to the wardrobe and starts pulling out her clothes. "I don't want to go!" She flings herself onto his bed, blonde hair flying. "I want to stay here!"

"I'm sorry," Nathan tells her firmly, shoving her dresses and underskirts into a duffel bag. "But this is not up for negotiation. You're leaving and that's final."

She sits up on the bed and gives him defiant eyes. "No," she pouts. "I'm not leaving. I'm not."

Nathan sighs as he turns back to the wardrobe. How could he have imagined prising his family out of this damn house would be such a chore? He can feel his daughter wearing away the calmness he has been trying so hard to cultivate. He bends down to gather up a wrapping gown that has fallen to the floor of the wardrobe.

When he turns around, Theodora is no longer on the bed, her footsteps echoing down the staircase. He rubs his eyes. Drops the gown on the bed and hurries downstairs after her, shouting her name.

The front door is hanging open, empty dunes stretching out into a mist-streaked haze. "Theodora!" he barks. "Come back here at once!"

Eva appears at his shoulder from inside the house. She is wrapped in her bonnet and cloak, pulling on her gloves, as though she were about to leave.

"Help me look for Thea," he says tautly. "Check the outbuildings."

Eva disappears around the side of the house, leaving Nathan to charge over the grassy rise and fall of the dunes. He rushes past pools and rock stacks; peers inside Eva's boat that's moored high up on the beach. The tide is rising, pulling the fringe of the embankment beneath the surface.

He calls Thea's name, again, again. Is answered with nothing but the bawl of the gulls and the restless sigh of the sea. Needles of sunlight prick through the clouds.

He marches over the moorland in the direction of the village, anger and frustration building. Footsteps sigh through the wet grass towards him. He turns to see Eva running in his direction, skirts in her fist. It is only when he looks back at her and sees the manor like a doll's house on the horizon that he realises how far he has gone. How much time must have past.

"Edwin says Jenny and Thomas are leaving." Eva gulps down her breath. "He says they cannot wait any longer if they're to catch the tide."

Nathan closes his eyes. His anger at his daughter is starting to turn into something more pressing. Something veering closer to fear. He does not want Thea here at the house. Has never wanted her here at the house. And never less so than right now, with the threat of conflict so immediate. But he cannot expect Edwin to put his own child in danger.

"Tell him to go," he says to Eva. "Tell him to get Thomas to safety."

She hesitates a moment, concern darkening her eyes. Then she nods and turns back to the house. Nathan's regret lingers only a moment before it's pushed aside by a growing desperation to find Theodora.

He strides towards the village, calling for her, his voice disappearing into the vast top end of the island.

"I'm leaving." Hugh appears at the top of the cellar stairs with a pack on his back and his greatcoat buttoned to his chin. His fiery hair is tucked beneath his blue wool cap.

Julia feels a jolt in her chest. She looks up, drawn away from her account book lying open on the counter. This is what she wants, she reminds herself—for her dangerous brother to be gone. This is what she had longed for from the minute Hugh had come barging into her shop demanding shelter. So why does she feel such a pang of dread?

"Where?" she asks. "When?"

"I'm heading south to join the rebels. The Lancashire Catholics have twenty thousand men preparing to fight. It's time for me to join them. I'm going to be more use to the cause down there than I am up here, waiting for information on the spies that might never come."

Julia hesitates. Is this some kind of twisted game? Is he testing her, to see if she will give up Joseph Holland's name in exchange for him staying away from the army?

She won't do it, she tells herself firmly. She cannot put Nathan in danger like that. But nor can she bear the thought of losing another brother to the Jacobite cause.

"Please, Hugh," she hears herself say. "Don't. It's far too dangerous."

He chuckles. "Are you saying you want me to stay here?"

"I'm saying I don't want to lose you too." Her voice wavers and she feels a sharp pain in her throat.

His eyes soften, catching her off guard. For a moment, she sees the elder brother she had looked up to throughout her childhood. He reaches for her hand. "I have to go, Jul," he says gently. "You know that."

And perhaps this is not about trying to squeeze information out of her. Perhaps he really has decided he is better off out of Lindisfarne, fighting with the rebel army.

She shakes herself out of her sentimentality. He is right, of course. He does have to go. Not for the cause, but for Bobby's sake, and her own. They are in far too much danger with him beneath their roof. If he is to pay for his choices on some mud-streaked Lancashire battlefield, then so be it.

Movement on the street catches her eye, and she drops Hugh's hand hurriedly. Flashes him panicked eyes. He darts down into the cellar, closing the door behind him just as the door to the shop swings open. The bell jangles wildly.

She welcomes her customers—the elderly wives of two of the herring fishermen; does her best to look as though nothing is wrong. She tries to breathe. Of course Hugh leaving is the right thing. Of course this is what she wants. It's the only way for her and Bobby to be safe. She hears herself churn out rote answers to the ladies' comments as they rifle though the shelves: *Yes, a lovely piece, isn't it. Sold to me from a woman up north. Yours for a shilling…*

She thanks them. Takes a moment to stand behind the counter and tuck the coins into her pocket book. The simple, everyday action feels jarring, somehow. As though day-to-day actions do not belong in this day. Her mind is racing with thoughts of Hugh's leaving; with Nathan's plan to confront Graveney. The writhing in her stomach seems to have become a constant fixture.

The bell above the door jangles again, making her look up. Julia freezes. And heat floods her body.

"Good afternoon, Mr Holland." She tries to keep her voice level. He's a boorish figure, seems to take up the whole doorway—though she feels fairly certain his size has been distorted by this sudden uptick in her fear. "Is there something I can help you with? Are you looking for anything in particular?" This is the best way forward, surely, to pretend this visit is nothing unusual. But it feels foolish. She knows, of course, that there is nothing routine about this visit. Joseph Holland has never come to her shop before. She cannot quite make sense of why he is here. She knows he has had his suspicions about her for many weeks—but what has brought him here now?

"Miss Mitchell." He nods brusquely. Does not answer the rest of her questions, just begins to stride wordlessly between the shelves. His footsteps are slow and rhythmic against the flagstones. Julia hears her pulse roaring in her ears. She hovers by the counter, uncertain of what to do.

Holland approaches the staircase. Nods towards the cellar. "Have you more wares down there?" And at once, Julia realises the reason for his visit. He has caught sight of Hugh, no doubt. In the street, perhaps. Or walking into her shop.

Striding in through the front door like he hasn't a care in the world. No doubt Joseph Holland knows her brother is a wanted man. A Jacobite criminal.

No doubt he wants him punished.

"The cellar is private." She speaks loudly, clearly, in hope that her brother will catch her words. What Hugh can do about it, she has no thought. There is no way out of the cellar other than the stairs Holland is at the top of.

Holland looks down the dark throat of the staircase. Julia's heart thunders. What is he planning to do? He is clearly expecting to find her brother at the bottom of the stairs. Is he carrying a weapon in his pocket? Dizziness swings over her.

"I said, the cellar is private." She lurches towards Holland, in a desperate, thoughtless attempt to block his way. Her words come out too loud, too uneven. Before she can make sense of it, the cellar door blows open and Hugh is flying towards them. A pistol shot echoes in her ears. And Joseph Holland falls, suddenly, heavily, blood beading from the wound in his chest onto her cellar stairs.

CHAPTER TWENTY-TWO

"Is he the one?" asks Hugh. "The government spy? The one who was threatening you?" He tucks his pistol into the pocket of his coat. Clenches a fist to stop his hand from shaking.

Julia nods, hand clamped over her mouth. She can't pull her eyes from Holland's lifeless body. Blood is blooming in the centre of his chest, radiating steadily outwards. His glassy eyes bore into hers; steel-grey, she notices distantly, with flecks of midnight blue. The skin around them is paper-thin, almost translucent.

Bile rises in her throat.

"Can we expect anyone else?" asks Hugh.

"I don't think so. Nathan says the other spies are not from the island." The words spill out before she can hold them back.

"All right. Good." Hugh clambers over Holland's body to stand at the top of the stairs. "Help me get him down here."

"You can't keep him in the cellar." Julia's words come out

sounding faintly hysterical.

"We'll get him out of the house," Hugh says firmly. "But we need to wait until dark." His voice sounds distant. Distorted. Julia feels panic weighing down on her. She presses a hand against the wall in a desperate attempt to steady herself.

"Come on, Julia." Hugh's impatience snaps her out of her haze. He leans down to take hold of Holland's shoulders. "Take his legs. I can't do this on my own."

Julia glances edgily out the window, then leans down and takes hold of Holland's boots. The mud on the soles is still cool and wet. It sticks to her fingers as she lurches down the steps beneath his weight. Blood on the cellar stairs, she thinks distantly. He has left his blood to stain her cellar stairs.

The distant jangle of the bell above the door makes her chest seize. In her panic, she had forgotten to lock the shop. She looks at Hugh with wide eyes.

"Go," he says, shoving the body into the cellar. "See who's up there. Keep them away from the stairs."

Julia stumbles dizzily back up to the shop. Blood on the stairs, yes. And on her shoes. And likely other places she has not even stopped to consider. She needs to get whoever is in the shop out of here as quickly as possible.

She stops abruptly when she sees Theodora Blake in the middle of the shop. She is without her bonnet or cloak, her blonde hair wild and her cheeks pink. She is crouching in front of the counter, stroking the cat, who has appeared from somewhere unknown.

"Theodora?" Julia manages. "What are you doing here? Are you alone?"

Theodora keeps stroking Minerva. "I want to see Bobby.

And I want to stay here. Papa says I have to go away with Miss Jenny. Back to London. I hate London. I'm not going."

Julia blinks. "Bobby is at the dame school," she manages. She takes a step towards Theodora, blocking her view of the blood-spattered staircase. "Where's your father?"

She shrugs. "Don't know."

Julia reaches a hand towards Theodora's shoulder, but stops. She sees it then; the blood on her fingers. The crimson splatters on the edges of her apron. Has Theodora noticed?

Before Julia can follow that thought far, the door flies open and Nathan barrels inside. He grabs hold of his daughter, pulling her from the floor and wrapping his arms around her, even as he hurls out an avalanche of scolding.

He looks at Julia. And he sees it at once, she has no doubt. Sees the blood on her fingers. On her apron. Blooming across the top steps of the cellar. A fresh look of fear passes over his eyes.

"Theodora," he says stiffly, "go and look at the bookshelf for a moment. I'll not be long."

Chastened by his scolding, she slinks off towards the back corner of the shop.

Nathan looks up at Julia with expectant eyes. "What happened?" he murmurs. "Are you hurt?"

She shakes her head, unable to meet his gaze. She knows she needs to give him something; cannot just let him see all this without providing an explanation. But what explanation can she possibly give that will not implicate her brother? She knows that Nathan will not turn Hugh in; knows he would not do that to her. But she also knows that if Nathan finds out what she has been hiding, the fragile threads of trust between them will unravel completely.

"Nothing's happened," she hears herself say. "You just need to get Theodora home."

Nathan drops his voice even further. "Are you in trouble? Is someone here? Holland…" The intensity in his eyes makes her chest ache. Barely a whisper: "Nod your head if I'm right. If you need my help."

At the mention of Holland's name, Julia's stomach rolls. She wants nothing more than to throw herself at Nathan and tell him everything. But all she can think of is how wild with anger Hugh would be if she gave him away. And how thoroughly things with Nathan would be destroyed. She shakes her head. "There's no one here. Nothing's happened."

"Julia," he says. "Please." And she reads it all in Nathan's eyes: the disbelief that she might be keeping this from him. That after all they have managed to build, she might be keeping silent when there is blood splattered across her apron, shoes, stairs.

He reaches for her, then hesitates. Pulls away before he makes contact. Julia feels a deep pang of self-loathing. It's not his fear that is keeping him from touching her, she realises. It's his suspicion. The reality of it burns.

"Nothing?" Nathan says. "There is nothing you wish to tell me?" He holds her gaze for a long time; wordless, imploring.

"No." Julia's voice is trapped in her throat. "There is nothing I wish to tell you."

And almost as if it were a tangible thing, she feels Nathan's hard-fought trust in her shatter into pieces.

Nathan barely speaks on the way back to the house. He keeps his hand tight around Theodora's to prevent her from racing away again, and the rigid contact does little to slow the hammering in his chest.

He is far too angry at Theodora to conjure up any coherent sentence. And as for what he feels towards Julia, well, that's not quite anger. Closer to betrayal. Definitely bewilderment. And a sizeable helping of pain. He had thought they had managed to find trust for one another. Openness. Something that went far deeper than lies.

But then he thinks of his visit to Elias Mitchell. Thinks of *militiamen were watching us*. And he thinks of the blood on Julia's fingers. There has never been trust between them, he thinks. There has never been truth. Not really.

Perhaps, in standing up to John Graveney and his men, he is making the biggest mistake of his life. Because he knows that this decision to stay and fight, against every grain of sense in his body, is just as much about Julia as it is about him needing to take control of his own life. And perhaps Julia Mitchell has been the biggest mistake of all.

Blood on the cellar stairs. Blood on her apron. Blood on her hands.

Perhaps in the right situation, he could have looked past all of that. He knows the Rising, and their entanglement with Ward, has led them all to do things they would never have considered themselves capable of. But he cannot look past her silence, her secrets. How can they have any future together if she can look him in the eye and lie, with her fingers stained scarlet with blood?

A big part of him wants to go back to the curiosity shop. Wants assurances that she is safe. Wants to keep begging for answers. But he knows there is little point. He could see it in her eyes. Whatever she is keeping secret, she has no intention of sharing with him.

And so. Right now, he needs to turn his thoughts away from Julia, and towards getting his child safely off the island before men with pistols appear at his door. It's where his priorities always ought to have been. How could he have let himself focus on anything else?

The tide is flooding the embankment, and he knows he is far too late to catch Jenny and Thomas. They will be tucked up safe in Bamburgh by now, away from the threat of John Graveney and his men.

Give in. The thought knocks against Nathan's head. *Give Graveney what he wants.*

But even in the face of Julia's silence, the prospect is sickening. He will not be forced from this house for the second time in his life. He will not be that man; constantly shaped by the wills of others.

As he approaches Emmanuel Head, he catches sight of Eva, still searching the rocky coastline on the eastern side of the island. At the sight of them, her shoulders sink in relief, and she strides over the uneven grass to catch them. And as far as Thea goes, he has one last option. Once last flimsy chance at keeping her safe.

"Go inside and fetch your cloak," Nathan tells his daughter sharply. "You're going to Longstone with your aunt."

CHAPTER TWENTY-THREE

Harriet has been waiting on the corner near the tavern for hours, and she is sure people are beginning to ask questions. Men are throwing looks her way as they enter the narrow street. She can just imagine what wild thoughts about her and her family are tearing through their heads.

The sun is beginning to sink. There is a deep chill on the air, darkness pushing out the crimson blaze at the bottom of the sky. Evening is drawing close, and she knows Edwin will be impatient to leave. Perhaps he will go without her. Is it foolish to hope she might be so lucky?

She huddles into her cloak, blowing against her gloved hands to warm them. Her stomach rumbles with emptiness. She peeks around the corner, watching a steady stream of men flow in and out of the tavern, in various states of disarray. No sign of her father yet. But he will come. She knows he will. Especially now, with so much conflict in the air, he will come here to collect any word from Highfield House.

It's almost night when she finally sees him. His head is down and he strides right past her, a deep frown of concentration creasing his brow. She watches him disappear into the tavern, then return moments later, tucking a folded note into the pocket of his justacorps. She steps around the corner and walks beside him as he cuts his way through the village.

Surprise flickers across his eyes at the sight of her. "Were you waiting for me?" he asks.

"Yes." She tugs her cloak tight around her body as wind whirls off the water. Above their heads, the first stars glitter in a brutally clear cobalt sky. "My husband wishes to take me back to London. He believes it is too dangerous here, given your men are after the house."

Ward doesn't look at her. "He is right. Especially given your brother has apparently decided to stay and fight."

"Stay and fight?" Harriet nods towards his coat pocket. "Is that what that note was about?"

Ward nods. He reaches into his pocket and hands her the page. She unfolds it curiously.

It's Nathan's handwriting, but the words do not sound like they come from her brother: *request assistance* and *confrontation* and *I intend to stand my ground.*

Harriet knows this is just bravado. Knows that if it comes down to it, and Graveney and his men appear on the doorstep with pistols waving, Nathan will crumble. He will hand over the deeds to the house and flee Holy Island with his shirttails flying.

Nonetheless, she is curious as to what her father sees in this.

"Are you going to help him?" she asks. "If Graveney and

his men try to take the house by force, will you fight them?"

He looks at her sharply. "How do you know about Graveney?"

Irritation flickers through her at how similar he sounds to Edwin. "I listen," she says, forcing an airy tone into her voice.

Her father smiles wryly. "You eavesdrop."

Harriet shrugs, feigning nonchalance. She tries to look behind his eyes; tries to determine whether he is angry at her admission. She cannot read him, she realises dully. She has never been able to read him. She wonders if Henry Ward is always this adept at keeping his emotions hidden, or whether this is just a skill he has cultivated around her.

He stops walking and looks at her squarely. "What do you think I ought to do?"

Harriet feels something flip in her chest. She cannot remember the last time anyone asked her opinion on anything. Perhaps her father is just doing this to humour her. But she cannot quite make herself care.

She takes a moment to consider her answer. "I do not want my brother to die," she says. "And without the help of you and your loyal men, there is every chance he may."

Ward nods slowly. He begins to walk again, but doesn't speak. What is he thinking, Harriet wonders? There's a blankness to his eyes, and she cannot see behind them. She knows Ward's crew is divided. Knows he does not have the authority he once had. She also knows he is not about to admit this—especially not to her.

"Will you take me somewhere?" she asks suddenly. "On your ship?"

"I'm afraid that's not possible," Ward says stiffly. "I would not be able to ensure your safety."

"You took me aboard your ship before."

"Things have changed since then. Your brother has antagonised Mr Graveney by refusing to hand over the house. I'm afraid that would make you a target. Besides, there's little time for pleasure outings. I ought to pay your brother a visit. Discuss these dangerous plans of his."

Harriet nods, unsurprised, but faintly disappointed. She continues to trudge beside him as he leaves the village and steps out onto the path across the moorland. Wind skims through the grass, and in the fading light the dunes seem to ripple like water. Harriet teeters over the uneven ground, wishing she had thought to bring a lamp. She has been away from the house for far longer than she anticipated.

She glances at her father, willing him to offer her his arm. He continues to walk with his hands folded behind his back.

He glances at her curiously. "Where did you wish me to take you?" he asks, after several moments of silence.

Harriet considers the question. In truth, the request had been more about spending time with her father, and outrunning the evening so she would not be dragged away by Edwin. She had known it was unlikely to lead anywhere. But she says, "I should like to see the Farne Islands. I want to see where my sister lives."

Ward smiles wryly. "I imagine you'd be rather disappointed to see that miserable pebble your sister has made her home. As disappointed as you might be with her choice of husband."

Harriet laughs a little. "Well. I can't fathom why she would want to make her life out there. But she does seem to love her husband."

Ward frowns slightly and something passes across his

eyes. He looks back at Harriet. "They've not told you, have they."

She raises her eyebrows. "Told me what?"

Ward digs his hands into the pockets of his coat and walks with his head down, a frown darkening his features. "About Finn Murray and your half-brother Oliver."

CHAPTER TWENTY-FOUR

Harriet has searched the house. Thrown open every unlocked door, charged into every room. There is no sign of her sister.

So Eva has left. Absconded back to Longstone to be with her wretched rogue of a husband. Harriet feels rage pounding behind her eyes.

Edwin's footsteps thump along behind her as she flies down the upstairs passageway. "Are you listening to a word I'm saying?"

He's rambling something about tides and wagons, she thinks. But no, she's not listening. All she can think about is the way her sister has betrayed the family. How could she knowingly marry the man who had taken their brother from them? How could she keep such a thing a secret? "Where is Eva?" she demands. "Has she left?"

"Yes, Harriet," Edwin says tautly. "She's left. And so has your son. I've had Jenny take him to Bamburgh. At least his nurse has some damn concern for his safety."

Harriet nods faintly. Supposes she ought to feel some guilt

at this. But Thomas is safe in Bamburgh. What more could Edwin want? Surely he knows their son is better off in Jenny's care than her own.

She turns to face him in the gloom of the hallway. A single lamp flickers on the wall outside their bedroom, but it does little to light the house's long shadows. "I asked my father if he would commit to supporting Nathan," she says, forcing an evenness into her voice. "He told me he was undecided. He is downstairs speaking with Nathan now."

Edwin sighs. "I suspected as much. Nathan is a fool if he thinks he has any chance of succeeding." He throws open the door to their bedroom and grabs her smallest trunk from the floor. "Put your cloak back on. We're going to the harbour. Eva has taken Thea to Longstone to try and keep her safe. I'm sure they'll have you too."

"No." The word falls out before she is even aware of it. The thought of sailing out to that cursed island makes her blood hot. All Eva's talk about wanting Harriet in her life. All the while holding such a secret to her chest. Did she truly imagine the truth would never come out? That they might just carry on with their lives as though nothing had happened?

Harriet's anger at Nathan is just as blinding. Her father had told her he had gone to Nathan, telling him of all Finn had done. Imploring him to put a stop to Eva's wedding. How could Nathan have just sat back and watched her marry that bastard? How could he be so spineless?

"I'm not going to Longstone," she hisses.

Edwin rubs his eyes wearily. "Do you not understand what's happening, Harriet? Graveney told Nathan he has until tomorrow to hand over the deeds to the land. It's not safe for you to be here. And I don't want to see you in any more danger." He is trying to keep his rage down, Harriet notices. And for all his resentment, she can tell he still cares about her. She hates that this is the case. It makes her feel far too guilty. "Besides, you just told me you needed to see your sister."

"I am not going to Longstone," she says again. "Ever. I'd rather take my chances with Graveney and his men."

In the light of the firebasket, Theodora is prancing around the edges of the rockpools, squinting into their dark-gold surfaces, her doll tucked under her arm. She looks back at Eva and Finn, who sit watching her from the cottage steps. "I think I see a fish!" she announces.

Eva forces a smile. She shivers. The night is vividly starlit and bitterly cold.

"What were you thinking?" Finn whispers. "We can't keep her safe here. What if Ward comes again?"

"I had no choice. Nathan was desperate. It's far more dangerous for her to be in Highfield House tonight." Eva shuffles across the cold stone of the step to press her body closer to Finn's. Nerves are roiling inside her. Before she had left the house, she had begged Nathan once more to reconsider standing up to Graveney. Her words had had no effect. "I'm so afraid for him," she admits.

Finn nods, not looking at her. He rakes a hand through the hair hanging loose on his shoulders. Scrubs a hand across his eyes. There's regret in him, Eva can tell. Though she cannot determine why.

She says, "What are you not telling me?"

Finn turns away from her for a moment. Lets out a breath. Finally, he looks back to face her. "It's my fault Nathan's decided to fight. I told him about the treasure ships." He sighs. "It was a mad thing to do. I wanted to help him, but I should have kept quiet. Because I know Ward's not going to support him."

The knot in Eva's stomach grows a little tighter. "How do you know that? Did Ward say something to you?"

Finn doesn't speak at once, his eyes fixed to Theodora as she bends to trail a hand through the rockpool.

"Finn," Eva pushes. "Tell me why."

He sighs. Rest his elbows on his knees and lowers his head, his hair falling forward over his face. "The night Ward came here to Longstone, he told me he'd only fight Graveney and his men if I agreed to re-join his crew. I told him I'd not do it." He glances at her, as though trying to gauge her reaction. Eva sees a wordless apology in his eyes.

She wraps her hand around his upper arm, pulling him closer. It feels as though she cannot get him near enough. "Why is he so desperate for you to re-join his crew? I know you know more than you are letting on."

He lets out a long breath. "He wants me away from you," he says bluntly. "Because he thinks that's what your ma would want. And he thinks it's the decent thing to do. He doesn't want you to spend your life with the man who killed your brother."

Eva feels a violent pain in her throat. She blinks back the tears that suddenly threaten behind her eyes. She thinks of Nathan, standing guard in that vast, creaking house. Counting blindly, foolishly, on Henry Ward's assistance. Assistance that will not come unless Finn agrees to leave her.

She had imagined being forced to make this choice between her husband and her family. But she had not imagined it would come like this.

"What did you tell Ward?" she asks, hearing the waver in her voice.

"I told him I wasn't going to leave you. But I don't know how Nathan will manage without Ward's help."

Eva swallows past the lump in her throat. "Nathan has made his own choices." She shifts on the step to meet Finn's eyes. "Henry Ward does not have the power to determine who I spend my life with." But even as she speaks, she recognises the cold reality of it: Henry Ward may well have the power to choose whether her brother lives or dies.

A wave swells over the edge of the island, catching the hems of Theodora's skirts. She yelps, and bounds away from the rockpool.

"Let's go inside," Eva tells her, climbing to her feet. She tries to inject a little brightness into her voice. "It's getting far too cold to be out here." She herds Theodora into the cottage, then turns back to Finn as he stands to join them. She catches his hand and tugs him close. "Please don't go with Ward. Whatever he thinks my mother would have wanted, and whatever he thinks is right, your place is here with me." She pulls the door closed behind them, muting the sound of the sea. Cannot shake the thought that she is sending Nathan to the gallows.

CHAPTER TWENTY-FIVE

"This is your final decision then?" Ward asks. The note Nathan had written him is sitting between them on the dining table. Nathan looks down at his own words: *request assistance... confrontation...* He feels oddly outside himself.

He sits rigid in the chair at the head of the table. His father's chair—no, *his* chair. "Yes," he says. "It is. I am not going to sit back and be forced from my home. If Graveney wants the house, he will have to fight me for it." He curls his hand around the arm of the chair. Despite all his self-encouragement, he is finding it hard to dig up the confidence he needs. "Can I count on your support?"

Ward leans back in the chair to Nathan's left. The vast wooden table stretches out before them, empty but for the misshapen scrap of the note, and a single spluttering candle. Nathan had sent Mrs Brodie back to the village earlier today. Had promised to fetch her again once the danger had passed. He had not let on that such a thing was no certainty. Couldn't bring himself to speak the words. In any case, he does not know how much his housekeeper is aware of, and he would prefer to keep as many of the details away from her as possible. The last thing this family needs is to be the topic of more rumours floating around the village.

Ward steeples his fingers. "Will it make a difference to what you do?"

Nathan knows it ought to. Without the support of Ward and his men, all he can hope for is for Graveney to see the pointlessness of putting a bullet in his chest. All of a sudden, his invincibility does not feel so secure. Refuse to hand over the house, and perhaps Graveney will kill him out of mere anger and frustration.

"I know you want Graveney gone," Nathan tells Ward. "I know you want the threat against your captaincy gone. And I know you want to leave Holy Island to hunt for these Spanish treasure ships."

Ward smiles wryly. "I see Finn Murray has been in your ear."

"I also know you loved my mother," Nathan says. "And I'm sorry for the way she betrayed you. But you know this is what she would want you to do."

Something passes across Ward's eyes and he swallows visibly. Tugs at his dark cravat.

Nathan leans forward, aware he has caught a hold of something. "Besides, this is not just for me. You want Graveney gone too. And surely you don't want his men coming here to the house, putting your own daughter at risk."

Ward clasps his hands in front of him on the table. He looks down into his folded fingers. Nathan wonders what he is thinking behind his deliberate façade of blankness. Of Abigail, surely. Of Harriet. At least, he hopes that's what he's thinking. Surely this is the only way to get Ward to do what he needs him to do.

For a long time, neither of them speak. Nathan can hear the distant tick of the clock on the mantel of the parlour. Hears heavy beams creak above his head. Ward stares into the flickering flame of the candle. In the dim light, his cheeks are shadowed, and he suddenly looks like an old man.

"You are right," he says finally. "I don't want my daughter at risk. And I do want to do what I think Abigail would have wanted, regardless of how she betrayed me."

Nathan shifts in his chair, the drum beat in his chest intensifying.

"Abigail would not have wanted Graveney in our daughter's life," Ward says. "But she did not want me in our daughter's life either. That's why I'm not going to help you fight Mr Graveney." Nathan opens his mouth to protest, but Ward raises a hand, silencing him before he can get a word out. "Your mother would not want you fighting. She would want you and your family out of this house. She would want you to get to safety. You know she would."

"Graveney won't kill me," Nathan says, too desperately. "He needs me alive." The words come out softer than he hoped. He wonders if he is starting to doubt them.

"He does need you alive," Ward agrees. "But there's nothing to say he won't retaliate if you refuse to do what he is asking. And what about my men? What about me? Graveney does not need any of us alive. Are you willing to risk our deaths for your own cause?"

And for the first time, Nathan sees behind Henry Ward's eyes. He sees that there is fear in him, just as there is fear in himself. This refusal to fight, Nathan realises, it accounts to a failure for Henry Ward. That bold and daring privateering captain who had appeared at the house during Nathan's childhood, he is on the verge of losing his ship to stronger men. Perhaps there are more similarities between the two of them than Nathan had initially realised. Perhaps they are both just weak, unremarkable men, trying to cope as best they can with their failures.

"I'm sorry," says Ward. "I know this is not the answer you wished for. But I've made up my mind. I suggest you get out of this house as soon as possible. Leave now, while you still can."

"I can't leave. My daughter is out on Longstone. I'll not go without her."

"Get out of the house," Ward says again. "Find secure lodgings off the island tonight. You'll find someone to take you out to Longstone for your daughter in the morning. Leave in the dark so Graveney and his men can't see you from the ship. And take the deeds to the house with you. With luck, you can return here in a few years' time, if that is really what you wish to do."

Nathan feels something sink inside him. A sense of heavy resignation. He knows Ward is right. He is not the kind of man who fights. He is the kind of man who runs.

He cannot deny that Holy Island has cast its spell on him, with its pink light and rising waters. But he also knows it is Julia Mitchell who has done the most spell-casting. Heartsplitting Julia, with her gold-dust eyes and blood on her hands.

Yes, he thinks. Running is the wise thing to do. Running. Hiding. Because really, if he is honest with himself, has he ever been destined for anything else?

CHAPTER TWENTY-SIX

They come almost as if he willed it. With Nathan Blake's daughter sleeping beneath their roof, there are lamps moving in the firelight. A longboat sliding soundlessly towards Longstone.

As if he willed it.

No—as if they have been watching. Watching the island, or watching Eva return from Lindisfarne with Theodora in the skiff, Finn doesn't know. Either way, it does not matter.

He stands on the jetty, watching the longboat approach. It is not fresh dread that he feels, because he has been expecting this. Has been carrying around this awful premonition since Nathan's daughter first stepped onto this island. She is currency, he thinks. She is the treasure that will make her father bend to John Graveney's will.

Ought he rush inside and wake Eva and Theodora? Hurry them into the skiff and try and escape? Try and weave through the reefs in the dark, with men on their tail? It's a suicidal mission—if it doesn't end with them all in Ward and

Graveney's hands, it will end with them all at the bottom of the sea.

They are easy targets here; he always has been.

As the men draw closer to the firebasket, Finn sees their faces; hard, empty eyes. Eyes of men who are following orders. Ward is not among them—not that Finn expected him to be. He assumes this longboat of men left the *Eagle* on Graveney's bidding, without the captain's knowledge.

"Open up the house," says one man as he climbs from the boat. He holds a pistol out in front of him.

Finn plays things out in his head. Refuse and the man will surely pull the trigger. He suspects these men who sail under the black flag will have no issue with doing so. So, refuse and he will die. The men will step over his body and climb inside the house and they will find Eva and Theodora sleeping.

He goes silently to the cottage. Climbs the stairs, five men trailing. Pushes open the door.

The cottage is dark, lit only by the stripes of light the firebasket paints as it strains through the half-open shutters. Embers glow orange in the grate. The men follow Finn inside, the floorboards creaking beneath their weight.

"Why are you here?" he asks, though he doesn't need to. When the answer comes—"the girl"—it is both terrifying, and desperately predictable.

"Take me," he says. "I'm the one Ward wants." But even as he speaks, Finn knows this is not about Ward. Ward's control is slipping. These men are here at Graveney's bidding. And he himself is of little value to them.

He looks around him in the dim light for anything that could be used as a weapon. A fire poker, perhaps, but he is still outnumbered. And one blow is likely to be replied to with pistol fire. Eva will wake, will rush out here, and they will fire at her too.

And then they will take Theodora.

"I'll fetch her," says Finn.

One of the men follows him towards the bedroom. Finn steps inside the dark room, a pistol held between his shoulder blades. He sees the small shape of Theodora, curled up in bed beside Eva. Both are breathing deep and even with sleep. Finn leans down and scoops Theodora out of bed, his fingers brushing against Eva's. A bitter irony, he thinks, that tonight she has finally succumbed to sleep. Or maybe it's a blessing. Maybe she's safer this way.

He holds his breath. He knows how lightly she will be sleeping. Knows how easy it would be for her to wake up, panic, retaliate. How easy it would be for these men to fire their pistols.

Finn's heart lurches. Because he cannot let these men take Thea to the ship alone. His only choice is to go with her. And he knows that once Ward has him aboard the *Eagle*, he will not let him go.

He looks down at Eva, her dark hair spilling out across the sheets. He wants to wake her. Wants to explain. Wants to tell her he is sorry, and that he loves her, and that he will come back to her as soon as possible. But he cannot put her in danger like that. Not with these men clustered in the doorway, pistols moving in the darkness.

He takes Theodora's cloak from the end of the bed and wraps it around her, her stockinged feet dangling down past his hips. And he steps quietly from the bed, forcing himself to turn away from Eva.

He must go with the men. Must go to Ward's ship. And

somehow, when all this is over, he will find his way back to his wife.

How he will do that, he cannot think about. Because if he thinks too hard on it, he will not do what needs to be done.

"I'm coming with you," he tells the men. "It's what your captain wants."

The men eye each other. Finn can see their indecision. Surely they must have foreseen this. Did they really imagine he might just stand back and watch them take a child from this island?

He wishes he had a chance to at least leave Eva a note. Telling her what has happened. Promising her he will return. He ought to have been more prepared. After all, he had seen this coming. But he just has to trust that she will understand. Surely once she sees Theodora gone, she will know.

He is walking towards the door before the men can argue. Before the need to turn back overwhelms him.

CHAPTER TWENTY-SEVEN

Theodora wakes when the longboat is surrounded by sea and the firebasket is little more than a glow on the horizon. She shifts on the bench beside Finn, where she is curled up beneath her dark blue cloak. She sits up suddenly. Her eyes widen as she takes in the men around her, the shifting longboat, the coal-dark water, as though struggling to make sense of whether she is still caught in a dream.

"Come here, Thea," Finn says, voice low. "Stay with me."

She shuffles across the bench so her shoulder presses against his side. For long moments, she doesn't speak, just alternates her gaze between him and the other men in the boat. None of them are looking at her, Finn realises. All of them have their eyes down, as though unable to look at what they have just been a part of. Finally, Theodora says, "Where are we going?"

"We're going to see the ship," Finn tells her.

"The ship outside my house?"

He nods.

"Why?"

"Because that's what these men want us to do."

There's a careful balance here. He needs Theodora to trust him. Doesn't want her to be afraid. Does he let her think he's the one behind this trip to the *Eagle*? The one responsible for tearing her out of bed in the middle of the night? Will that cause her to fear him? Or to trust that everything will be all right? He's not been in her life long enough for trust like that, Finn realises.

"Is it an adventurer's ship?" she asks, her voice still thick with confusion and sleep.

"Aye. Something like that." He glances back at the firebasket. It's beginning to burn out now. He ought to be out in the shed with a shovelful of coal.

That ache in his chest, he can't go near it. Not now, with Theodora here. He knows that once he is aboard the *Eagle*, it will be near impossible to leave. Ward will not allow him to escape a second time. The only way he will make it back to Eva is if Graveney succeeds in overthrowing Ward as captain. Finn can't bear to think what that would mean for the Blakes.

But he cannot think of Eva; cannot think of how she will react when she finds out he and Theodora are gone. All he can do right now is focus on keeping them both alive. On getting Thea back to her father.

They are on the ship too quickly, among shadows and dark wood and men moving in circles of lamplight. The *Eagle* feels old and worn, as though its best days are far behind it. How had he ever been awed by this ship, Finn wonders? How had he ever seen beauty in it? He is surprised he had ever been that naïve and foolish, even as a child.

211

Theodora looks around, wide-eyed, her stockinged feet silent as she crosses the tarred slats of the deck. She looks sickeningly out of place in her thin white nightgown, cloak wrapped around her shoulders and blonde hair tangled around her cheeks. Ghostly, almost. Finn can't tell if she's scared or intrigued. He keeps a firm hand around her wrist.

He sifts through the lamplight of the deck, searching for Ward. But it's an older man that comes towards them now—John Graveney, he expects. Finn does not remember Graveney from his time in Ward's crew. But he had seen this man arguing with Ward at the tavern on Lindisfarne several weeks ago—no doubt about Abigail Blake's cursed letter.

Graveney glances at Theodora; glares at Finn. He turns to the men who had brought them from Longstone. Speaks to them in inaudible words.

"I want to speak to the captain," Finn says tautly.

"This isn't the captain's business."

Finn grits his teeth. "Take the lass back to her father. You know he'll hand over the house in exchange for her safety."

"In good time." Graveney's voice is coarse and abrupt. "But let's give Nathan Blake time to discover his daughter missing."

Theodora takes a step towards Finn. He feels her shoulder press hard against his hip. Feels her hand clutch a fistful of his greatcoat. And yes, she is afraid now, he can tell. Perhaps made so by the mention of her father's name. He wraps an arm around her shoulder, trying to steady her. He feels her shivering hard.

"Take us below," he says. "It's far too cold for her to be out here in her nightclothes." Where in hell is Ward? Is he even aboard the ship?

Graveney calls to one of the men who had brought them from Longstone. Murmurs to him in words Finn cannot catch. But before the men can act, the saloon door blows open and Ward steps out onto deck. Surprise flickers across his eyes at the sight of Finn and Theodora. "What is this?" he demands. "Mr Graveney?"

Graveney doesn't respond. Just continues speaking to his men.

Finn meets Ward's eyes. "Take us below."

Ward nods silently. He calls across the deck to his steward, who gestures to Finn to follow him into the ship.

Finn glances back over his shoulder at Ward. He needs to speak with him urgently. Needs his help to get Theodora back to her father. But the captain is locked in a heated conversation with Graveney and his men.

Finn debates whether to stay on deck. No, he decides. He needs to get Theodora out of the cold, and he does not trust any of these men to be alone with her. He trails the steward down through the passages, stumbling as Theodora presses herself a little too close to his side.

There's a strange silence to the ship. Once, the *Eagle* had been full of shouted voices, banter, laughter. Now it's a place of whispers. Finn had not noticed it when last he was aboard. He'd been too preoccupied by the prospect of death—and by the prospect of Eva learning he had killed her brother. It's a silent kind of tension, wrought by a divided crew. A thread about to snap. He can only hope he is no longer aboard when it does.

The steward unlocks the door to the great cabin and steps aside, allowing Finn and Theodora entry.

"Tell Ward I need to speak with him urgently," says Finn.

213

He hopes, as he speaks, that the steward is loyal to Ward. Hopes he is not another Jacobite seeking to punish the Blakes for their mother's crimes.

The steward nods his grey head, giving nothing away. He pulls the door closed. Turns the key in the lock.

Finn glances around the great cabin. The air feels too thick, too close, too tainted with familiarity. The windows at the stern of the ship are boarded up, and the sight of it makes his chest ache. He knows this was Eva's doing; knows she had smashed the glass and leapt into the sea, risking her life so she might help him escape a keel-hauling—with the fresh truth of Oliver's death ringing in her ears.

———————◇———————

Eva opens her eyes. It is dark—too dark. There is only ever this kind of darkness on Longstone when the rain is thrashing too hard for the firebasket to be lit. But she does not hear rain. Just the steady exhalation of the sea.

She reaches into the blackness for Theodora. At the feel of the empty bed, she lurches forward, scrambling for the tinderbox on the bedside table and calling Finn's name.

The silence is achingly deep. Her hand trembles as she lights the lamp and carries it into the living space. She calls for them again. Pans the lamp around the living area. There is the soup pot on the hook, the remains of supper growing cold. There are Theodora's black buckled shoes, lined up in front of the hearth to dry. Her doll lies abandoned on the table, eyes staring blankly into the darkness. Rocks and candles and twine on the mantel. Everything as they left it. No sign that anyone else has been here.

But Eva knows instinctively what has happened. Knows Finn was right to fear having Thea on the island with them. Knows that she had never truly been safe here. None of them have.

She rushes back to the bedroom and throws on her clothes and shoes. Grabs the lamp from the table and stumbles down the steps at the front of the cottage. Darkness consumes her, the meagre pool of lamplight powerless against the blackness of the island. Stars explode overhead, but the thin crescent moon provides little light. Just the faintest glow of orange from within the firebasket, a candle against an ocean of dark. All around her, she hears the restless sigh of the sea; hears the distant barking of seals. Hears her panicked breath rushing in her ears. Tonight, Longstone terrifies her.

She hurries out to the skiff and flings loose the mooring ropes. Forces aside the sudden fear of the dark, and everything that might lie beyond it.

CHAPTER TWENTY-EIGHT

There is not a cell in Julia's body that is surprised to be here, out on a dark ocean with her eldest brother, condemning Joseph Holland's body to the sea. Somehow, she has always known that having Hugh around her would lead her somewhere like this; deep into the heart of the Rising, where she never wanted to go.

She has fought it for so long; trying to keep Bobby blind and deaf to all that is happening; hiding her brothers' presence from everyone. Speaking in lies to a man who has made her feel the way no one has before. And for what? Bobby knows far too much. She surely has no way of ever rebuilding things with Nathan. And she literally has blood on her hands.

Julia had not said a word to her brother as they had carried Holland's body towards the anchorage, wrapped in hessian stolen from the fishermen's huts. Had not said a word to him as he had sailed them out here, to this gulf of dark water between Holy Island and the Farnes. Out here, Nathan had told her, Donald Macauley's body lies. And Joseph Holland is to meet the same fate.

Hugh piles stones into the hessian pall containing the body. Julia turns away, unable to watch. "All right," he mumbles. "It's ready. Help me."

Julia keeps her eyes averted. "Cover him. I don't want to see."

Hugh sighs. On the edge of her vision, she sees him folding the hessian back over Holland's face. When she dares to look back, his thick legs are still visible in their mud-caked boots. She closes her eyes and lifts the dead weight of Holland's legs. Together, she and Hugh slip the body over the gunwale. The boat tilts and Joseph Holland vanishes.

For several moments, they sit without speaking. Julia says a silent prayer for the dead man. With its mainsail furled, the dory is tugged along on the current, out in the direction of the Farnes. Julia squints. The Longstone firebasket is dark tonight. Everything is dark. She wonders if she ought to be concerned.

But then she sees light. The glow of a lamp on the sea. It's faint, candle-like, but drawing closer. Less than a mile away, perhaps. She panics. They cannot let themselves be seen. Never mind that Holland's body is sinking to the bottom; if she is caught out here so close to midnight with her criminal of a brother, they will be under no end of suspicion.

Hugh curses under his breath and lurches for the mainsail sheet. Tugs on the line to open the sail to the wind. Julia turns to look over her shoulder. The skiff is Finn Murray's, she thinks. She lifts the lamp; squints into the dark.

It's Eva at the tiller, alone in the boat without a cloak or bonnet, and flying out far too close to the reef. Julia can tell something is very wrong. She knows Eva is level headed, sensible. An inexperienced sailor, she assumes, but still not the kind to behave so recklessly. Certainly not one to sail out here so late at night. Especially not alone.

"Get closer to her," Julia orders. "She's in trouble."

Hugh snorts. "We're not getting close to anyone. You don't think they'll have questions?"

"She'll not turn us in." Julia knows this with certainty. Distrusting of her or not, Eva will not turn her in for a crime she herself had committed. "Eva!" she calls. "Come about at once!"

Eva whirls around at the sound. She stumbles against the gunwale, but makes no attempt to back the mainsail and slow the boat. Julia tries to shove Hugh aside, elbowing her way towards the tiller.

Hugh curses under his breath. Something changes in his eyes—an acknowledgement, perhaps, that Julia is doing this with or without his consent, and that it will be easier if he plays along. He nudges her aside, taking the tiller.

The fishing boat flies over the swell, dark water sputtering up into Julia's eyes. She holds her breath as the dory careens out towards the reef. Lets out a sigh when Eva's boat begins to curve away from the Knavestone.

Hugh eases the dory up alongside Eva's skiff. The two small boats knock and grind together. Julia scrambles over the gunwale of the dory, landing heavily on her knees in the skiff.

"Are you all right?" she asks Eva, climbing to her feet.

Eva nods faintly, breathless.

Julia takes the tiller, easing the skiff into open water. She watches the lamp of Hugh's fishing boat fly off into the darkness. Watches her brother disappear with it. She swallows a swell of pain. Tries to make herself believe she will see him again. That one day soon, Hugh and Angus will be sitting at her supper table, telling Bobby about their enormous haul with the herring fleet. She can't make it feel like anything other than a lie.

Once they are clear of the reef, Julia looks back at Eva. "What's happened?"

Eva is huddled on the bench now, trembling, her eyes red and swollen. Her words are garbled with tears; hard to make out. Finn, she says; and Theodora; and, "We have to get to Ward's ship."

"No," Julia tells her, reining in her own panic. "That's madness. You know it is." And she steels herself against the tide of emotion that rises when she says, "We have to tell Nathan."

Nathan tells himself history is not repeating. Tells himself this is nothing like the circumstances in which he was forced from Highfield House as a child. This time, his leaving is a choice. A reluctant one, but an informed choice, nonetheless. He will leave the house, sensibly and safely, and attempt to sell the place from London.

The right thing to do. Because he is not the kind of man who fights. He is the man who had railed against his family coming here. Who had drowned in panic when Eva and Theodora had first appeared on the doorstep of Highfield House. He is the kind of prudent, rational man who is going to do everything he can to get his family to safety.

He throws his clothes into a duffel bag. Without a wagon, they will have no way of transporting their trunks into the village tonight, but at least he will not be reduced to running with nothing but the clothes on his back, like his mother was twenty years ago.

"You're making the right decision," Edwin says from the doorway.

Nathan can't look at him. Edwin is a reminder of the life he will be reduced to now. A life of pity and charity. For a moment, he understands his mother's need to break the law to ensure her family's security.

"Are you and Harriet ready to leave?" Nathan asks, not turning around.

"If I have to carry her out of here over my shoulder, then that's what I will do," Edwin says wryly. "I've locked her in the bedroom in the meantime. In case she has a thought to try to disappear again."

"Does she know her father has gone?" Nathan had watched Ward leave the house; knows he had done so without a word of farewell to his daughter. Had Ward simply decided things were easier that way? Or had he been so distracted by the conflict on his ship that it did not cross his mind to seek Harriet out?

He doubts it; suspects Ward's leaving had more to do with his knowledge that Abigail had never wanted him in their daughter's life. He knows Harriet would be devasted to learn of such a thing.

"I've not told her," says Edwin. "And perhaps it's best for her that I don't. Let her think I'm to blame for tearing her away from this place without the chance to see her father one last time. At this point, I don't think she can despise me much more."

Nathan turns to look at Edwin then; gives him sympathetic eyes. "Perhaps things will be different once you're back in London," he says. "Perhaps we can all begin to see clearly again."

Unbidden, his gaze drifts to the telescope Julia had given him, lying in its box on the bed. It would be foolish to take something so bulky with him, but he cannot bear the thought of leaving it behind.

He takes it to the window and pushes back the curtains. It is only when he brings the telescope to his eye that he realises he is using it to see Ward's ship.

No. He does not want this gift tainted by Henry Ward.

He places it back in its box. Considers shoving it in his duffel bag.

Leave it, he decides. For better or worse, when he runs from Holy Island, he will run from Julia too. And the only way he will survive that is if he does his best to forget her. If he's honest with himself, the two of them have never been destined for anything else.

Nathan buttons his bag. "I'll meet you downstairs shortly. Just give me a moment."

Edwin nods. Disappears from the doorway without another word.

Nathan feels a deep grief as he walks down the passage. It's a sadness he never imagined this house would be able to wrangle from him. This house has been in his family for five generations. He hates that it will be lost on his watch.

Maybe this was what had caused his mother to flee so abruptly—this reluctance to leave, even with the knowledge that she had no choice. Maybe hesitation had left her frozen, until Henry Ward's ship had appeared through the windows and she had run out of time.

He understands. Understands, now, the power this house has to creep beneath your skin. It's the windows that open onto the sea; the roll of the dunes on every side. The depth of the darkness when the lamps are dimmed and the universe unfolds above rows of smoke-stained chimneys.

He goes to his study. The room had belonged to his father, and his grandfather before that. He runs a hand over the smooth wood of the desk. Whoever buys this house will end up with all his family's belongings. He will have no chance to empty it. No chance to return. The deeds to the house will also give the new owners shelves of books his father had read, the dressing table with the mirror his mother had peered into so many times. Nathan can still picture Abigail sitting on her stool, running a brush through her long, dark hair. Pictures her eyes meeting his in the mirror when he would peer around the doorframe in an attempt to catch a glimpse of her.

All right, my love? he hears her say. *There's no need to hide.*

Despite his anger at his mother, the memory still feels precious.

He hates the thought of strangers walking through his family's past. Of them discarding the house's contents as meaningless junk. A strange thing, he thinks. Was that not exactly how he had viewed all this when he had first been forced up here by Henry Ward? Pieces of a life he had done his best to forget? He had been quick to bundle up all the moth-eaten clothes and tarnished jewellery and cart it off to the church's charity collection. Now everything feels impossibly valuable. He takes his father's penknife from the desk drawer. Tucks it into his pocket.

He steps from the study and closes the door behind him. Then he takes out the ring of keys and unlocks the door to Oliver's room. Steps inside.

The room is dark and cavernous, emptied of furniture when he had torn up the old floorboards while on a search for the letter. The dark is deep, but Nathan realises suddenly that the dread he has always felt in here is gone. Somehow, in the wake of admitting how he really felt about his brother's death, the room has lost its power. Become nothing but an empty shell. Hollow. Surrounded by empty walls.

A cruel irony, Nathan thinks, that he might have landed in such a place now, when he has no choice but to leave the house without looking back. As though Oliver is managing one last callousness, before Nathan lets him go entirely.

CHAPTER TWENTY-NINE

The door of the great cabin clicks open and Ward steps inside. Finn looks up at him from his seat at the table. A deep frown creases Ward's forehead, a look of unease in his eyes.

Finn nods towards the bed, where Theodora is curled up asleep beneath her cloak. "Was this your doing?" he demands.

"Of course not." Ward turns the key in the lock. "You know me better than that."

"But you just let your men sail out to Longstone and take her from her bed?"

Ward fixes his gaze on Theodora. "I had no idea my men were on Longstone. I've been at the house. Trying to convince Nathan Blake to give up this foolish fight."

"I'm sure taking his daughter will do it."

Irritation flashes across Ward's eyes. "I told you, I had nothing to do with that."

"And yet it's got you what you want. Here I am, back on your ship, just as you wanted."

Ward slides off his coat and hangs it on the back of his

desk chair. "It's the right thing to do, Finn. But I did not force you to do it."

"What choice did I have? You think I'd just let those bastards take Nathan's daughter?"

Ward smiles thinly. "Seems I did teach you a little decency after all." He goes to the cupboard beneath his desk and pulls out a bottle of whisky. Holds it up to Finn in offering.

"I'd rather keep a clear head, if it's all the same to you."

Ward ignores his sharpness. He fills a glass and sinks into his desk chair. "I had nothing to do with the men taking Nathan's daughter. I regret that that happened. I regret that my crew has become so lawless."

"You took a ship full of men from the Republic of Pirates. What did you imagine would happen?"

Ward doesn't respond. Finn watches as he brings his whisky glass to his lips. A faint tremor there. Ward is growing old, Finn realises. Weary. The captain he remembers would never have hidden away in his great cabin like this, while other men sought to take his ship. Sought to harm the family of the woman he loved.

Perhaps it's being around the Blakes that has made him so weary. Perhaps it's the knowledge of Harriet; the confirmation that Abigail had not loved him as he had loved her. This can come as no surprise, surely. Finn knows that, after the night Oliver died, Ward never saw Abigail again. How could he have imagined she did anything other than flee to escape him? Escape the poisonous influence of captain and crew.

And now what? Is Ward to sit back and let these men take as they wish from Abigail's family? There's a resignation in his eyes that suggests this is exactly what he plans to do. Once,

Ward had told him that to spend a life at sea required nothing less than great passion for the cause. And Finn can sense that, as far is Ward is concerned, this passion is running thin.

But he thinks of the spark in his former captain's eyes when he told him of the Spanish treasure ships. That passion might be running thin, but it has not disappeared completely.

"Keep your word, Ward," Finn says finally. "I re-join your crew, you fight Graveney. Was that not the deal we made? Get Nathan's daughter home and get your men out of the Blakes' lives." These are dangerous words, Finn knows. Because he has no intention of staying here on the ship. He desperately hopes he can be back on Longstone before Eva even notices him gone. But with each passing minute, that is becoming less and less likely. Either way, he needs Ward to believe he is here to stay. Needs him to agree to this deal he had proposed.

"I told Nathan Blake to leave Holy Island," says Ward. "He has agreed."

"That's because he thinks his daughter is safe on Longstone," Finn hisses. He leans forward, smacking a hand into the table, a desperate attempt to spark Ward back to life. "You've always claimed to be a man of honour. You need to do as you promised. Fight these men." Finn watches the indecision pass over Ward's face. "Is this really what you want?" He gestures to Theodora. "To be the captain of a crew who stoops to such things?"

Ward takes another sip of whisky, hard eyes looking out across the cabin. Finn can tell this is not the first time he has considered such things. After a long time, he nods slowly. "You're right," he says. "This is not what I want. And regardless of your reasons, you are here as I wished. I know I

cannot ask you to do what is right, if I do not do the same."
He stands abruptly and clenches his jaw. Finn watches the
muscles tick. "I shall tell my men to prepare for engagement."

Finn feels a tug of guilt. *I cannot ask you to do what is right.*
He is deceiving Ward, there is no denying it. He is here on
the ship now, just as Ward wished. But at the first
opportunity, he will run back to his wife.

Ward goes to his desk drawer and produces a pistol. Sets
it on the table in front of Finn, along with a handful of extra
shot.

Finn glances down at it. He's not touched a weapon since
he had sailed with Ward as a boy. Back then, he'd felt drunk
on the power it gave him. Now, he wants nothing to do with
the thing. Still, he can't deny that with the ship about to erupt,
he feels a little safer with its cold metal between his fingers.
He slides it into the pocket of his coat, along with the
ammunition. Nods towards Theodora. "I'm taking her back
to the house." Ward opens his mouth to speak, but Finn
continues, "I gave you my word I'd stay. But you can't keep
her here if you're about to open fire on these men. Once she's
safely back at the house, I'll return."

Ward looks at him with doubtful eyes. He's right to, of
course. Because Finn has no intention of returning. How he
can he do anything but keep sailing on to Longstone and
climb back into bed beside Eva?

But the thought is chased away by a sudden reality: escape
from Ward again and he and Eva will continue to live with
one eye on the horizon. They will continue to live in fear of
stray bullets and lights on the sea. Eva will live at the window
with her eyes on the water. She will spend her life sleepless;
wondering, waiting, worrying. And it will only be a matter of

time before Ward comes for them again.

He will come back to the ship, Finn realises suddenly. Ward will have what he wants.

He will come back, because he cannot do anything else. He cannot let Eva spend her life at that window, staring out over the sea. He cannot let her days and nights be consumed by worry. Cannot put her through any more of this unbearable anticipation.

He cannot condemn his wife to a life lived in fear.

The sudden reality of it makes his stomach lurch. His body turns hot, then cold and he grips the edge of the table to steady himself.

"My steward, Mr Slater, will go with you," Ward says pointedly. "See that you keep your word." He slides his justacorps back over his wiry shoulders. "I'll speak to my loyal men first. Then draw the rest of the crew up onto deck. Give you a chance to get the girl off the ship unnoticed. I'll have Slater ready the longboat."

Finn nods dizzily. Watches after Ward as he slips out of the cabin.

He waits. Listens. More voices. Footsteps. A muffled shout from somewhere far above. Everything seems distorted. Too loud. Too soft.

When he turns around, he sees Theodora standing a few yards behind him. The sight of her makes him start. He had not even heard her getting out of bed. She scrubs a hand across tired eyes.

"Are we still on the ship?" she asks blearily.

"Aye." Finn takes her cloak from the end of the bed and slings it over her shoulders. "But we're going to leave very soon, all right? So we've got to get ready."

Theodora looks up at him with wide blue eyes. She nods silently, fumbling with the buttons on her cloak. Finn makes his way across the cabin and presses an ear to the door. It's quiet in the passage now; he can hear the distant hum of voices from up on deck.

He touches the pocket of his coat, feeling for the pistol. Theodora hangs back, knotting her hands in her cloak. "Come on now," Finn says, voice low. "Quick as we can, aye?"

She nods. Hurries towards him, and reaches out to grip a fistful of his coat. Finn turns the key and steps out into the passage. And it's instinct guiding him, up this ladder, down that passage, past closed doors and groaning bulkheads. Because he remembers the hatch behind the mess tables that will take them out to the poop deck. Hopefully there he will find Slater and the longboat waiting.

He guides Theodora through the passage and up the ladder, reaching over her head to shove open the hatch. "Up here," he says. "Careful now. Hold on tight." She climbs slowly, feeling her way through the dark. He can make out little more than her fragile outline, moving steadily up the rungs, her nightgown glowing against the blackness. Finn scrambles up after her, squeezing his body through a hatch he last climbed through as an eleven-year-old child.

The deck is crowded and noisy, with men clustered towards the bow of the ship. Finn is dimly aware of Ward speaking heatedly to Graveney, but barely pays them attention. He cannot consider the prospect that this ship will be his life now. That these men are the people he will spend his every day and night with. All he can focus on is getting Theodora back to her father.

He cannot think of any of it. He just helps Theodora into the longboat and climbs in beside her, nodding to Ward's steward to row them back towards Highfield House.

CHAPTER THIRTY

Nathan hears a thunderous rap at the front door. He fears
he is too late in leaving; fears Graveney and his men are here,
a day early to catch him unaware. He snatches the deeds to
the house from inside his bag before hurrying down the stairs.
He had hoped to run without handing them over, but if he
opens the door to waving pistols, he sees now that he will
have no choice.

But when he pulls the door open, it is not Graveney or
Ward, but Eva and Julia that fly inside, frantic and
windblown, with wild hair and fear in their eyes. He cannot
make sense of why they are here; why they are together; what
he is supposed to feel in Julia's presence. And they are both
talking at once, words so tangled Nathan can barely make
them out. But: *Theodora* he hears; and *ship*. And every thought
of fleeing suddenly vanishes from his mind.

From the water, the house looks as otherworldly and grim as it always has. A stone hulk against the emptiness of the dunes. Lamps are blazing in several of the windows, but they cast no more than meagre circles that do little to light its mass. At least, Finn thinks, when all this is over, he will never have to step inside the place again. The thought brings little comfort.

He feels his heart stutter. There's a boat on the embankment—his skiff. Eva must have brought it here when she discovered him and Theodora missing. He had hoped—naively, he sees now—that she would not get entangled in this. That she would sleep away the night, and know nothing of it until Theodora was safe and the *Eagle* was long gone. He cannot bring himself to think of what she had gone through, waking to find them gone, sailing in the darkness, drowning in panic.

He finds himself staring up at the windows, hoping for a glimpse of her. If Eva is here, Nathan must know that Ward's men have Theodora. What is he planning to do? Finn knows he has to get Thea back to her father before anyone acts rashly.

He tears his eyes away from the glass. If he sees Eva, he will never do what needs to be done.

He looks at Theodora. Her eyes are on the house, her small hands clasped tightly around the edge of the bench. She is gnawing on her lip, eyes wide and glistening. Finn turns to Slater. "When we get to shore, I need you to take Theodora back to the house."

"What about you?"

"I'll take the longboat around the point. Keep an eye on the ship."

Slater gives a humourless chuckle. "Sorry, lad. I've orders to keep an eye on you."

Finn scrubs a hand across his eyes. "Come on, man. Just do as I'm asking. Please. I'm just trying to stay the hell away from the house. I can't—" He stops abruptly. Refuses to speak of it. "Please just do it," he says again.

Slater lets out a sigh; glances back over his shoulder at the ship. Then he nods resignedly. A wave pushes the longboat closer to the beach and Slater clambers out, splashing softly into the dark water. He reaches over and lifts Theodora out of the boat. Finn hears her murmur. He can't look at her. Can't look at the house.

He shuffles onto the bench seat left empty by Slater and takes up the oars. He pulls the longboat around the point as quickly as he can, hiding the house from his line of sight.

A burst of gunfire. Finn whirls around to look back to the ship. He hears shouting drift across the water.

He pulls on the oars, further out to sea for a better look at the ship. He sees lamps bobbing, tracing through the darkness. Men are pouring into the longboats from the *Eagle*, he realises. Boats are beginning to pull towards the house. His stomach plunges. Have Ward and his men been defeated? Has Graveney discovered Theodora is gone? Has he chosen to come for Nathan before he can run?

And he cannot hide, Finn realises. If Graveney and his men are coming to the house, he cannot just sit back and watch. Especially not now Eva is inside.

It was not clarity he was seeing with before, Nathan

realises. Because he is seeing with clarity now. A singular focus. He must get Theodora out of the hands of these men. The house, the money, the letter—nothing else matters.

He hears pistol fire coming from the direction of the water. Cannot allow himself to think about what that might mean.

"Take me out to the ship," he says to Julia. "I know it's dangerous. But I wouldn't ask it—"

She nods before he can finish. She had prepared herself for such a request; he can tell by the hardness in her eyes. He murmurs his thanks.

On the edge of his vision, Nathan sees Edwin tucking his pistol into his pocket. He is grateful for the support.

"I'm coming with you," says Eva. "I have to find Finn."

Nathan throws open the door and steps out onto the dunes. There is no way, of course, that he is going to allow Eva to climb into that boat with them, but right now, he does not have the time to argue.

The sight before him turns his body hot, then cold. Longboats are cutting through the water towards the house. Lamps glowing, men shouting, shots flying. He hears a distant cry of pain.

A conflict between Ward's fractured crew, but Nathan knows this house—and his mother—is at the centre of it all.

There's a deep, boiling fear there, at his edges. But right now, all he can focus on is the tiny shape at the water's edge. His daughter, stumbling over the dunes in her nightgown, with a man by her side. Eva shoves her way past Nathan and rushes forward, letting out a stifled cry when she realises the man is not her husband.

Nathan flies towards Theodora, scooping her into his

arms. Tears are flooding her face, falling harder with each echoed pistol shot. She clings to his neck, wraps her legs around his waist, buries her wet face against his neck. And for a moment, there is nothing beyond this; no men fighting, no boats approaching, just pure unbridled relief. Then the feel of her in his arms is too much, and dizziness threatens to overwhelm him. He sets Theodora down beside Eva. Tries to catch his breath. She wails harder at the loss of him.

"Take her upstairs," Nathan tells his sister. "Get her inside." His words come out in pieces: *the passage. Behind the priest hole. Oliver's room.*

Eva's arm goes thoughtlessly around Theodora's shoulders. But she starts to protest. "I can't. I have to—"

"Please, Eva. She's terrified." Nathan glances back over his shoulder at the approaching men. "We'll find Finn. I swear it."

Eva blinks back a fresh rush of tears. Another argument on her lips, then finally, a faint nod of acceptance. She hurries Theodora inside the house.

Nathan turns back to Julia. "Go with them." His voice is husky. "Get inside. Get to safety." She meets Nathan's eyes for a long moment, then follows Eva into the house without a word. Closes the door behind her.

Nathan reaches into his pocket, his fingers closing around the deeds of the house.

"Let's go," Edwin hisses, standing at his shoulder. "If we leave through the servants' entrance we can make it into the village—"

"It's too late to run." If they try to escape now, they will be easy targets out on the exposed dunes. Nathan knows he has to stay here with his house. Has to trust this place will protect them.

He curses Henry Ward for refusing to fight. Curses himself for refusing to run, until it was too late. And he curses his mother for not having the foresight to know where her crimes would lead.

But when he looks out to sea once more, Nathan realises he was wrong. Henry Ward is here among these men, a pistol in his hand, on his feet at the bow of one of the longboats. Shouting orders. Directing men. Fighting for them, as Abigail would have wanted.

But just like Nathan himself, Ward has made his choice far too late. Because the first of the boats are sighing against the shore. Men leap out into the shallow water. And John Graveney strides steadily up the beach.

CHAPTER THIRTY-ONE

Eva rushes up the stairs, clutching Theodora's hand. Down the hall to the room at the end of the house.

The priest hole. The passage.

She has never seen them. Has only ever heard stories of them: Nathan crawling through the walls to find Julia's brothers hidden in the attic. Finn using the passage to escape, the night of Oliver's death.

The door creaks as she pushes against it, but it swings open willingly. Has she ever been inside this room before? The question is there dimly; poorly timed at the back of her mind. Certainly not since she had returned to Highfield House as an adult. As a child? Her memories of Oliver are fragile, built mostly on fear. She cannot imagine having willingly gone into his bedroom.

It's dark inside; feels airless, somehow. Eva imagines she can smell the decay of neglect, though she knows it can be nothing more than her own fear and racing imagination. Knows this was one of the first rooms Nathan and Edwin restored.

She hurries to the window and looks out. Lights on the water; boats moving through moonlight towards the house. Beside her, Theodora is sobbing messy tears, clutching at Eva's skirts, feet sliding over the floorboards in her dirty stockings.

Eva squints through the glass. There are men crossing the embankment now, but she does not see Finn.

She swallows down a swell of grief and goes to the fireplace, a beastly black shape in the dark. Eva pushes against one wall panel, another, another; a desperate attempt to find the priest hole. And at once, her thoughts are back with Finn; with his panic, his fear, as he had scrambled to find the hiding place in the wall in the wake of Oliver's death. Her chest aches. And the house moves beneath her hands, the panel twisting open to reveal the hidden space behind.

Theodora's eyes widen. Her crying halts as she stares into the chasm inside the wall. Eva knows Nathan has always forbidden his daughter from coming into this room; has always kept it locked. Had he opened it just for this purpose, she wonders distantly? Had he seen this necessity coming?

Eva goads Theodora into the hiding place. Murmurs words of encouragement she cannot make herself feel. She pushes the wall panel closed, trapping her niece inside. Theodora pounds against the wall, howling out her protest. Eva feels a sharp pang of guilt. But she cannot stay here. She needs to find her husband.

Theodora's shrieks echo through the panelling as Eva hurries back to the window. It is still too dark to see much beyond inky shapes, but she sees the flashes of pistols, hears shots fly. Men on the dunes now too, coming towards the house. Coming *for* the house.

She hurries for the door. Turns at the sound of the priest hole groaning open. Theodora spills out and rushes towards her.

"Get back inside," Eva manages, but Thea is howling, hysterical, gasping for breath. Behind them, glass shatters, spraying into the dark room. A stray shot, sent from the beach, careening up into the house.

Eva stops herself on the way to the door. She cannot go out there now, not even to find Finn. Running into pistol fire and putting herself in danger will only cause more trouble for everyone.

She grabs Thea's hand and rushes back towards the priest hole, keeping low to avoid any more wayward shots. She pushes on the panel beside the fireplace and burrows into the wall, losing herself in the darkness within the innards of the house.

<hr />

"Hold your fire." The order comes from Henry Ward; Nathan knows that voice all too well. This voice does not come from the fearful man who had sat at Nathan's dining table and told him to walk away. It comes from the man who had threatened him into returning to Lindisfarne, the man who had made him believe he held his life in his hands. Nathan wonders which version of Henry Ward is real.

And for all the conflict on that ship; for all the power that John Graveney seems to hold, Ward's words silence the fire. Men are still brandishing swords and pistols, but there's a sudden motionlessness. A held breath. The stillness that falls over the beach feels impossibly deep.

Nathan hears his pulse roaring in his ears. His legs feel weak beneath him, his vision pulsing at its edges. He is going to die—of that he is suddenly certain. Never mind that Graveney needs him alive. Never mind these deeds in his pocket, worthless without his signature and seal. To think that that would save him suddenly feels like the greatest of naiveties. Because Henry Ward may have rediscovered his authoritative voice, but Graveney is facing Nathan with a pistol in his hand, and the beach is already stained with blood. Men have fallen across the embankment, others slumped in the longboats.

To his left, Nathan catches sight of Finn, striding up the beach towards the house. Ward steps in front of him, presses a palm to his chest, holding him back.

Several of Graveney's men face Ward and his supporters, weapons held out in front of them. Silent; waiting for a signal to strike. And this held breath, Nathan realises, this fleeting peace, it's all for him. These men are waiting to see what he will do. Waiting to see if he will relinquish the house. If he will plunge his family deeper into poverty. If he will live his life at the will of another man.

"Mr Blake," says Graveney. "I trust you've made your decision."

My decision, yes. Relinquish the house. Plunge his family into poverty. Live by another man's bidding. But when he opens his mouth to answer, Nathan's rational thoughts disappear. In their place is that fierce single-mindedness that had consumed him with the news that Theodora had been taken. By the man that stands in front of him.

My decision. He reaches for the deeds, barely registering that it is not the paperwork he is pulling from his pocket, but his pistol. A singular focus. Clarity.

He hears the shot echo in the stillness. Barely realises he is the one to have pulled the trigger. And with a blissful sense of being outside himself, he watches Graveney fall.

CHAPTER THIRTY-TWO

Nathan waits for the responding shot. Waits to die. Because surely they will come for him now, these men who had rallied around Graveney; these fellow Jacobites who had helped him try to take the house. He feels himself being shoved backwards, pulled away from the conflict. Feels himself pitch sideways, stumbling against the damp earth of the dunes. Shots fly and swords collide. Nathan's thoughts are clattering too violently to make sense of who had pulled him out of the throng of men. Ward, perhaps? Or Finn? A stranger glad to see Graveney defeated? He cannot make sense of why he has been deemed worth saving.

His vision is swimming, his body hot. He can make sense of little beyond the humming in his ears and the lifeless body of John Graveney lying on the embankment. And the fact that Henry Ward is here, fighting, as Nathan had requested. He has no thought of what had made Ward change his mind. But right now, he has no thought of anything.

He crawls towards the house. Does not dare attempt to

get inside, in case anyone tries to follow him. But he hunches behind the rise of a dune, hand clenched around his pistol. He knows there's little point—the barrel is empty; he has made his shot. And he may die for it yet. But somehow, he feels safer with the weapon in his hand. It makes him feel like something more than a man who runs.

Men fall, and shout, go loudly to their deaths; and after minutes, or hours, of distorted time, there is silence. Henry Ward marches across the beach. His deliberate stride suggests the blood splattered across his shirtsleeves is not his own. Victorious? Nathan supposes the fact he is alive would suggest as much. Ward reaches into his pocket and slides a fresh round of ammunition into his pistol. And for a moment, Henry Ward is the fearless adventurer Nathan had seen him as back when he was a boy. That mythical figure who had appeared sporadically at the house, as though he had been magicked in from an adventure tale.

"Take the fallen back to the ship," Nathan hears him say. "Prepare them for burial." Ward's gold-buttoned figure drifts in and out of focus.

Nathan turns his gaze to the sky. It's vividly clear tonight; an eruption of stars. *Pegasus, Sirius, Scorpius.* The constellations help him breathe.

His eyes draw downward to Graveney's body, lying a few yards away on a curve of a grassy dune. His chest is ink-dark with blood. The moon is too thin to light the details of his bearded face, and Nathan is glad for that reprieve. Easier to carry a death, he sees now, when the evidence is not so illuminated.

A close murmur snaps him out of his daze. To his side, he sees Edwin hunched over. Sees the hand clasped to his side.

Sees the blood trickling out between his fingers, beading black on the grass of the dunes.

Finn's body is blazing. He has not come so close to conflict since he was Henry Ward's cabin boy, and as a child, he had had little sense of his own mortality. Now, he is surprised to find himself still living.

He hunches over, tries to catch his breath. Feels his boots sink into the pebbles of the beach. The pistol in his hand feels hot, though he does not remember firing. Cannot tell if the heat is just his imagination, or if he had pulled the trigger without being aware of it.

And fired at who, he finds himself wondering? A victory to Ward and the Blakes retain their home. A victory to Graveney and Finn has a path back to Eva. He knows it doesn't matter. His own undefined loyalty has had no bearing on anything.

He cannot help but be surprised that Ward has come out of this victorious. Alive. Or maybe he can. Maybe he had underestimated Ward. Maybe the bold and forthright man Henry Ward had been twenty years ago is still in there somewhere.

Maybe the prospect of an undisputed captaincy has been enough to bring him to the surface.

Finn glances across the beach. Ward's back is turned, and he is locked in conversation with several of his men.

Now.

Finn lurches towards the house. He sees the irony in his desperate need to be inside that damn place. To walk that staircase again. To feel that worn banister beneath his hand. To stand in Oliver Blake's bedroom and see the monstrous fireplace looming before him.

Ward catches him on the fringe of the embankment. Takes a firm hold on his arm. "I kept my word, Finn. I expect you to do the same."

To hell with your word, he wants to say. What right does Henry Ward have to keep him from his wife?

But Ward looks into his eyes for a single, charged moment, and Finn sees it all.

He thinks of the broken windows in Ward's great cabin. Thinks how close he had been to losing Eva the night she had thrown herself into the sea to escape the ship. He thinks of her watching out the window for Ward on their wedding night; thinks of all her broken, anxious sleeps on Longstone, as she waits for that ship to reappear.

Is this truly the life you want for your wife?

She is better off without him; this Finn knows for certain. Safer without him. And in time, she will come to see that she is also happier without him.

At least he will leave knowing she is at Highfield House with her family, and not alone out on Longstone.

He pulls his arm from Ward's grip. But he can't take his eyes from the house. None of Graveney's men had made it inside, and Graveney himself is dead now. Eva will be safe in there.

But Finn knows she will come looking for him. She will climb into the skiff and sail out to Ward's ship, and she will put herself in danger again by trying to find him.

He cannot let that happen. Eva had almost died the last time she was on Ward's ship. He cannot let her sail out there a second time.

He strides across the embankment towards his skiff. Pulls the spare shot from his pocket and slides it into the pistol.

He holds his breath. Pushes aside his hesitation. This has to be done.

He fires into the hull of his boat. Wood splinters. And threads of dark water creep inside.

Finn closes his eyes for a second, trying to breathe. Then he shoves one of Ward's longboats out to sea and climbs inside, before he falters and changes his mind.

CHAPTER THIRTY-THREE

Inside the priest hole is dark, and dark, and dark. Eva hears Theodora's soft murmuring, hears her own rapid breathing, hears the creak of old boards above her head. She hears no more pistol fire.

She pushes on the wall panel and stumbles out into Oliver's empty bedroom. She hurries through the dark to the window, broken glass crunching beneath the soles of her shoes. Salty air gusts through the shattered pane, blowing her hair back from her face. Eva sees only in shadows and lamplight, but she can tell the shooting has stopped.

She sees men on the beach, milling about towards the boats. Henry Ward is there, but she cannot see Nathan, cannot see Finn. Does the fact that Ward is alive mean he has been victorious?

Either way, she can wait here no longer.

Finn must be out there. Either he had fought with Ward's men, or he is on the ship. The prospect of him being among the dead is one she cannot even bring herself to consider.

And no matter what deal he had made with his former captain, Eva is not about to let him leave her. Who is Henry Ward to act as a judge upon their lives?

The skiff is still waiting on the embankment. She had made it aboard Ward's ship once before. And she will do so again.

She murmurs something to Thea that even she herself can barely make out, then she is flying down the staircase. She hears voices, murmuring, groaning, coming from the direction of the parlour, but she cannot find space to think about what this might mean. As she runs out of the house, she hears Nathan call her name from inside the parlour. Distant gratitude to hear he is alive, but she doesn't stop moving.

Outside the house, men are carrying lifeless bodies towards the longboats. Piling them into the boats like they are nothing more than sacks of wheat. Eva dares a glimpse at the dead men's faces. She can make out little in the darkness. But Finn is not among the dead, she tells herself. He cannot be. She will not even allow it to be a possibility.

She stumbles towards the skiff.

"Don't be foolish, Eva."

She whirls around at the sound of Ward's voice. Anger burns inside her. "Where is Finn?" she demands.

"He's returned to my ship."

Eva lurches forward, but Ward steps in front of her, blocking her way.

"Do you really think you can get out there without any of my men catching you?"

Fresh tears escape down her cheeks. "Why are you doing this to him?"

"I did not do anything. It was his own choice. He could have stayed on Longstone. He chose to come to the ship."

"Because your men took Theodora!"

"Because he knows this is what's best for you. And your family."

He is wrong, of course. Has always been wrong. About all of this. And if this is what Finn truly believes is best, then he is wrong too. This is not what is best for her. This is not what is best for her family. And this, Eva feels certain, is not what her mother would have wanted. Abigail would not have wanted this grief, this pain, this utter sense of loss for her daughter.

She stumbles across the embankment, her eyes not leaving the lamplit ship. Sailing out there alone, without Ward catching her, feels impossible. But she has to try. She needs to get to Finn. Needs to tell him he is making a mistake. Needs to tell him she would happily spend every night waiting for Ward to appear, if only he would come back to her.

She shoves hard against the skiff. Hears it groan and scrape against the pebbles of the embankment. She throws her weight against it again, but it refuses to be lifted by the tide.

She looks down. Sees the dark pool of sea gathering in the hull. Pain strikes her chest. Fury at Ward that makes her vision blur. Because this is his doing, surely. This is no accident. No wayward shot. This is his way of showing her he is in control.

She whirls around in search of him. Sees him march across the beach in the opposite direction, not looking back at her, as though she is not even worth another thought.

A soft knock at the bedroom door and Harriet stops pacing. She unwinds her fingers from her shawl.

"Why are you knocking?" she says bitterly. "It's hardly as though I can let you in." She hears the waver in her voice, wrought by the constant echo of pistol fire outside the house—and the utter helplessness of being locked in here like an animal.

For your safety, Edwin had claimed. She's no fool—she knows he had locked her up to keep her from running away again. Even the windows of her bedroom had kept her blind to all that was unfolding; looking out over the dunes behind the house, rather than out towards the sea.

The key turns in the lock. And it's Nathan that stands in the doorway. The coffee-brown waves of his hair hang loose on his shoulders, and there's a slightly wild look in his eyes. A hotness to his cheeks. And more there too—remorse, and regret, perhaps. Or is it pity?

"What happened?" Harriet asks.

He tells her in a soft, guilt-ridden voice about the bullet Edwin had taken to the side, about the way Julia had gone to the village for the barber surgeon. *We're doing everything we can*, he is saying; and *please try not to worry*.

Harriet listens with an odd sense of detachment. She waits for the horror she sees in Nathan's eyes to pass itself onto her. Instead, it seems to dissipate. "And my father?" she asks, her voice coming out far more level than she expected. "Is he still alive?"

"Yes."

"Was he hurt?"

"No. I don't believe so."

She hears herself murmur with relief. Feels the knot in her belly loosen an inch. Harriet smooths her skirts. "He fought Graveney and his men? As you asked him to?"

Nathan looks down. "Yes. He did."

There are things he is not telling her, Harriet is sure. She doesn't care. She is just grateful her father had helped her family. She wonders if her request for him to do so had had any influence on his decision.

"Where is Edwin?" she asks finally.

"In the parlour." Nathan looks up at her, his eyes alight with guilt. "The barber surgeon is with him."

She nods.

"We're doing all we can, Harriet," he says again, more feverishly this time. "With luck he will be all right."

She follows Nathan dutifully down the staircase. It's quiet downstairs now, apart from Edwin's muffled grunts sounding through the closed parlour door. The air is tinged with gunpowder and sea. Harriet stands with her back pressed to the wall of the hallway, staring at the parlour door.

What is it she ought to be feeling? Sadness? Anger? Relief? She can't tell. All she knows is that she ought to be feeling *something*. Something other than this emptiness.

No—emptiness; it's not right. It's just an absence of the things she ought to be feeling.

She turns at the sound of footsteps. Ward is standing in the entrance hall, looking like he belongs here. He is without his hat, a long strand of greying hair hanging loose from his queue. A spray of crimson paints the arm of his shirt, but she can tell by his movements that the blood does not belong to him. There's a glow in his eyes that Harriet has not seen before. A look that would make her afraid of him, if he weren't her father. Perhaps it makes her afraid anyway.

She swallows heavily. Nods towards the parlour. "Who did this to my husband?"

"I can't be certain. One of Mr Graveney's supporters, I assume. Retaliating in response to his death."

Harriet raises her eyebrows. "Edwin killed Mr Graveney?"

"No," says Ward. "Your brother did."

And of all the things that could have happened out there tonight, this is the outcome Harriet had least expected. She cannot imagine what might have driven Nathan to do such a thing. The last she had heard, he had had his bags packed and been ready to run.

"I'm sorry about your husband," says Ward.

Harriet doesn't reply. Possibly not trusting herself to make the correct reply; a reply that might suggest she has some humanity, some decency in her.

Footsteps clop across the parlour. Ward glances towards the sound, before turning back to her. "Harriet," he says, "may we speak in private?"

She nods. And she finds herself leading him down the passage to her workroom. She lights the lamp on the mantel and closes the door behind them.

Ward glances around the half-empty room. Harriet wishes she had her paintings in here to show him. Without them, the room feels impossibly bleak. Soulless. She and Ward face each other in the gloom. Neither attempt to sit.

"My crew and I are leaving," Ward says. "We've business in the New World."

The New World. Even with her limited knowledge, Harriet knows this is a dangerous, months-long journey. She feels something sink inside her.

"What kind of business?" she asks.

"Business that, with luck, will deliver my crew the wealth I promised them. The wealth they will not get from your family."

"I see." Harriet looks up at him hopefully. "When will I see you again?"

He is silent for a long moment, before turning away from her expectant eyes.

The realisation swings at her. "You're not coming back here, are you."

"No," he admits. "But surely you're not either. Do you not intend to return to London?"

Return to London? Is he truly speaking of such things when her husband may well be dying? Does he truly have no qualms about disappearing on her when she is on the verge of becoming a widow?

"You would leave me now?" she demands. "When my husband may well be on his death bed—at the hands of your own men?" Her words come out dripping with drama and childishness, but she doesn't care. At least Edwin's state has managed to conjure up some flicker of emotion in her. "Is that all I mean to you then? You'd rather chase gold than be a part of my life?"

She is just like him, she sees now. This is where her selfishness comes from. Her inhumanity. Her mother was right to leave him, she thinks. She was right to hide their child from him. Right to lie to her about who her father was.

Anger bubbles beneath her skin. It makes her hands clench into fists. Makes her want to strike him. She is seeing him for the first time: that man Eva and Finn had been so wary of. That man Nathan had fought to keep out of their lives. At first, she had assumed their fear came solely from their secrets, and the power Ward had to spill them all. But there is more to it, she sees now. Henry Ward is a man who will always put himself first. Even tonight, when he had risked his own life to rid them of Graveney, he had no doubt only done so because it would give him back a secure captaincy. "You're a selfish bastard," she hisses.

Ward's eyes flicker with surprise. "Harriet," he says. "Please calm yourself. There's no need for such hysteria."

She glares at him. She hates this façade of his she is unable to break through. Hates that she has no idea who he truly is. Does it even bother him a scrap that he is to sail out of his daughter's life, never to return? Did it ever even faze him to learn about her in the first place? Once, she had believed so. Now all she feels is doubt. Betrayal. A sense of being discarded. "How can I behave otherwise when you are acting with such selfishness and greed?"

"Is that why you think I'm doing this? Out of greed?"

"It's the truth, isn't it?"

Ward goes to the window for a moment and peers out onto the embankment. Harriet can see the faint glow of his ship just beyond the glass. After a moment, he turns back to face her. "Listen to me," he says slowly, carefully. "You know your mother never wanted you and I to be in each other's lives. And I'm choosing to respect her wishes." He sighs. "She was right to keep you from me. Look at all that has happened to your family with me in your lives." He glances down, and for the faintest of moments, she sees a genuineness in his expression. "In all honesty, I thought it best for both of us that I leave without a word. But then your husband was hurt, and I—"

"I don't care what Mother wanted!" Harriet cries, desperation welling inside her. "You cannot just disappear! I barely know you!"

Ward folds his arms and gives her hard eyes, forcing her into silence. "I care about you, Harriet," he says, his voice suddenly empty of emotion again. "But do not let yourself be fooled into thinking you have a say in what I do."

She presses her lips into a thin line. She had not grown up with any male figure in her life, beyond her older brother, less than a decade her senior. But with Henry Ward's eyes on her, scolding, scrutinising, she suddenly feels like a reprimanded child. And that is not a feeling she welcomes. She has enough of this from her husband.

She stares at her father for a long, wordless moment. She means nothing to him, she sees now. How can she? A man who cared for his daughter would never willingly cut himself from her life, regardless of what her mother would have wanted. She has been nothing to Henry Ward but a momentary interest.

"That's it, then?" she asks coldly.

"Well. I would hope we would manage an amicable goodbye." He reaches out a hand towards her, but she steps away. Ward swallows visibly, but holds her gaze. "Regardless of all that has happened, I am truly glad I came to know of you," he says.

Harriet grits her teeth. "I wish I could say the same."

CHAPTER THIRTY-FOUR

Finn watches from the deck of the *Eagle* as the longboats return. On the empty ship, the sigh of the sea against the hull is magnified, and he hears the ratlines clatter in the faint breeze. He stares down at the lifeless figures piled at the back of the longboats.

Now Ward has turned to piracy, Finn knows it will not be long until the rest of this crew follow these men into death. Whether his life will end on the gallows or with a bullet to the chest, he has no idea—but a life under the black flag is rarely a long one.

The ship begins to fill. The line of bodies at the gunwale grows. Finn stares past them to the glow of the lamps in Highfield House. Beyond the dark mass of Lindisfarne, the Longstone firebasket has burned itself out.

He watches Ward climb aboard the ship. Tries to force down a wash of hatred.

The remaining men gather around their captain. Forty souls left living; fifty, perhaps. Two thirds of the crew or

256

more. The victory over Graveney has brought the unyielding look back to Ward's eyes. It's a look Finn remembers well.

"Mr Graveney is dead," Ward says. "And Abigail Blake's letter has not been found." He looks around the group, meeting the eyes of the crew. "I regret I cannot offer you the immunity I promised. But I intend to travel to the New World to uncover the cargo of two fleets of lost Spanish treasure ships. Anyone who does not wish to join us in Florida is free to leave now." His eyes meet Finn's pointedly, making it clear the offer does not extend to him.

Finn thinks of running, of jumping, of swimming back to shore. And he thinks of the pistol fire that will surely follow. Thinks of the men that will come to Highfield House, to Longstone, in search of him. Ward has kept his word. And now he needs to keep his.

When no one leaves the ship, Ward finds his navigator among the crowd. A course to the New World. It is suddenly hard to breathe.

"Prepare the dead for burial," Ward tells several of his men. "We will hold the service in the morning, once we are in deeper water." He turns towards the saloon.

Finn pushes through the cluster of men towards Ward, catching him before he steps inside. "I saw you go to the house," he pushes. "Did you see Eva? Is she safe?"

"She is," says Ward. "Safe with her family."

Finn nods. He knows he ought to be grateful for this—and in many ways, he is. But the pain of it is almost unbearable. She shouldn't be in that house with her family. She ought to be out on Longstone with him.

But the moment the thought comes to him, he catches its untruth. Eva is far better in the safety of her family than she has ever been with him. What has their life together ever offered her beyond danger and fear? What right did he have to make her his wife when he could not even give her a safe home?

Ward clamps a hand to Finn's shoulder. "Join me in the great cabin."

Right now, Henry Ward is the last person in the world he wants to be around. But he knows that steely tone in Ward's voice. Knows he does not have a choice in the matter.

Ward unlocks the door of the great cabin and steps inside, Finn following reluctantly. He opens the cupboard beneath his desk and produces the bottle of whisky he had been drinking from earlier. Fills two tin cups and hands one to Finn.

"Do you really imagine I want to drink with you right now?"

Ward ignores the question. He sits at the head of the table and brings his cup to his lips, staring up at Finn.

There is no other option but to sit. He does. And then he drinks. Just a mouthful. He knows he needs to keep a clear head around Ward now, in case he does something foolish. But he also needs something to calm that desperate ache in his chest.

The whisky only makes it worse.

"I'm sorry," Ward says after a moment.

Finn snorts. "No you're not."

"I am. I'm sorry that things came to this." Suddenly there's a distant look in his eyes. Finn wonders what he is thinking. Of Abigail? Of Harriet? "And I'm sorry I took you to Highfield House that night in the first place. I've always blamed myself in part for Oliver's death."

"Why?" Finn says gruffly. "You only took me there because I was unwell."

"No. That's not why I took you."

Finn frowns. "What are you talking about?"

Ward shakes his head. "It doesn't matter. It's all in the past."

Finn laughs coldly. All that has happened and Ward is still talking in riddles. He doesn't care. Whatever Ward's reasons, he cannot think on them. It will only lead him to madness. He gulps back another mouthful of whisky. "I need your word," he tells Ward, "that you will never go near Eva again. Or her family."

Ward nods, and Finn sees a sincerity in his eyes. "You have my word, Finn. You know you can trust me."

He nods. Because yes, in spite of everything, he knows that Ward is telling the truth. He is a man who does not lie. A man who sticks by his word. And despite the grief pressing down on him, that is some small consolation.

Ward meets his eyes. "You are doing the right thing, Finn."

He grits his teeth. The right thing? He is abandoning his wife mere weeks after they had married. But he also knows he has no choice.

He wishes he and Eva had the seemingly endless years he had once imagined they would have. Years in which he could ask for the answers to all the trivial things he is yet to learn about her. Whether she had slept well before she had begun to keep the light. Whether she has ever been to Scotland. Her favourite season. Cats or dogs.

But they do not have endless years. Or even a single trip around the sun. Not even another night of keeping the firebasket burning together. But it's best this way. Eva is free of Ward now, and safe with her family.

He will give her back her unbroken nights' sleep. Will let that towering cottage on Longstone turn to a ruin, and the future he had imaged with Eva along with it.

Grief pushes at his chest. "Please," he says, swallowing past the pain in his throat, "we need to leave as soon as possible. If she can see the ship from the house, she'll try to come after me. I've damaged the skiff, but she'll find some way…"

Ward gives him the faintest of smiles. "She's a lot like her mother." He gets up and goes to the desk in the corner of the room. "My navigator is plotting our course as we speak. I'll give the men instructions to sail out of the bay in the meantime." He pulls a ream of papers from the desk drawer and tosses them on the table in front of Finn, placing a quill and inkpot beside them. Finn glances down at them. *Articles of the pirate vessel* Eagle.

Something turns over in his stomach.

Ward looks at him pointedly. A look that tells him to keep his word and sign his name. He leaves without speaking again.

Finn stares down at the articles. He uncorks the ink pot and dips in the quill. Tries to find the courage to put the nib to the page.

CHAPTER THIRTY-FIVE

Wartime now, thinks Harriet. And militiamen are everywhere. There are always soldiers in the streets, their eyes and ears open for Jacobite plans. They are easy to find in the alley outside the tavern—almost as easy as it had been to leave the house without anyone noticing.

Well, who was there to notice? Jenny and Thomas are away on Bamburgh; Nathan trying to pace away his guilt. Theodora, Harriet assumes, is still tucked away on Longstone with her secret-keeping aunt and uncle. And Edwin, well, he is alive, and she supposes there is gratitude there. But it's a shallow gratitude; overshadowed by the relief of how easy it was to slip out of the house and approach the authorities.

Harriet lifts her chin and strides up to the soldiers with as much deliberateness as she can manage. It's a difficult thing, given how much she is shaking. Shaking with grief, with anger, with a sense of betrayal. Shaking with the magnitude of all she is about to do. She barely notices when a raft of men spill out of the tavern towards her, hollering about *ladybirds* and *lift your skirts*. She just puts her head down and keeps walking.

She wishes she had never met Henry Ward. Wishes she had never gone searching for Samuel Blake's headstone. Wishes for her old ignorance.

For a while, being Ward's daughter had felt special. But that's not what she is. Not to him. She is nothing compared to an ocean of gold.

The two militiamen turn as she approaches.

"I've information," she tells them. Her voice trembles slightly. "About a pirate vessel leaving these waters. They took the cargo of the East India ship *Albion* off the coast of Nassau. And plenty more besides."

CHAPTER THIRTY-SIX

Harriet tries not to think about what she has done. She focuses on the soft sigh of her footsteps against the earth, the way the light of her lamp bounces over the dunes. The silver thread of moon in the clear sky overhead.

Reporting her father's ship is not bringing her the satisfaction she thought it would. Just a dull sense of self-loathing. And inevitability, perhaps. It feels as though this was always how things were destined to end between her and Henry Ward. After all, this was what her mother had wanted: for them to not be in each other's lives.

Since she had met her father, Harriet had been racked with anger at her mother. But now she has chosen Abigail's side.

Would her mother be proud of her for what she has done? Harriet wants to believe it. But she cannot quite see beyond the regret.

Movement on the embankment catches her eye. Harriet's heart flutters; she is on edge after all that has taken place tonight. It's her sister, she realises. And that fact does nothing to slow her racing heart.

At once, the thoughts of turning her father in are gone, burnt away by rage at Eva and all she had sought to keep from the family. She cannot make sense of why her sister is here— had Eva been here at the house the whole time Harriet had been locked away in her bedroom? Why is she not on Longstone with Theodora? Harriet pushes the questions away. She cannot make herself care about the details.

Eva is huddled on the water's edge, her knees pulled to her chest. She is staring blankly at her little boat. It seems to be languishing on the rim of the embankment, lame against the pull of the waves.

"What are you doing here?" Harriet hisses. "I thought you were on Longstone."

Eva doesn't answer. Her eyes are glassy and unfocused. Harriet wonders if her words have even registered.

After a long silence, Eva says, "Where have you been?"

Harriet's fingers tense around the handle of the lamp. She is not about to explain herself to Eva. Why should she? "Did you know it when you married him?" she demands suddenly. She holds out the lantern, spearing light into Eva's eyes.

Eva turns away. Her shoulders round and she hugs her knees tighter. Pieces of dark hair fall across her eyes. She doesn't look surprised. As though she has been waiting for this truth to find its way out. "Yes," she says finally. "I knew."

Her flat admission catches Harriet off guard. Something has happened, surely, but she cannot bring herself to care. "Did you really think you could go your entire life without any of us finding out?" she demands. "Or did you simply imagine we wouldn't care?"

Eva doesn't respond. Doesn't argue. Just rests her chin on

knees and continues staring out at the water. Darkness there now. For the first time in weeks, the bay is empty of Henry Ward's ship. Perhaps the *Eagle* has sailed far away, Harriet thinks. Perhaps the *Eagle* will not be caught. The thought feels naïve. Too hopeful. Or is it hopeless? She can't tell anymore.

"Oliver was a dangerous bully," Eva says finally. There is no fire to her words. None of the hostility Harriet was expecting. "Finn was just defending himself."

Harriet snorts. "Is that what you tell yourself to make it all right? Or is that what your husband tells you?"

Eva doesn't look at her. "You did not know Oliver. You do not know what he was like."

"And you did? How old were you when your husband killed our brother, Eva? Three? Four? Young enough for your memories to have turned into what you want them to be."

Eva looks at her squarely then, and Harriet sees her eyes are bloodshot and swollen with tears. The sight catches her off guard. Eva is rarely one for outward displays of emotion. "Well," she says finally. "You do not have to worry yourself over my husband any longer. He left. On your father's ship. Because he thought that was what was best for me."

Harriet's stomach falls. "On my father's ship?" she repeats. Her mouth turns dry and she feels her heart hammering against her ribs. But this is what Finn Murray deserves, isn't it? To hang at Execution Dock beside her father?

Yes, she tells herself. What he deserves.

She can't quite make herself feel it. But what's done is done.

She swallows heavily. "I'm sorry, Eva," she says. Her voice comes out so soft she is not sure her sister even hears her.

Without waiting for a response, she turns and makes her way inside the house.

CHAPTER THIRTY-SEVEN

When he wakes the next morning, Nathan's first thought is that he has killed a man.

His second thought is that Julia had not returned to the house after sending for the barber surgeon.

The barber surgeon's outlook, Nathan supposes, had been as good as he could have hoped for. Ball removed cleanly from flesh and muscle only. As yet no sign of infection.

The guilt of it is almost impossibly heavy on Nathan's shoulders. After all, Edwin had only been out there to support him. But Nathan cannot bring himself to regret the events of last night. Cannot bear to think what might have happened to Theodora if he and Edwin had fled from the house as they had planned.

When the sun has risen and the tide drained, Nathan takes Thea over to Bamburgh in a wagon and brings Jenny and Thomas back to the house. Fetches Mrs Brodie from the village. The house settles into a sluggish rhythm, with Edwin bleary with opium on the settle in the parlour, Harriet sitting dutifully at his side, and Eva locked away upstairs with her wordless grief.

And so. Edwin is alive, and Graveney is dead; and these things make it possible for Nathan's thoughts to veer towards Julia.

His heart is overbeating as he makes his way to the curiosity shop. And not in that dizzyingly pleasant way that being around her usually elicits. No, this time is far more laced with dread. A fear of what he might see when he steps through that door. Blood on her hands. Lies on her tongue. Nonetheless, he can't deny the pull to see her. To try and wrench an explanation out of her. Last night, he had believed his only choice was to flee Holy Island and never see her again. Now this chance to stay has been given to him, he knows he ought to be grateful. But he cannot quite make himself feel it.

He is not surprised to find the shop closed. How can Julia let customers inside with blood staining the stairs of the cellar? He knocks on the side door, caught between a desperate need to see her, and a deep desire to run away.

Julia opens the door without speaking. The shadows beneath her eyes suggest her night had been as sleepless as his.

"You thought it best to leave without a word last night?" he asks.

"Did you wish me to stay?"

He holds her gaze for a long second. Does not know the answer to that question.

Julia steps aside, gesturing for him to enter. Nathan expects to be led down to the cellar, or be herded into some lightless corner of the alley. But she leads him upstairs to her living quarters.

Nathan's gaze travels around the tiny space. A small round table is crammed up beside a threadbare settle, two bowls and teacups dumped into the trough by the hearth. Though the fire has burnt out, the room still carries its warmth, and the stale smell of burnt porridge. Two narrow beds stand side by side against the back wall, blankets tossed messily across them.

"I'm sorry," Julia says huskily. "It's a little small. And untidy." Nathan sees a flicker of shame in her eyes. A part of him wants to reach for her, pull her to him. Tell her she could live in a cow shed for all it bothers him. But right now, he cannot let that part of himself win. He has far too many questions that are in dire need of answers.

"You've never brought me up here before. Why now?" He wonders if it's some kind of peace offering. An attempt at letting him in, after all she has been keeping from him. Or maybe she has reached the point where she no longer cares. A point they can no longer come back from.

Julia doesn't answer. Doesn't sit, or offer him a chair. She just hovers by the table, picking at a scrap of dirt beneath her thumbnail.

"Joseph Holland was not in his cottage," Nathan says finally. He had gone to Holland's cottage on his way to the shop this morning, seeking confirmation of the suspicions he had begun to gather. Not that he had truly needed it.

"Is that some thinly veiled accusation, Nathan?" Something flickers behind Julia's eyes. "If there is something you wish to ask me, why not just do it?"

"I did that yesterday. And you refused to speak to me."

She lowers her eyes, her fleeting boldness disappearing.

"How could I have spoken openly when your daughter was around?"

Nathan takes a step towards her. Softens his voice slightly. "My daughter is not here now."

For long moments, there is silence. Julia opens her mouth to speak, and then seems to change her mind. Nathan clenches his hands; wills her to talk to him. He is choosing to take her bringing him up here as a sign she wants to resurrect what was between them. He wants that too. Desperately. But they cannot resurrect anything with silence.

He tries to swallow his frustration. "Did Holland hurt you?" he asks finally.

Silence.

"Where is his body?"

"It's gone."

"Did you kill him?"

Julia looks up to meet his eyes. "Is that what you think me capable of?"

"No," Nathan says, without hesitation. "I don't." Thoughts of his own seconds behind the trigger flash through his mind. He had never imagined himself capable of killing another. Perhaps he is wrong about Julia too. "In any case, I know you are not capable of removing his body from your cellar all on your own." He looks at her squarely. "I assume from the blood on the stairs that that is where he ended up."

Julia doesn't respond.

And the removal of Joseph Holland's body, Nathan realises then, is just one in a long line of pieces that do not quite add up. Her reluctance to take him upstairs before now, her insistence on speaking in the cellar, the sound of hidden people moving around inside her shop. Pieces he has been

270

doing his best to ignore, in favour of the way Julia makes him feel. He cannot be that naïve fool any longer.

"Who has been here?" he asks suddenly. "One of your brothers?"

His guess is not wrong; he can tell by the look in her eyes. He can see her thoughts churning, as though debating whether to be open with him. Is that really where they are at now? Have they ever been anywhere other than this?

Julia lets out a breath. She goes to look out the narrow window, keeping her back to Nathan. "Hugh returned to Lindisfarne not long after the siege at the castle," she says finally. "He told me I was to keep him at my shop, down in the cellar. I told him again and again that it wasn't safe. But he had no interest in hearing it. He said he needed to be on Holy Island to do his part for the cause."

"You were adamant that you would not let your brothers stay with you," Nathan says tautly. "Need I remind you, you hid them away in my attic. And then cast them off on Eva and Finn."

"I know. And I never wanted…" Julia trails off. Rubs her hand across her eyes. Finally, she turns to face him. "Hugh… He's different to Michael and Angus. He takes what he wants. Does not ask questions first." She sighs. "I wish I had the strength to tell him no. But I've always felt indebted to him, after all he did for me and Bobby. And he's a changed man now. Since his wife and son died, all he cares about is seeing the Rising succeed. He'll not listen to reason. And he doesn't care what anyone else wants. He wouldn't even let me tell Michael and Angus he was staying with me."

"You ought to have told me," Nathan says. "You know I would have supported you. I would not have told anyone he was here." He hears his voice harden. "Or did you not trust me enough to do that?"

Julia closes her eyes. Her silence is all the answer he needs.

"Well," he says tightly, "in that case, you ought to have kept your distance from me."

Tears slide off Julia's chin. "I could not do that either."

A chaos of emotions roils inside him. Nathan digs his hands into the pockets of his coat, so he will not be tempted to reach for her. "Did you tell your brother that Holland was spying for the government? I assume that's why he killed him."

"No." She looks at him squarely for the first time, her eyes dark and intent. "I swear it. Hugh tried to get the information out of me. But I refused to tell him. I knew it would put you in danger." She swallows heavily. "Holland came to the shop yesterday. Tried to force his way down into the cellar where Hugh was hiding. He must have seen him in the street, I suppose. Must have heard about the crimes he committed. Hugh fired at him the moment he saw him." She wipes her eyes with the back of her hand. "That's just the kind of man he is."

"Where is Hugh now?" Nathan asks.

"He left. Last night. He's gone to fight with the rebels in Lancashire."

Nathan nods. He sinks wearily into a chair at the table and stares into the unlit grate.

"What will you do?" Julia dares to ask. "Now Ward and his men are gone?"

Nathan doesn't answer. Doesn't have an answer. He feels stuck in limbo. He cannot leave Lindisfarne now, with Edwin in such a state, of course. But with luck, he will heal. He and

Harriet will return to London with their son.

And then?

Nathan cannot deny that, in spite of everything, he has grown attached to the idea of staying here on Holy Island. Returning to London, and struggling to rebuild his business leaves him more hollow than he could ever have imagined when he had first been forced up here by Henry Ward.

A foolish thing, he knows, after all the distrust he has faced from the villagers. But with Holland's disappearance, rumours about the man will spread, and he will soon be revealed as the island's government informant. With luck, the suspicion will be lifted from Nathan's family.

Joseph Holland... Unsurprisingly, the thought leads him straight back to Julia. If he walks away from her now, with this thing in pieces, how will he ever pass her in the street? The village is too small to hold two people who can barely look each other in the eye.

He knows Theodora will be devastated if he tells her they are leaving. And he has no thought of what effect returning to London will have on her. Will she go back to her unsettled, fearful self, plagued by nightmares and haunted by the loss of her mother? Nathan would rather face Julia every day than put his child through that again.

He stands up from the table too abruptly. "Is there anything you need?" he asks, well aware he has not answered her question. "I want you to be safe."

Julia shakes her head. And as Nathan makes his way towards the stairwell, silence feels like the only fitting response.

CHAPTER THIRTY-EIGHT

Harriet listens to the raspy timbre of Edwin's breath. Inhalation. Exhalation. She watches his chest rise and fall beneath his thin linen shirt. She must be grateful he is living, because if she is not, well, what kind of person would that make her? She cannot bear to think on it.

Her eyes drift to the dark pearls of blood staining the fabric of the settle. There is something oddly fascinating about them. They feel so utterly out of place; a symbol of violence against the mundane bleakness of the parlour. In any case, focusing on the bloodstains, and on trying to force the gratitude of Edwin's survival, stops her from thinking about her father, and whether or not he is in the hands of the authorities now. And whether her sister's husband is in chains alongside him.

Harriet has no thought of whether the authorities have found her father's ship. Unlikely, she tells herself. Surely the militia's priorities will lie with the Rising, and they will have brushed away her report of pirates in the bay.

Wishful thinking. Harriet knows she was not imagining the hard look in the soldiers' eyes when she told them about the *Eagle's* attack on the East Indian trade ships. No doubt the authorities will derive as much pleasure from seeing pirates on the end of a rope as they would a band of Jacobite rebels.

And if this is the fate that is to befall Finn Murray, it is best that Eva does not know of it. Best she live ignorant, at least now, while she can. Best she hold onto her distant scrap of hope for his return for as long as possible.

Of course, if her husband is to be put to death, she will receive word of it. But she will never know that her sister had been the one to send the authorities after the ship. Harriet will make sure of that.

It has been two days since she went to the militia. Two days since she had confronted Eva about her husband's role in Oliver's death. They have not spoken a word to each other since. Worst of all, it is not even a malicious coldness. It is just emptiness on Eva's part. Deep guilt on Harriet's. Her vigil at this makeshift bedside of Edwin's is far more about avoiding her sister than it is about keeping watch over her husband.

Harriet hears the distant sound of voices outside the house. Hears a muffled scraping and crashing coming from the direction of the water. She cannot see out in that direction from the parlour.

With a distant kind of curiosity, she goes to her workroom and peeks out the window. Sees two of the herring fisherman on the embankment with Eva, hauling that sorry-looking boat of hers up out of the low tide.

Footsteps thump down the stairs and Nathan strides

outside. "What is all this?" he asks.

Eva keeps her eyes on the boat. Harriet can just make out her words: "They've agreed to fix the skiff for me. I'm going home."

"Back to Longstone?"

"Yes."

Harriet is glad of it. Keeping her distance from her sister will be far easier, of course, with Eva marooning herself out on Longstone.

"Don't be foolish," Nathan says. "You cannot go out there alone. Please. Stay here with us."

Harriet holds her breath. Is relieved when Eva says, "No. I need to go back." As though it is not even a choice.

Harriet hurries back into the parlour before either of them catch her at the window. She returns to her chair at Edwin's side. Returns to watching his chest rise and fall.

It ought to be Eva that is feeling guilty, Harriet thinks. After all, she is the one who married the man who killed their brother. But she also knows that one word to her sister will send her tumbling down into this bottomless chasm of regret.

She stares at Edwin. His skin is pale, a sharp contrast to the dark hair that hangs limp and thready against his cheeks. A good chance of survival, the barber surgeon had said. Soon they will return to their house in London, with all their misery. She will be *wife* and *mother*, with her paintings burned, and there will be no escaping it all.

And if he doesn't survive? What would her life look like then? The townhouse would be hers, along with a comfortable settlement. No doubt she would be drawn back under Nathan's wing somewhat. But there are far worse fates. Nathan is soft and pliable. Far easier to manipulate than

Edwin. He would put a paintbrush back in her hand, without demanding she behave herself first. He would allow her to see her artist friends. Perhaps allow her to travel to Paris with Isabelle.

Harriet is not even aware of having picked up the cushion. And she is watching from outside herself as she lifts it Edwin's face. Holds it to his mouth and nose. Gentle pressure at first, a faux thing, testing herself, imagining what the act would feel like. And then a little more pressure. A little more. Edwin's body twitches. He lets out an opium murmur, and the floor outside the parlour creaks. Harriet darts a glance over her shoulder, the cushion tumbling to the floor.

Theodora is standing in the doorway, motionless, watching. She holds Harriet's gaze for a long, wordless moment, her lips parted, her eyes wide and unreadable.

Harriet tries to smile. Her heart is speeding and her body is on fire. Her hands tremble with the realisation of what she had just tried to do. "Thea," she says, too brightly, "go and tell Mrs Brodie that Uncle Edwin would like some more water."

CHAPTER THIRTY-NINE

Over and over, Julia had told herself this would always be home. She had fought for it when her father had thrown her from his house—he had been the one to leave Lindisfarne, unable to bear the shame of her and her bastard child. She had held her ground. Fought for this place.

But she knows now that she was wrong when she claimed she would never leave. Because Lindisfarne has stopped feeling like home.

People are beginning to speak of Holland's disappearance. There are whispers about a man who lived alone; and those whispers, predictably, are leading to stories that he had been spying for the government.

Julia has not heard any suspicion cast in her direction. But that does not stop her from feeling guilty every time she passes another villager in the street. And it does not stop her from fearing that soon the suspicions will turn to her. All it would take is one glance at the blood she has been unable to fully remove from the cellar stairs, no matter how many times she scrubs them.

She stands in the middle of the curiosity shop. This life she had built from nothing. But she knows every time she hears the bell above the door ring now, she will think of Joseph Holland stepping inside. Will hear the echo of Hugh's pistol shot.

Worst of all, she knows she will think of Nathan. Of the way he had held her, kissed her, told her he planned to stay here and build a life with her. And she will think of the pleading look in his eyes when he had come to her shop the day of Holland's death. Will think of her own stony silence, and the unbearable look of hurt in Nathan's eyes.

Julia knows she cannot stay here. Her brothers have all left now, and she will follow them. Will leave no trace of her family on Lindisfarne, beyond her mother's grave. She cannot walk the streets with held breath every day, in fear of passing Nathan. Nor can she expect him to leave, given how hard he had fought for Highfield House.

She turns in a slow circle, taking in the cluttered shelves of her shop. The gold-embossed books, the gnarled and tarnished candleholders, the gaudy brass trinket boxes and that old pair of cavalier boots. Where to even begin packing up such a place? Is she to take these wares with her? Cart them across the country in an attempt to start again? Or just walk away, and leave this part of her life to be forgotten?

In the back corner of the shop, she finds an old wooden travelling trunk. She carries it over to the bookshelf. Begins to pull the titles from the shelf and place them inside. This, she supposes, is as a good a place to start as any.

Though he knows he should not be surprised to see it, the sight of Julia packing up the shop is a knife to the chest. Nathan has tried to stay away, but he keeps being drawn here. Cannot even make sense of why he has come here today. When he had left her yesterday, it had been clear there was to be no fixing things.

He knows the wisest thing is to walk away. Not ask questions. Accept that this is the way things are supposed to be.

He finds himself knocking anyway. Seeking what? Closure? An explanation that will make this make sense? Make it less painful, somehow? He doubts such a thing is possible.

Julia unlocks the door without a word.

"You are closing the shop?" he asks throatily.

"I'm leaving Holy Island."

Hearing her say it out loud makes his stomach fall. This is not the way things ought to be. Nathan knows how much she loves this place. He steps inside, closing the door behind him. "Because of Holland?"

Her eyes are glistening, but there is a hard look about her, as though she is refusing to let her emotions run away. "In part," she says. She swallows visibly. "In part, because of you."

Her honesty makes his chest ache. He stares at her for a long time. A part of him wants to beg her to reconsider. Cling to her. Keep her here. But something keeps him rooted in place. Something more than his fear.

"You know I'm right to do it," she says.

And he nods. "Let me be the one to leave," he says huskily. "This is your home. You told me once that you never wished to leave this place. I do not want you to do that on account of me."

"This is your home too," she says. "I know you forgot that for a time. But I think you have remembered it now." She lowers her eyes. Drops her voice. "It is best for me to leave. Before anyone begins to suspect I had anything to do with Holland's disappearance."

He reaches for her suddenly. Pulls her into him, feeling the warmth of her body against his own. Surely this has to count for something, the fact that he can hold her like this. Can feel his heart beating hard against his chest with something that is not fear or dread.

And yes, it does count for something. But it is not enough.

He closes his eyes for a moment, drinking in her nearness. When will he ever feel this again, he wonders? This need to be close to a woman. Perhaps never. But the two of them are an impossibility.

Julia pulls back and looks at him squarely. "I loved you," she says. "For what it's worth. I just want you to know that." She swallows visibly. "I love you."

"I loved you too," says Nathan. He cannot bring himself to consider whether he still does, after all this. Because if he reaches the wrong conclusion, he will try and make her stay.

"I'm sorry," he says.

Julia nods. "So am I. But this is how it is."

"Yes." He releases his grip on her. Clasps his hands together so he is not tempted to reach for her again. "It is."

Having no choice in the matter makes it easy to find

courage. Harriet knows she cannot stay here, after all Theodora has seen; after all she has done to Eva. She cannot stay here and wait for Edwin to recover, for that colourless life in London to become a reality.

There's a simplicity to her leaving.

The deep darkness of the island is lit only with a single candle, and its light barely makes it to the corners of this vast, empty bedroom. There is something unnerving about being in this room alone so late at night. Something that makes her think of all the death and loss this house must have seen.

She slips her coin pouch inside her stays. It is still heavy with the money Michael Mitchell had paid her for her journey to Lesbury. It will be enough to get her off this island. Back to London. To Isabelle's garret in Lambeth.

Harriet knows Isabelle will keep a roof over her head for as long as she needs it. Until she finds a way to turn those coins into more. How she will do this, she cannot bear to think on. In her dreams, she does it by selling her artwork. In reality, she knows there are other horrors that are far more likely.

Still, she cannot stay. Simplicity.

She blows out the candle and feels her way through the blackness. She stands for a moment in the doorway, looking across to the nursery as her eyes adjust to the darkness.

This is the part of the equation that is not so simple. Or perhaps it is. Perhaps she just does not want to admit to that simplicity.

She touches the coins in her bodice. Enough to make it to London. But not enough to give a child a good life.

She pushes down anything that comes close to emotion. She does not open the nursery door. Does not peek inside at her sleeping son.

Edwin will recover, she tells herself. Thomas will have his father. And he is far better off without his mother. Always has been.

Simplicity.

With her bag on her shoulder, she walks down the stairs and out the door in the silence of the night, quietening the voice in her head that seeks to take away her courage.

CHAPTER FORTY

Longstone is where she needs to be. In spite of all she has lost, Eva has no choice but to be here. Because that firebasket must to come to life each night; must light the dark, to save lives.

It must be lit to atone for Oliver. To atone for Donald Macauley. And it must be lit because that is what Finn's father had wanted when he had built this place all those years ago, after his brothers had drowned on the Knavestone reef.

A thick autumn cold settles over the island, and Longstone becomes a place of silvery half-light. Eva goes to the mainland, to Lindisfarne, when she needs supplies: flour for bread, and vegetables for soup that all too often are left to curl and brown, neglected in the bottom of the sideboard. She mends hemlines and holes, exchanging them for coins that keep her fed and warm. She goes to Highfield House for Theodora's lessons; hears of Edwin's slow recovery, and Harriet's midnight escape. She sits through plea after plea from Nathan to return to the house and be with her family.

Though she is thankful her brother is staying on Holy Island, she grows tired of refusing his requests. Begins to go to the house with less and less regularity, until Nathan gives up and sends his daughter to the dame school.

And as she exchanges words with the villagers, Eva hears things: hears of the Jacobite defeat in Lancashire; hears of the bloodshed on the heathland of Sherrifmuir. She feels the gloom fall over Lindisfarne when the troops return at the end of the campaign year, broken and defeated, and mourning the dead. She feels their heaviness and their grief, and she carries it back to her island.

Each night, as she lights the basket, she thinks of Finn. Wonders where the *Eagle* has taken him. She tries to hold on to that scrap of hope of seeing him again, but it feels so unlikely. So far away. She knows the *Eagle* is on its way to the New World, with nothing surrounding it but sea. No way off the ship. No way back to England.

No way back to her.

The emptiness is profound; deep and quiet and silver-grey. The nights are never-ending; and the day, when it comes, is pale and weak. She sleeps with the sparse hours of daylight. Rises with the night.

And that emptiness, it's almost unfathomable, given she has also become aware of the life she is carrying inside her. A profound un-emptiness in this face of this great hollow. But this is something she cannot acknowledge. Not yet, with the days growing shorter and the winter closing in. No, she thinks, she cannot even begin to contemplate that future when she will no longer be alone on her island. When this wild place will no longer just be hers. Because if she thinks of it, she will only manage fear and grief and loneliness; none of the happiness she wishes she could feel. Right now, it is easier to feel nothing at all.

Right now, she cannot think further than the next long firelit night that lies ahead.

———⟨◆⟩———

News has reached them in the Marshalsea cell: Henry Ward has been taken to the Admiralty Court to face trial. The fall of a once-revered privateer. He will hang, of course; a warning to all those other privateers who have turned to piracy in the wake of this shallow European peace.

Ward's trial, Finn thinks, will be a spectacle. Not so much for the rabble he is locked in here with. Their trial will take place in two days' time—a foregone conclusion, he has no doubt. Each of these men had sailed from the Caribbean with Ward, lured by the promise of riches. And yet none of them have the pennies to do anything other than represent themselves. No choice but to put their own sorry defences before the court: stories of drunkenness, and regret, and lies of being taken from honest merchant ships by bloodthirsty pirates. Finn knows none of it will make a difference. In a few days' time, their bodies will be swinging over the Thames, to be washed by three tides of the river.

The cell is crammed with debtors and pirates, thick with the breath and grunts and snores of men. The stone floor is covered in straw. Buckets in corners and carpets of damp, foul-smelling muck. With a forgone trial laid out before him, Finn spends the nights with his knees hugged to his chest and an impossible weight bearing down on him. Floats in and out of hazy firelit dreams.

He hopes that somehow, Eva will learn what has happened to him. With his execution she will be free to marry again, free to start the life she ought to have been living. He longs to see her once more, if just for a moment. But even if he could somehow get word to her before he is to die, he would not want that for her. He does not want her last memories of their marriage to be of him climbing onto the scaffold.

Guards at the gate now. They unlock the door of the cell, the loud clatter pulling Finn from his thoughts.

He hears someone call his name. A guard, he realises. He can't make sense of it. Are they not all to go to trial together, this rabble of Henry Ward's? Perhaps he is delirious, his senses dulled by thirst, by fear, by grief.

He tries to stand anyway. His legs are weak and shaky from disuse, his calf aching dully behind the scar left by Martin Macauley's bullet.

With a vice-like grip around his arm, two guards lead him out of the cell, through narrow stone corridors with high peaked roofs. He shivers in the sudden cold. No one speaks.

They climb stairs. Walk more corridors. And a door is unlocked. A door to the outside world, Finn realises, as pale morning light trickles in, cold and smoky and stinking of the river. He gulps down the air as though it just rose off the sea.

"Henry Ward has confirmed you were a prisoner on the *Eagle*," says one guard. "He has confirmed your name was not on his pirates' articles."

And in his haze, and his grief, and his exhaustion, it takes Finn a moment to piece together these words. Takes a moment for him to understand that that foregone trial has fallen away. Takes a moment for him to realise he is free.

This is nothing but delirium, surely. How could it be anything else? But then Finn feels a silent laugh starting from deep within him, making his chest shake.

He thinks of sitting at the table in Ward's great cabin with the articles laid out in front of him, feeling the ship move, drawing him away from Eva. He thinks of the ink blots he had left on the articles, as his hand hovered over the page in indecision.

Thinks of the way he had tossed the quill aside at the shouts from the lookout—*enemy, three points to port…*

The prison gates clang open. Finn does not look back at the guards, or the sharp peaked roofs of the Marshalsea. Does not look back in case this is a dream, or the cruellest of tricks. How many men accused of piracy must have stood in the dock at the Admiralty Court and claimed they were forced aboard the ship? He supposes the words of the captain have far more weight than a desperate, accused nobody.

Finn knows he will not have the chance to thank Ward for this reprieve. And perhaps there's a part of him that does not even think he ought to be grateful. After all, Ward had been the one to force him onto the ship in the first place.

But he cannot help the lingering loyalty for the man who had once been like a father to him. For the man who had looked out for his safety; who had sought to allay his fears. For the man who had taught him a little decency. And he cannot help the lingering sadness that comes at the thought of Ward's approaching death.

It is a short walk from the prison to the river, through the winding cobbles of Southwark. The air is cold enough to make his breath plume, cold enough to coat the mud on the roadside with a thin layer of ice. Finn is dimly aware he ought to be freezing in just his shirtsleeves, but his pounding heart is making his body blaze.

Watermen's dinghies are tied up along the edge of the river, two small ketches moored alongside them. In the pink half-light of early morning, the river is coming to life, with a forest of masts already cluttering the water. Men shout to each other as they pile crates and barrels onto barges; a waterman winds at his mooring ropes as two women in patched cloaks holler down at him from the bank.

But that sloop, over there, unattended and loosely tethered, that would be all too easy to climb into. All too easy to free from its moorings and take down the Thames towards the sea. Ocean-worthy, no, but he can cling to the coast; guide it carefully back towards Northumberland. Nurse it out the Farnes. Sleep beneath the upturned boat. Wash in the ocean. Pocket apples and bread loaves when no one is looking. Find a coat and hat left unguarded.

No more thieving, he had promised Eva. Not a single lump of coal. But he steps into the boat and grapples with the mooring ropes anyway, certain she will allow him this one last transgression.

CHAPTER FORTY-ONE

It's only when Finn sees the bonfires glittering on the hilltops that he realises he has sailed into Northumberland on midwinter's night. Fragrant ribbons of peat smoke thicken the air, and from the water, he sees the fireflies of torchlights as villagers march back to their homes. He thinks of childhood midwinters; traditions his Scottish-born mother had insisted on. Milk left on the hearth for the friendly spirits; iron hammers and axes beside it meant to keep the nasty ones away. Memories he has barely thought of in years.

Back when his mother was alive, the year's midnight had been his favourite time of year. But alone on Longstone with childhood far behind him, midwinter had been nothing but eternal cold and dark.

Tonight, though, there's a restless thumping in his chest, half excitement and half fear. He is just a handful of miles from Holy Island now.

Never in his life had he imagined the sight of Highfield House might bring him joy. He is craving it with every inch of his being. But beyond that desperate desire to return to the house is a fear of what he might find. He knows there's every chance Eva and her family may have returned to London. Knows he might have sailed right past them on his way back up the country. But he needs to try the house first. Needs to hope they have decided to stay in Northumberland, now Ward and Graveney are gone.

But then he sees a light he was not expecting to see. Out on his right, high in the sky. Guiding ships away from the Farnes, and the black crenelations of the Knavestone reef.

Finn hears his own exhalation, overcome with fresh emotion. He leans on the tiller, turning the boat out towards Longstone.

He thinks of Eva with ash on her hands. Thinks of her huddling over the lamp with her needle and thread, dark hair falling over her cheeks. Thinks of her decorating the cottage in flour as she wrangles out another half-moon of bread.

And he thinks of her standing at the window, looking out over the sea. Watching, waiting.

He had gone with Henry Ward so she might be saved from such a thing. So she might spend her nights with her eyes turned away from the ocean. But he sees now that he has been foolish. Sees he has only given her more reason for sleeplessness. More reason to keep her eyes on the sea.

As he gets closer, he sees her, dwarfed by the firebasket, illuminated by its light. He sees her fly down the stairs of the cottage, charge out onto the jetty. Sees her standing on tiptoe, trying to reach out to sea, a hand pressed to her mouth as though she is afraid to believe.

Finn wills the boat onward. Wills it faster. Wills it straighter. Feels waves of emotion tighten his throat.

When he had first climbed aboard Henry Ward's ship as a nine-year-old child, it had been with the hope that he would never see the tiny spit of Longstone again. But he has never been more grateful for the blaze of the beacon, bright against the darkness, guiding him home.

Edwin has not come after her; Harriet feels certain of that. If he wished it, he could find her here at Isabelle's garret with little difficulty. Perhaps he does not yet have the strength to come after her. Perhaps one day he will appear at the door. She knows it's a possibility. Nonetheless, with each day that passes without sight of him, the knot inside her loosens a little.

Harriet feels safe here in London. Sheltered. The only window in this attic room looks straight up into the sky— only the birds and the stars can see inside. Tucked away with her paints, with her easel, with this woman she cares about so deeply, Harriet is beginning to see flickers of light in the darkness.

She thinks often of her son. Argues with herself, berates herself, and repeatedly comes to the conclusion that she had done what was best for him. Perhaps it's just an excuse. But convincing herself of its truth is the only way she can carry the shame. The only way she can let this life she has longed for bring her any joy.

But today, that life is bringing her no comfort. Today the knot inside her is as tight as ever.

Harriet buttons her cloak. Pulls on her gloves. Forces down a fresh wellspring of regret.

"Shall I come with you?" Isabelle asks. Her voice is calm and gentle, and there's a part of Harriet that wants nothing more than her company.

But she shakes her head. This is something she needs to do alone. And perhaps there is a part of her that does not want Isabelle to see the guilt she carries. Sometimes faint, sometimes blazing.

She has begun to tell Isabelle about everything that happened on Lindisfarne. In pieces, only—it is far too much to spill everything at once. With each fragment of the story, Harriet feels herself unravelling, opening. Feels the glacier inside her beginning to thaw.

But she is not ready to speak about sending her own father to the gallows.

Isabelle had not judged her when she had admitted to leaving Thomas behind. Had not judged her when, in a half-whispered voice, Harriet had spoken of holding that cushion in her hands. That dizzying outside-herself moment of lifting it to Edwin's face. But condemning her own father? Harriet fears that Isabelle would not see past this.

She slips her coin pouch into her pocket and murmurs her goodbyes, keeping her head down so Isabelle cannot see her eyes.

Harriet climbs from the waterman's boat not far from the Tower. The streets are heaving; boats knocking up against each other along the water. A grand procession is to take place, she has overheard, from London Bridge to Wapping, with the Marshall of the Admiralty carrying his silver oar. Her father, the condemned man, trailing behind. A final drink offered at the Turk's Head.

There's laughter in the air; raucous chatter, children running back and forth along the riverbank. It makes Harriet's skin prickle. Do none of these people understand that her father is to die? Sent to his death by his own jilted child?

Harriet pushes through the crowd. She fights the urge to turn back, and elbows her way past the wharves into Wapping. She follows the crowd past red brick towers, and warehouses echoing with thumps and voices. And she reaches Execution Dock; a floating pontoon just off shore, the noose swaying gently with the brown rise and fall of the river.

Harriet feels her stomach drop. Beneath her cloak and thick winter bodice, her skin is blazing.

She has never seen anyone put to death before. Has never seen the revelry in it; never understood why the end of life ought to be a source of entertainment. But she knows she needs to be here today. Knows this is her punishment. Once it is over and her father is gone, she will return to Isabelle and her painting and the quiet, sheltered garret with a view of the sky. She will try to remember that this life is making her happy.

The crowd chatters as it waits. Stories of hangings witnessed: men who took an age to die. Others whose bodies were rushed by the crowd, legs tugged downward to a quick and merciful death. Harriet's stomach turns over and she forces herself to breath.

The minutes tick towards twelve o'clock, beating away the seconds of her father's life. The knot in Harriet's stomach grows a little tighter. Will he see her here in the crowd? Will he know, somehow, that all this was her doing? That she, in a moment of unbridled childish rage, had sent the authorities after him? Had condemned him and his crew to their deaths?

Now she is off the island, calm and safe in Isabelle's company; now her decision to leave has been made and cannot be undone, Harriet is able to see with a little more clarity. She sees the foolishness, the childishness of her choice to turn her father in. And the regret is almost impossible to bear. Still, this is the choice she has made. And she must learn to carry it.

It is ten past the hour. Now twenty. With each distant rattle of cartwheels over the cobbles, the crowd turns as one. But the Admiral's procession does not appear. And the whispers are beginning. The rumours, the elaborate stories of last-minute pardons and jail breaks and escaped prisoners.

Harriet does not allow herself to believe them. Does not dare to, for fear of what this might mean for her, for her family. Does not dare to grapple with that flimsiest scrap of hope for a reprieve from the guilt that keeps her awake at night. Does not dare to imagine that her father, who had been privy to Jacobite secrets, might somehow have wrangled his way to freedom.

She does not allow herself to believe this, no. But that does nothing to change the empty swing of the hangman's noose, or the restless groans of the crowd. Does nothing to change the knowledge that her father will not cast a shadow over the Thames tonight.

ABOUT THE AUTHOR

A lover of old stuff, folk music, and ghost stories, Johanna Craven bases her books around little-known true events from the past. She divides her time between the UK and Australia, and can be very easily persuaded to tell you about the time she accidently swam with seals on Holy Island.

Find out more at www.johannacraven.com.

Printed in Great Britain
by Amazon